UNTIL THE HARVEST

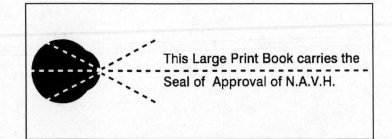

This Large Print Book carries the
Seal of Approval of N.A.V.H.

UNTIL THE HARVEST

SARAH LOUDIN THOMAS

THORNDIKE PRESS
A part of Gale, Cengage Learning

Farmington Hills, Mich • San Francisco • New York • Waterville, Maine
Meriden, Conn • Mason, Ohio • Chicago

Thorndike Press, a part of Gale, Cengage Learning.

LIBRARY OF CONGRESS CATALOGING-IN-PUBLICATION DATA

Thomas, Sarah Loudin.
    Until the harvest / by Sarah Loudin Thomas. — Large print edition.
    pages cm. — (Thorndike Press large print Christian fiction)
    ISBN 978-1-4104-8151-1 (hardcover) — ISBN 1-4104-8151-4 (hardcover)
    1. Large type books. 2. Domestic fiction. I. Title.
PS3620.H64226U58 2015b
813'.6—dc23   2015013729

Published in 2015 by arrangement with Bethany House Publishers, a division of Baker Publishing Group

Printed in Mexico
1 2 3 4 5 6 7 19 18 17 16 15

To Mom and Dad,
thanks for loving me —
always.

Let both grow together
until the harvest.
Matthew 13:24–30

1

Wise, West Virginia
New Year's Eve 1975

Henry Phillips sliced into the venison steak on his plate and savored the rich meatiness of it. Mom always cooked his favorites when he came home from college, and this Christmas break was no different. He'd been enjoying being home so much he almost decided against broaching the subject of his music for fear Mom and Dad would launch into their usual speech about his education coming first, but he was itching to share the latest news.

"Mort Jeffries asked me to come play at the Screen Door down on High Street. Guess I must've sounded pretty good."

His father raised one reddish eyebrow shot through with gray and chewed a bite of potato. "Oh?"

That was all the encouragement Henry needed. "Yeah, he heard me fooling around with my fiddle on campus one afternoon and said I should come sit in with the band. Guess he thought I was good enough to play a night or two. Even got some tip money out of it. Man, those guys can play." He put down his fork and used his hands to illustrate. "Mort gets that guitar going, and Benny plays the mandolin like he was born with it in his hands — almost as good as you. Sure wish you could come hear us."

His mother smiled and gave his father an inscrutable look.

"Son, you know we don't want you to let music distract you from your studies." His dad buttered a roll and took a bite. "You're talented in more ways than one, and getting an education should be your priority right now."

Henry tried not to roll his eyes. "I guessed you might say that, but somehow I thought — maybe this time — you'd see it's not just dreaming. I actually made some money. And Mort said if I'd commit to playing with them regular, he might be able to work out something steady."

Dad sighed. "We've been over this before —"

"Yeah, I know, and it's always the same. School, school, school. Maybe you don't think I'm good enough."

10

Mom reached over and squeezed his arm. Henry wanted to jerk away but knew it wouldn't help his case.

"I thought you were enjoying school." Dad leaned back in his chair and studied Henry. He had a way of looking at him that made Henry feel like he was reading his very soul.

"Yeah, I do like it. It's just . . ." He spread his hands wide, as though reaching for something. "I feel so connected when I play. It's almost spiritual or something, and the music flies out all around me, and . . . and I feel great."

Dad smiled. "I guess I know what you mean. Might be I should dust off my mandolin and see if we can't make some music together after supper." He glanced at Mom. "I know your mother would enjoy that."

"Does that mean it's okay if I play more regular? I know I can do it and keep up with classes." Henry tried not to sound too eager.

"No, that's not what I'm saying. I'm saying I know how you feel, and I know how hard it will be to put this dream on hold until you finish your degree." Dad folded his napkin and laid it beside his plate. "Music is one of the purest things this world has to offer, but I've never let it get in the way of my responsibilities. I know you won't, either."

Henry swallowed hard and pushed away his half-eaten steak. If his dad really understood, he'd know it was possible to get an education and play the fiddle at night. But he respected him too much to argue any more.

"Yeah, I understand."

Dad smiled. "Good, now go get your fiddle, and let's serenade your mother."

"Maybe tomorrow. It's New Year's Eve, and I promised the guys I'd go out with them tonight."

His mother frowned. "Which guys?"

"Oh, just some fellows from high school. Most of 'em are home from college like me."

"You be careful. Some of those boys drink."

"Mom, you know I don't drink."

His dad caught his eye and winked at him. "Our son's a good man, Perla. We can trust him."

She looked from her husband to her son as she smiled and stood to begin gathering dishes. "Casewell, you always did have a knack for thinking the best of folks, especially the ones you love."

He caught her wrist and tugged her closer, wrapping an arm around her waist. "Not always, my love, but I learned my lesson."

12

He kissed her elbow and released her.

Henry was sometimes embarrassed at how affectionate his parents were, but he guessed it might be worse. Some of his buddies' parents were divorced, and some didn't even talk to each other. He stood to go find the keys to his dad's old truck. Yeah, his parents weren't perfect, but it sure could be worse. And maybe they didn't have to know about it every time he played at the Screen Door.

Henry woke the next morning with an abruptness that frightened him. Was that a sound? Had someone spoken? He shivered, even though he was snug under two layers of quilts. The sun had begun to color the sky outside his window. He shoved up on one elbow and listened. The house was quiet — too quiet. And too cold. He shivered again, but this time it was the chill air slipping around his shoulders. Dad should be making noise by now, turning up the furnace from its nighttime setting, chatting with his mother while she started breakfast. Maybe they were sleeping in.

Henry swung his bare legs over the side of the bed and pulled on a pair of dungarees, shaking in the cold. He tried to credit his uneasiness to the late night ringing in the

New Year — it was 1976 now — and the nip or two of moonshine he'd sampled. He didn't much like alcohol, but it would have been unsociable to abstain completely.

He grabbed a sweatshirt with the name of his school emblazoned across it — West Virginia University. He'd need to head back in the next day or two. He'd begin the second half of his junior year on the seventh, but he had until the final day of break to turn in his paper on Soil Genesis and Classification. Man, who wouldn't prefer playing the fiddle to that? Just thinking about it made him want to crawl back under the covers, but the silence of the house was too much. He finished dressing and headed for the kitchen.

Mom sat at the table, her robe wrapped around her, bare feet tucked under her chair. Her feet looked almost blue. Confused, Henry laid a hand on her shoulder. She jumped up, sending her chair clattering to the floor. For a moment, Henry thought she was going to hit him.

"I've already called Al Tomlyn. He'll send someone shortly. I knew I should wake you, but I didn't know . . ." She glanced down at her tightly cinched robe. "I'd better put some clothes on." She shot a look at the bedroom door, and her face crumpled.

"Mom, what's going on?" His stomach churned, and it felt like his heart was trying to keep up with his speeding thoughts. "Why did you call the funeral home? Who died?" As the last word fell from his lips, the earlier feeling of disorientation closed over Henry like jumping into the swimming hole on a hot day. And he thought he might drown.

Turning toward the door to his parents' room, Henry took a tentative step. His mother grabbed his arm. "I can't go in there," she said.

"Can I?" Henry wasn't sure if he was asking his mother or himself. He took another step, and Mom released his arm. She tightened the belt to her robe, as though tying a tourniquet to stop — what? The pain?

Henry pushed open the bedroom door. His father lay in the bed, blankets tucked beneath his arms, hands folded neatly on his chest. For a moment, Henry breathed again, and then the wrongness of the scene penetrated his thick brain. His father would never sleep like that. Dad would never stay in bed past six in the morning. Henry glanced at the clock on the bedside table, and his shoulders sagged when he saw it was twenty after six. As if everything would be all right if it were only five fifty-five.

15

"Dad?" Henry's voice squeaked. He cleared his throat. "Dad, time to get up." He moved the last few feet to the bed and gently shook his father's shoulder. The icy dread that roiled his stomach earlier gripped his heart. He laid two fingers on his father's throat and felt his own pulse slow, as though trying to match what he was feeling — nothing. Nothing at all.

Mom stood in the doorway, watching dry-eyed. "Son, the men from Tomlyn's are here. Can you . . . ?"

Margaret Hoffman bustled around Emily's house, tidying things and making sure every surface gleamed. It wasn't only to please her sweet employer; it was because every woman in the community — including Margaret's own mother — would traipse through here just hoping to catch a speck of dust, an unmade bed, or a dirty dishrag. Emily was easy to please. It was the rest of the world that gave Margaret a hard time.

She sighed and put the last of the breakfast dishes away. News traveled fast, especially when it was as sad as Casewell Phillips dying in his sleep. And as soon as the ladies of Wise could throw together a casserole or a cake, they'd be knocking on the door with their condolences. Poor Emily. Margaret

16

couldn't think of anything harder than losing a child, no matter if he was six or fifty-six. She squared her shoulders. Well, she'd been working for Emily since she was sixteen — five years now — and if there was anything she could do to be a comfort, she would be more than glad.

"Margaret?" Emily walked into the kitchen, bracing herself against the backs of chairs like an old woman. She was nearly eighty, but she'd always behaved as though she were much younger.

"Yes, ma'am? Do you need something?"

"I do. Somehow I'm not sure how to dress for . . . this." She waved a hand vaguely in the air. "People will start coming any minute. Won't they?" She turned wet eyes on Margaret, as though she had the power to change things.

"Yes, ma'am, I expect they will. The house is about as ready as I can make it. Now, let's see about getting you dressed in something nice."

Margaret hooked her arm through Emily's and led her to the bedroom. She sifted through Emily's closet, finally pulling out a plaid skirt and a simple blouse. "I think this will be about right. You can wear one of your sweaters over it. I don't think it's supposed to warm up much today."

"Oh, thank you, sweetheart. I'm not normally at sixes and sevens like this. But you know that. Don't you?"

"Oh yes. It's not like you to be unsure of yourself." And it wasn't, thought Margaret, but losing a child so suddenly would set anyone off. They didn't even know when Casewell died exactly. Was it in 1975? Or 1976? What would they put on the tombstone?

A knock on the back door, followed by the squawk of worn hinges, interrupted her musing. She'd been meaning to oil that door.

"Must be family," Margaret said. "I'll go tend to it while you finish dressing."

Emily nodded and rummaged through the drawer where she kept her underthings. For a slip, Margaret hoped. Emily would be mortified if she forgot a slip in her present state of mind. But she'd likely be even more mortified if Margaret hovered over her like a child.

Closing the bedroom door, Margaret walked into the family room and found Henry standing with his head down and shoulders slumped. She'd heard he was in from college but hadn't seen him. Normally, she wouldn't be seeing him now. Emily always insisted on doing for herself over

18

holidays so Margaret could be with her family. Not that she much enjoyed being with her family, except, of course, with Mayfair. Her sweet little sister was always a bright spot.

"Hey, uh, Margaret? Right?" Henry straightened up a bit.

Margaret nodded. "Your grandmother is getting dressed. She's a little fuddled this morning."

"We all are," Henry said, and for just a moment Margaret caught a glimpse of anguish, but then his face shuttered closed again. "Mom thought I should bring Grandma over to the house. Make it easier on everyone."

"That's sensible," Margaret said. She wondered if she should go on home but felt a surge of desire to be a help to the Phillipses' family. "I could stay here and send anyone who stops by on over to your place."

Henry's brown eyes warmed, and he almost smiled. "That'd be great. Thank you."

They stood staring at each other, and Margaret became aware of how she must look. She'd thrown on a worn blouse over green polyester slacks when Emily called early that morning. She knew she'd need to tidy the house so selected something shabby.

Now she almost wished . . . But why? To impress a college boy who had been a year behind her in school? He wasn't likely to notice her even on a good day, at least not for the right reasons. She had a round face absolutely covered in freckles, and a figure her father indelicately referred to as "good for childbearing." Plus, her hair tended to frizz. None of which would impress the tall man in front of her with his wavy chestnut hair and broad shoulders. He scuffed one foot on the rag rug, and Margaret jumped.

"I'll go check on Emily."

Henry nodded and focused on a picture of his family that was sitting on the mantel. Margaret followed his gaze. The photo showed his parents with Henry and his sister Sadie on either side. Casewell looked like he'd been pleased with the world on that particular day. Margaret hoped he'd felt the same right up until he went to sleep the night before.

After the funeral, Margaret tried to get her parents to take Mayfair home instead of subjecting her to the crush of mourners at the Phillipses' house, but they wouldn't hear of it.

"She needs to be exposed to crowds like this," Margaret's mother said.

Her father nodded as his lips tugged down. "She's twelve now. We can't treat her like a child forever."

Margaret sighed. No wonder it was hard for her to think of these people as Mom and Dad. Wallace and Lenore Hoffman were typically more concerned about appearances than they were the well-being of their children. Mayfair would retreat into her books for a week after being forced into a social situation like this. She could manage sitting in church between her mother and older sister, but circulating in a house full of people would be too much. Why couldn't her parents see that?

Mayfair's shoulder touched Margaret's as they got out of the car and walked toward the house. An impromptu parking lot had been created in a nearby pasture, and Lenore picked her way through the grass like she expected to encounter cow manure at any moment. Wallace tried to take his wife's elbow, but she shot him a look and jerked her chin in the air. Margaret wondered what they were fighting about now.

"There are too many people," Mayfair whispered.

"I know, sweetie." Margaret tucked her sister's hand into her own and pulled her tight against her side. "Maybe we can find a quiet spot for you to read. Did you bring a book?"

Mayfair reached into the patch pocket of her skirt and pulled out a well-worn copy of *Anne of Green Gables.*

"Good for you, coming prepared." Margaret's praise raised a timid smile. "Just remember, the angels are holding hands all around you. Nothing can hurt you while they're here."

Mayfair gave a jerky nod and turned her head so she could watch the people entering the house through her peripheral vision. Margaret ached for her sister, wishing she could make life easier for her. Who knew? Maybe there really were angels, although she doubted it. She reached into her purse and felt for the handful of hard candies she always carried. If Mayfair's sugar dropped too low, she'd need something fast, and Margaret prided herself on always being prepared.

Henry ducked his head and aimed for the front door. He'd had enough of hearing about what a wonderful man his father was, how he was with Jesus now, and how he'd had a weak heart ever since he was born and was lucky to have lived this long. If anyone knew how great Casewell Phillips was, it was Henry. Someone even commented to his mother that it had been a blessing for Dad to die in his sleep. That was when Henry's hands balled into fists, and his heart began to beat a drum in his head. It was leave or hit someone, and he didn't want to disgrace his mother. Although he was getting closer and closer to not caring.

Bursting through the screen door, Henry nearly collided with two women scrunched together there. He started to push past them and then recognized Margaret, the girl who worked for his grandmother.

"I suppose you've come to spout platitudes like everybody else," he said. "Well, save it."

Margaret's cheeks turned scarlet, and she put an arm around the shoulders of someone he realized was little more than a girl. "That's pretty fancy vocabulary for somebody without any manners. Guess you learn big words like that in college."

He stopped short. There had been no call for his outburst, but he was too ashamed to back down. Instead, he continued the attack. "You have to be pretty smart to get into college in the first place. Let's see, which school did you go to?"

Margaret leaned in so her heavily freckled nose was inches away. "I'm going to assume that grief is making you act out of character. Now, you can either go on, or you can help me find a safe place for Mayfair while I check to see if your family needs anything."

Henry opened his mouth to tell her where she could go when his eyes met the girl's. They were more gold than brown and something about them stopped up his words. He felt a sudden deep longing, though he wasn't sure for what — his father, he supposed. Dad would never treat guests like this. Tears pricked his eyes and the beating of his angry heart slowed, as though matching some rhythm outside him. And all at once he wanted — more than anything — to make this girl happy.

"What do you mean, 'a safe place'?"

"Mayfair's kind of shy around people. I was hoping I could tuck her somewhere out of the way until it's time to go home."

"Dad's workshop." Henry spoke without thinking. He hadn't been in the shop since the last time he was home at Thanksgiving. He didn't really want to go there now, the memories would be too close, but the desire to help Mayfair outweighed his misgivings.

He led the two girls to the shop and pushed open the door. It was heavy, but the

24

hinges were well-oiled. Dad would never leave it any other way. He wondered what would happen to the tools and supplies now that his father was gone but quickly shifted his thoughts back to Margaret and Mayfair.

A small potbellied stove sat in the center of the room with two chairs pulled up to it. Dad always said it was practical to use the waste from his labors to heat his workshop. Henry opened the little door and found a fire already laid. By his father, no doubt. He choked on sorrow, not sure he could do this. Not sure he could set fire to something his father had touched only a few days ago.

Mayfair brushed his hand, and he felt the warmth from her fingers. "I'm not cold." Her voice was quiet but had a clarity that was almost musical. He wondered if she could sing.

He leaned toward her and smiled. "Dad would have my hide if I didn't make his workshop comfortable for guests." He looked back into the grate. "He laid that fire for you. The least you can do is enjoy it."

His hand shook as he lit a long match and held it to the crumpled paper under the kindling. Mayfair touched his elbow, and the shaking stopped. Flames started to consume the paper and wood. He reached into a box and added some larger pieces of scrap lumber.

"You'll be fine here," he said. "I don't think anyone will bother you."

Mayfair smiled and slid onto one of the wooden chairs. She pulled a book from her pocket and was immediately absorbed. He saw Margaret tuck a piece of candy into her sister's palm.

"Only if you need it," she said.

Henry walked Margaret back toward the house.

"I thought you were leaving," Margaret said in a way that made him think she was still stinging from his earlier greeting.

"I was, but I'm over it now. I guess people mean well." He looked toward the house and the steady stream of people coming and going. "Dad would expect me to stay."

"Parents expect a lot of their children," Margaret said, her lip curling back.

"Do your parents expect a lot of you or Mayfair?"

Margaret shot him a look that he couldn't read. "Both, I guess."

"I like your sister."

Margaret finally relaxed and shoved her hands in the pockets of her jacket. "So do I."

Henry noticed she was wearing a skirt

with knee-high socks and brown shoes. He wondered if her legs were cold. He opened the front door for Margaret and earned a small smile. Man, she even had freckles on her lips.

2

"Are you packed yet?"

Henry took a big bite of oatmeal to delay answering his mother's question. She quirked an eyebrow at him.

"Son, I asked you a question."

Henry gulped his milk. "I thought maybe I'd take a semester off," he said.

His older sister Sadie snorted and rolled her eyes. She always had an opinion.

Perla cut a look at her daughter, then turned her attention back to Henry. "What in the world for? It's not like there's anything you need to do here. Your education is too important to shirk."

"I've talked to most of my professors, and they understand. All I have to do is get ahold of Dr. Stanley to see if he'll excuse my final paper. Then I can just pick up next August. I might even be able to take extra classes so I can still graduate in four years." Henry carried his empty bowl to the sink and ran water into it. "You and Grandma need a man to take over here — to keep things up, maybe earn some money." He swallowed hard. "With Dad gone, I figured I'd better stay a while." He squared his shoulders and stood up straighter.

"You'll never make anything of yourself without a degree," Sadie said. She had just gotten her first job as a librarian at a university up in Ohio. Apparently they'd been very nice about giving her a week off for the funeral. Henry thought she was kind of full of herself at the moment, but she could be all right. If she wanted to. He reminded himself that she loved his father, too, even if he'd only been her stepfather.

Mom rubbed her temples and reached for her coffee cup. "I think you should go back, but if you can get approval from all of your professors, I suppose it'll be all right for one semester."

Henry let it rest at that. He was trying to behave as though he cared about school for his mother's sake, but honestly, what did it matter? What did anything matter anymore? He'd keep going through the motions for her sake, but he wasn't sure he'd ever go back to school. It occurred to him that he'd be free to pursue his music now, but that thought caused a stab of pain, and he brushed it aside, as well.

Later that day, Henry called Professor Stanley about his paper on Soil Genesis and Classification. Stan the Man as the kids called him was a real stickler, but Henry was confident his father's dying would move even a crusty old guy like Dr. Stanley.

"Hello?" Dr. Stanley always sounded curt.

"Dr. Stanley, this is Henry Phillips. You've probably heard that my father passed away recently, and I'm planning to take a semester off to take care of my mother. Which means I won't be able to get my paper in after all."

Silence stretched and just as Henry started to say something more, Dr. Stanley cleared his throat. "I'm sorry to hear about your loss, but I'm sure your father would want you to meet your obligations in school and in life. The paper should have been completed by now and will be due as scheduled." There was a rustling of papers. "If you intend to pick back up in an ensuing semester, you'll need this credit completed. I'm looking forward to reading your work."

"But there's no way I can get it done considering everything." Henry heard a whine in his voice and tried to regain his composure. "I'm sure we can work

30

something out."

"Henry, without that paper, I'll be forced to give you a failing grade. As I said, I look forward to reading your work. Please give my condolences to your family." He heard a click and then a dial tone.

Henry stormed out of the house and slammed through the door of his dad's workshop. Gordon Stanley was a jerk. Like the fool had any idea what Dad wanted for him. It was the last straw. What did he think he was going to do with a degree in agriculture, anyway? Be a farmer like his grandfather? He'd been hearing stories about John Phillips all his life, and somehow he'd thought it might be cool to follow in his footsteps. But what difference did a degree make? His grandfather died young. His father died young. He would probably die young, too.

So why not go ahead and flunk out of school and just live his life however he wanted? The worst thing that could happen would be dying, and apparently that was going to happen regardless. He picked up a wood chisel and considered what kind of damage he could do with it.

A half-finished footstool sat on the workbench. Henry settled the point of the tool against the top and grabbed a mallet.

He whacked the chisel, and it bit deeply into the wood. Henry hit it again, and a chip went flying. He looked at the marred surface of the stool and felt hot tears rise. He flung the tools down and cursed.

Henry gripped the edge of the worktable until he felt his fingernails sink into the wood. It hurt. He tried to focus on the pain, finding it preferable to the guilt, anger, resentment, and slurry of other emotions threatening to drag him under. He'd always followed his father's advice — done what was expected of him. Maybe it was time he made some decisions of his own. Maybe it was time to stand on his own two feet.

A Mason jar stood on the counter with a handful of finishing nails inside. Henry thought back to the night his father died and how Charlie Simmons supplied the Mason jars of moonshine his buddies drank. He'd gone to school with Charlie, who played a mean guitar — used to really like him. Maybe it was time to reconnect with his old buddy. Henry eased his grip, ignoring the blood oozing from a torn cuticle. Now that was a good idea. Charlie might be the solution to several of his problems.

"Why you feel the need to have a job is beyond me." Lenore examined her manicure and seemed to be satisfied. "Your allowance should be more than enough to meet your needs. You ought to be going to school."

Margaret sighed. She'd almost been ready to leave the two-story house in the middle of town for the peace of Emily's house in the country when her mother wandered into her room.

"I like working. It gives me a feeling of satisfaction. And Emily Phillips is a lovely person." Why did she even try to explain herself?

"But domestic work — it's beneath you. And it's an embarrassment to me."

"Helping people should never be beneath anyone." Of course her mother would be embarrassed by her. But that would likely be the case no matter what she did. It gave her a certain perverse pleasure to aspire to a life her mother disdained.

Lenore made a derisive sound, then brushed her nails against her perfect white blouse. "Well, the least you can do is take Mayfair with you. I kept her out of school again today — she looked flushed — and she's certainly more suited for menial work. Goodness knows she isn't likely to have much success in this world. Between her idiotic diabetes and her attitude, it's a wonder she's made it this far."

Mayfair sat curled in a window seat in the room the girls shared. Margaret didn't know if her mother was even aware her younger daughter was present. Not that she'd speak more kindly if she did. Margaret wanted to point out that her parents had probably somehow passed diabetes down to Mayfair, but she knew better than to try to get her mother to take responsibility for anything.

"I don't mind going." Mayfair's whisper softened Margaret's heart. She'd be only too glad to have her sister along today, and Emily adored the child. It had been two weeks since the funeral, and the older woman's sorrow still hung about her like a too-large dress. Mayfair seemed to cheer her.

"There, now. Maybe I'll be able to get something done with both of you out from underfoot." Lenore sailed out of the room and down the stairs.

Margaret looked at her sister. "Has she ever done *anything*?" The pair giggled. "Grab your stuff. Emily will be glad to see you."

When they walked through Emily's back door, they overheard her on the telephone.

"No, I understand. Send him over anyway. Maybe some time on the farm will be good for him. I can surely find plenty for him to do." She paused, listening. "Yes, he'll have to be willing to do it, but maybe it'll be easier for his ole granny than for his mother. Young people are often like that."

Margaret made some noise so Emily would know they'd arrived. Was Henry the mysterious "he" coming over to work on the farm? She remembered how vulnerable he looked lighting the fire in his father's workshop. Stoic and sad all at once.

Emily came into the room as Margaret and Mayfair hung up their coats and removed their boots.

"Leave those wet shoes on the rug there. It'll sop up any dampness. Mayfair, I'm so glad you came. You're not sick, are you?" Mayfair shook her head. "Excellent, you can help me make some oatmeal cookies." Emily reached out and gently squeezed the girl's arm, knowing a hug might be overwhelming. "Henry's coming, and I'm sure he still eats enough for two men his size."

Mayfair smiled and headed for the kitchen. Emily turned to Margaret. "Perla's having a time with that boy. Seems he got into some trouble last night. I won't go into the details, but I think the two of them need a little time apart." She placed a hand in the small of her back and stretched. "Getting too old to keep up with the young people, but I'd do just about anything for that boy." A gleam lit her eyes. "He can clean out the chicken coop." She shot Margaret a meaningful look. "I don't expect you to help him, but if he's willing to talk, it might do him good to have someone more his age to listen."

Margaret schooled her expression. She had no intention of mucking out chicken poop with Henry. Although his father *had* just died. She supposed she should be digging deeper for some Christian charity.

"I thought he'd be back in school," she said by way of not answering Emily.

"Apparently he got mad about some professor expecting him to keep up with his assignments in spite of his loss. Perla says he isn't going back this semester." She squeezed her eyes shut for a moment then opened them again. "Time and the Lord will set him right. We just have to put up with him until then. I'm sorry you have to see his bad behavior, but I know you're a kind girl and won't hold it against him."

Fifteen minutes later, Henry slammed through the back door. Margaret paused in her scrubbing of the bathroom sink when he thundered into the house. She heard Emily speak to him, then he reversed his trip with a similar amount of noise and bluster. When the door slammed the second time — he went back out, she assumed — Margaret heaved a sigh and marveled that someone Henry's age could be so immature.

Emily appeared in the doorway. "You've got it shining in here," she said, admiring the spotless fixtures. "Henry's out in the chicken coop. Might not be the time to join him, but maybe you'd be kind enough to check on him in twenty minutes or so?"

Margaret nodded. She'd check to make sure he hadn't killed any chickens, if nothing else. She and Mayfair could go gather the eggs in a little while. Her sister always enjoyed being around animals of any kind.

After finishing in the bathroom and changing the sheets on Emily's bed, Margaret went looking for her sister. She found her nibbling an oatmeal cookie and reading *Little House in the Big Woods* for the umpteenth time.

"Only one cookie, Mayfair. Want to help me gather the eggs?"

Mayfair lit up. She placed her half-eaten cookie on a cloth napkin and ran for her shoes and coat. "Let's take Henry some cookies," she suggested as she went.

"He's been cleaning out chicken mess.

He's too dirty to eat right now."

"Take him a wet washcloth." Mayfair slid her arms into her jacket. "A warm one."

Margaret rolled her eyes. If it had been anyone other than her sister suggesting such a thing, she wouldn't even consider it. She got an old washcloth out of the linen closet and dampened it in water as hot as she could stand. It would cool quickly. Mayfair took up a plate of cookies, and they walked out to the chicken house.

Henry sat on the ramp the chickens used to come and go, muttering to himself.

"We brought you cookies," Mayfair said.

He looked up as though someone had just offered to rob him of his chickens at gunpoint.

"And Margaret has a cloth for you to clean your hands."

Margaret stuck out the cloth. Henry took it, rubbing it over his hands like he'd been hypnotized and told to do it.

"It's warm," he said.

"We knew you'd be cold." Mayfair smiled and handed him the plate of cookies. "And hungry."

He handed her the soiled cloth and bit into a cookie. "Good," he said through the crumbs.

"Emily and I made them." Mayfair

sounded pleased, and Margaret realized this might be the longest conversation she'd heard her sister have with anyone outside the family.

"How're you coming with the coop?" Margaret asked.

Henry looked over his shoulder. "Guess I'm about halfway. Probably hasn't been cleaned out since my grandfather died forty years ago."

"Surely your father . . ." The words died on Margaret's tongue. Well, that had been insensitive.

Henry stiffened. "I'm sure he did. It was just a way of talking." He shoved the remainder of a cookie in his mouth and handed the plate back to Mayfair. "Guess I'd better get back to it." He shot Margaret a look she chose not to interpret.

"We're just here for the eggs," Margaret said and moved to the side where she could enter and check the laying boxes. Mayfair balanced her plate on a rock and scurried ahead of Margaret. Inside, she carefully collected the few eggs, even reaching beneath two hens still on their nests. Margaret didn't like to do that, since a hen pecked her on the back of the hand one time. But the chickens let Mayfair reach beneath them as though they wanted her to have their eggs.

Job finished, the sisters walked back to the house leaving Henry to chip bird mess off the roosts. Margaret felt bad for him. It wasn't a nice job, and somehow she felt she'd made it worse for him. If only he weren't so — what? Angry? She wasn't sure, but whatever it was, it made Henry Phillips hard to be around.

3

Henry wasn't sure how much money his parents had or how his father had left things, but he figured Mom would need some help now. He could always get a job in fast food or bagging groceries, but he had an idea he could make money more easily than that. And Charlie Simmons could be his ticket to quick cash.

The first few nights he rambled around with the Simmons boys, he snuck out his window after he thought his mother was asleep. But she knew what he was up to — at least he was pretty sure she did — so he opted to stop trying to hide it. The previous night he'd strolled out the front door at ten, telling Mom not to wait up for him. The look on her face made his stomach clench, but he chose to ignore it. She should be grateful he was willing to take risks in order to provide for her. A man had to do what a man had to do.

Of course, he hadn't really wanted to hike through the woods to break up a rival family's still in the dark of night. He hadn't really enjoyed running through the woods, tripping, falling, banging his knees, and having shots fired over his head. Henry knew the Simmonses were one of only a few families still running bootleg liquor and maybe breaking a few other laws, but he was determined to prove he could handle anything they dished out. He had to, if he wanted a fair cut of the profits.

When Mom sent him to Grandma Emily's to help out this morning, he'd been secretly relieved. Not that he'd show it, but he felt somehow anchored on his grandmother's farm. He felt safe, like he had a purpose. Not to mention connected to Dad. They'd spent a lot of time over there together, helping his grandmother with the garden or the few animals she kept.

He remembered one time when they were weaning the milk cow's latest calf. He was only ten or so and liked messing around with the calf while she was in the stall next to her mother, scratching her behind the ears and petting her wooly head. Daisy didn't think much of it, but there was little she could do.

Then he'd been in the calf lot one day

when Daisy ambled in for the evening milking and saw her chance. He'd had his back to the annoyed cow when she charged, and his father roared, "Stop," in a voice like thunder. Poor ole Daisy skidded to a stop, and he'd escaped into the barn just in time to avoid a trampling. Dad ran shaking hands over his shoulders and down his arms. He'd laughed a little and said he'd take a boy over a milk cow any day and warned him to stay clear of Daisy. Thinking back on it he wondered that Dad hadn't yelled at him for being in the calf lot when he shouldn't have been, but his father had never been one to yell or berate. He just gently admonished.

He sat on the ramp leading up to the now much cleaner chicken house and swallowed past the lump in his throat. Chickens scratched near his feet, even though there wasn't much for them to peck at this time of year. But they went over and over the ground around the coop just the same. He envied their mindless pursuit. They weren't agonizing over what to do with their lives. They were simply looking for something good to eat.

His stomach rumbled on cue. He wished he had some more of those oatmeal cookies Mayfair brought out. The one he'd eaten had been delicious, but then Margaret ruined his appetite. That girl seemed way too uptight. Probably a real prude — all prim and proper. But she did look out for her little sister, and Henry liked Mayfair. Something about the younger girl made him feel like he should take care of her.

He stood and dusted the seat of his britches. It was probably lunchtime by now, and Grandma was sure to feed him well. Although he was almost too dirty to go inside. Once he warmed up, he'd probably reek of chicken manure. But who cared? It wasn't like he had anyone to impress. Margaret might be cute if she loosened up, but that wasn't likely.

Henry ambled down to the house and kicked his work boots off at the front door. He stepped inside in his stocking feet and shrugged out of his jacket. He probably should have left it outside, too, but he dumped it on a hook near the door instead.

He heard laughter from the kitchen. Margaret and Mayfair were singing along with the radio. It sounded like Captain and Tennille doing "Love Will Keep Us Together." He peeked around the corner and saw Margaret singing into a wooden spoon while Mayfair danced next to her. They joined in together on the last chorus and collapsed into giggles. Henry had been determined to

44

hang onto his foul mood but smiled in spite of himself.

"Not bad," he said, walking into the room.

Mayfair ducked behind Margaret and smiled shyly past her sister's shoulder. Margaret blushed in a way that almost made her look pretty. Even with all those freckles. Maybe if she did something with her hair. . . .

"Lunch is just about ready," Margaret said, reaching for the radio knob as John Denver came on.

"Wait, I like this one." Henry bumped Margaret's hand as he turned up the volume.

He listened to the opening lines, then jumped in with "Thank God, I'm a country boy." By the end of the second verse, Mayfair joined in. Margaret looked a little surprised but joined her voice to the din with the third verse. They made such a racket, Emily came into the room, saw what was what, and added her soprano. They were all dancing and carrying on by the time the last notes died away. Henry wished for his own fiddle so he could play another chorus or two.

Emily flicked off the radio as laughter replaced the music. Mayfair positively glowed, Margaret looked more relaxed than

Henry thought possible, and for a moment he forgot he was mad at the world.

"Well, now, that was a fine way to start our lunch off," Grandma said. "You're all good singers, though I can't say much for your dancing." They laughed some more. "Henry, go wash up, and we'll have us some of this fine potato soup Margaret has cooked up."

As Henry scrubbed his fingernails with a soapy brush, he let the pleasure of singing in his grandmother's kitchen sink in a bit. He almost wished he could stay here. He didn't care if he ever saw the Simmons boys again. He could quit school for good and run his grandmother's farm. She had the chickens, and they could get a pig to raise come spring. Maybe even a milk cow. Now that would be good. Margaret probably knew how to make butter — she seemed like the kind to have a knack for those sorts of things.

Henry stopped scrubbing and dropped the brush in the sink. He rinsed his hands and dried off. But then again, his mother needed him. And anyway, all that taking care of animals would be a lot of work. And it would definitely tie him down. He'd end up losing the chickens to foxes, the pig would get foot rot, and the cow would go dry. Farming was a whole lot of trouble, and he reckoned life was hard enough. The heck with John Denver and his stupid song.

As he dragged back into the kitchen, Margaret dished up soup and put bowls on the table, along with a loaf of warm soda bread and a jar of peaches that probably came from the tree down at the cold spring. Well, the world didn't much suit him at the moment, but that didn't mean he couldn't enjoy lunch.

As they sat, Emily folded her hands and bowed her head. Margaret and Mayfair did the same, but Henry didn't feel like bowing before a God who would take his father. He watched the women as his grandmother said grace.

He had the feeling Margaret wasn't all that into praying, either, but Mayfair seemed completely absorbed. She clasped her hands and her thumbs almost touched her nose. She squinched her eyes as Emily thanked God for the food, the hands that prepared it, and finally for Henry, who had been such a help. Henry wanted to bat the prayer away as if it were a cobweb drifting over his face, but he sat still out of respect for his grandmother.

Once the prayer ended, Henry tasted his soup. Man, it was good. Rich and buttery.

He broke off a hunk of bread and slathered it with apple butter. Margaret might not be a barrel of laughs, but she sure could cook.

"Oh, it does my heart good to see a man eat after he's worked all morning." Emily patted Henry's arm. "Your grandfather was lean, but he'd eat a whole pan of biscuits if I let him. He'd even pass up dessert for biscuits and jelly. That man could eat."

Henry thought his grandmother looked almost as proud as she would if she'd just said, "That man saved a child from a burning building."

Grandma turned to Margaret. "Will you help me make a casserole this afternoon? It's my week to take something to Angie Talbot."

Margaret agreed and added some more soup to Henry's bowl without asking. He started to get annoyed but decided to eat the soup instead.

"Angie Talbot. Didn't her twin sister die a while back?" Margaret asked.

"Yes, poor thing. She's always kept her feelings to herself, but I know it was hard on her. Of course, Frank Post is over there most every day, but he's old as the hills himself."

Henry considered how ancient you had to be for his grandmother to think you were old as the hills. "How old is he?"

"Oh, both of them must be near about ninety. I think they were sweethearts once a long time ago. Or maybe it was Liza he was sweet on." Emily sopped up the last bit of her soup with a piece of bread. "I doubt anyone remembers. At any rate, the members of Laurel Mountain Church take turns looking after Angie. One of those visiting nurses comes in just about every day, but we like to see to our own." She cocked her head and looked at Henry as if she was trying to decide something.

"If you're up to it, you could spend some time walking the old fence line this afternoon to see what needs fixing. I've been thinking about getting a cow."

Margaret made a sound like she was going to speak, but Emily kept talking.

"Before I make up my mind, I need to know if that fence will hold an ornery old milk cow. You think you can manage something like that?"

Henry had thought he might go home and sleep the afternoon away after his rough night, but suddenly, walking the fields in the thin January sunshine seemed like a much better idea.

"I reckon I could."

"Good. About the time you finish, we

should be ready to go over to the Talbot place. You can drive us."

Margaret acted like she was going to say something again, but Emily shot her a look. "Let's gather these dishes and get started on that casserole. Henry, take some cookies with you."

Mayfair scurried to wrap cookies in a napkin for Henry. She ducked her head as she handed them over. "Can I come with you?"

"What?" Henry wasn't sure he'd heard the girl.

"I want to come, too," Mayfair said, peeking out from beneath long lashes. "Like Laura helping her Pa on the prairie."

"Mayfair, you stay here and help Miss Emily and me." Margaret sounded annoyed.

"Oh, let the child go." Emily made shooing motions toward her grandson and Mayfair. "She could do with the fresh air."

Margaret made a sour face but didn't stop Mayfair as she ran to put on her boots and jacket. Henry didn't especially want her along but decided it would be worth it just to annoy Margaret. He made sure the girl had mittens and a woolen hat, and they headed out into the bracing air.

"Honestly, Emily, I'm not sure Mayfair

needs to be spending time with Henry. I know he's your grandson, but he doesn't impress me as super stable right now."

Emily's eyes flickered. "What do you mean?"

"Well," Margaret went to the refrigerator to pull out chicken and vegetables for the casserole. "He was rude at the house after the funeral."

"I thought he found a spot for Mayfair."

"Only *after* he nearly bit our heads off."

"I suppose you might excuse a young man for being testy on the day he buried his father." Emily pulled a two-quart casserole dish out of a cabinet and handed it to Margaret. "What else?"

"He's throwing away his education, and I hear he's been spending time with the wrong crowd." Margaret felt a tingle of triumph, shadowed by shame. She shook it off.

"He still has time to finish school. Could be he just needs to settle himself and get used to his father's being gone. Goodness knows, it's going to take me a while. As for the wrong crowd, I'll have to agree with you there, but I think it's important we not judge someone by the company they keep." Her eyes twinkled. "Jesus spent plenty of time with questionable people — tax collectors, prostitutes, lepers, beggars. Henry could do worse."

Margaret puffed her breath out in frustration. "I know you love him, but maybe you're too willing to see past his flaws."

"Oh, Margaret, I forget how unsentimental you can be." Emily patted her on the arm, and Margaret wanted to shake the kindness off. The only time her parents were nice to her was when they wanted something. She had to remind herself not everyone was like that.

"But if you ignore his flaws, how is that going to help him improve?" Margaret thumped pie dough on the counter and began to roll it out like she was smoothing out all of Henry's shortcomings.

"Not ignore the flaws, but love the person in spite of them. There's a difference," Emily said.

Margaret turned back to the refrigerator to hide her confusion. She didn't quite understand what Emily was talking about, but she decided not to write it off completely. Maybe she should be more gracious about having Henry around. It would give her a chance to watch Emily and her grandson and see how people who loved each other were supposed to act.

4

Henry walked the fence line, mentally not-
ing areas that needed repair. He carried a
small bucket with fencing nails, a hammer,
and a wire stretcher. Mayfair trailed along
behind him, saying little and lending easy
companionship. He was surprised by how
much he liked having her with him. Maybe
it was because she didn't chatter on and on
but just kept him quiet company.

Stopping to stretch a bit of wire that had
come loose, Henry set the bucket at his feet.
Mayfair swooped in and handed him a nail
and the hammer as he needed them. He
grinned at his silent helper. Maybe this was
what it was like to have a kid. He imagined
himself with a son one day, and then he
thought about how he used to follow his
own father around. He'd probably been
more hindrance than help, but Dad always
put up with him. He felt a lump forming in
his throat and blinked rapidly, telling himself

it was just the cold stinging his eyes.

Mayfair brushed his arm as though she knew he was struggling and wanted to brush the pain away. And oddly, it did ease a little. He found he could think about his father without wanting to cry or hit anything. Maybe the pain would get easier in time.

A figure appeared over the rise and moved toward them. Henry stopped what he was doing and leaned on a fence post, watching. It was a man, but he didn't recognize him right off. The man raised a hand in salute and recognition dawned. It was the sheriff.

"Howdy, Henry," Sheriff Pendleton called out. "Fine day for mending fence."

"A mite chilly," Henry said, trying to appear relaxed but going stiff inside. "What brings you all the way out here?"

"Stopped off at Perla's place. She said you were over here working for your grandma. Saw you as I drove in and thought I'd walk on out. No need to bother Emily."

Henry's stomach knotted. "Bother her with what?"

"Well, seems Charlie Simmons ended up in the emergency room with a bullet in his leg sometime late last night. I heard you were out with those boys yesterday evening and wondered if you knew anything about it." The sheriff pushed his hat back on his head a notch and looked at Henry like he was a steer at auction. "Charlie says he and his brother were messing around target shooting. You part of that?"

Henry swallowed hard. He'd heard gunfire as they took off through the woods the night before, but they'd scattered and gone their separate ways. He hadn't known anyone got hit.

"Was he hurt bad?"

"Oh, he'll live, but he might limp a while. Hope it'll be a reminder to be more careful in the future."

Henry stood there, hammer forgotten in his hand. He sorted through possible stories, but he wasn't much of a liar.

"Were you with those boys last night?"

"Yeah, for a while. But I didn't see anyone get shot." That was true enough. It'd been dark, and he'd been running too hard to see anything.

"Don't suppose they were messing with the Waites? Seems those two families have something purt near to a feud going on these days."

"Yeah, they don't seem to get along, but I wouldn't know much more than that."

The sheriff put his hands on his gun belt and leaned toward Henry a bit. It seemed he was done fooling around. "Son, I don't know what you're up to, but your daddy was one of the best men I ever knew. He wouldn't care for you getting mixed up with a bunch like those Simmons boys. I'm going to drive on back into town now and consider this case closed." He leaned in closer. "But if I have to reopen it, I'd better not find you in the mix. Got me?"

Henry nodded. "Yes, sir."

The sheriff turned and strode back across the field. Henry let his shoulders sag and realized he was clenching the hammer as if it might get away from him. So Charlie got shot. He guessed he'd been in more danger than he realized. He turned to Mayfair and shrugged.

"Don't know what that was all about," he said.

She looked sad, but then she usually looked that way. He grabbed the bucket and continued down the fence. "Better get back to work."

As they worked, the fear that washed over Henry at seeing the sheriff faded, and he began to think he'd put one over on the old guy. He hadn't given anything away, had stood up under the questioning without betraying his friends.

Henry straightened his shoulders and patched two more sections of fence. He was

56

a man now, and no one, including the sheriff, was going to tell him what his father would have expected of him.

"I'm cold." Mayfair's voice brought Henry out of his own head. He'd just about forgotten her.

He glanced over his shoulder. Her nose shone red and her eyes were watering. She looked about frozen. "Better get you on back to the house," he said. He started to wrap an arm around her shoulders, but she shied away like a skittish colt. He started to protest that he was only trying to warm her up, but the look in her eyes stopped him. What was it? Disappointment? He wasn't sure, but whatever it was, she needed to get warm.

"Come on, then," he said. "Let's go see if that casserole's ready to deliver."

Margaret could have wrung Henry's neck when she saw how he let Mayfair get so thoroughly chilled. She pulled a chair up to the stove, still warm from the cooling casserole, and gave her sister a mug of hot tea with a little honey. She gave some to Henry, too, although her mother would have described the delivery as ungracious.

Once Margaret was satisfied that Mayfair would be fine, the four of them piled into

Emily's massive Oldsmobile with Henry behind the wheel. Emily insisted on riding in the backseat with Mayfair. Margaret sat stiffly beside Henry, trying not to slide toward him in the turns. He seemed focused on the road ahead of them, although she thought she detected an undercurrent of worry.

"You're a good driver." Margaret decided to try forgiving Henry, though she had to make herself do it. She told herself it was Christian to forgive.

Henry sort of grunted. Well, so much for reaching out in Christian love. She spoke to Emily over the back of the front seat.

"How's Angie been since Liza died?"

"You know, I didn't think she'd live long after her sweet sister passed, but she seems to be all right. Although I was visiting last week, and she talked about Casewell and Perla's wedding like it happened yesterday instead of twenty-some years ago. Then it seemed like she couldn't remember what day it was. She had a confused air about her." Emily looked out the side window. "Guess that happens if you live long enough."

"And Frank stays with her?"

"No more than is proper. They're both single people, you know."

Henry snorted, and while Margaret thought it was rude, her reaction was similar. Who cared if two old people spent every possible moment together? What harm could come of it?

Henry pulled into the driveway and stopped alongside the front porch. Margaret hopped out and picked up the warm casserole dish from where it nestled in the floorboards between her feet. Mayfair carried a basket with a loaf of light bread, a jar of apple butter, and half a pound cake.

"You know, we made that apple butter in the Talbot sisters' kettle. I think just about everybody in Wise has borrowed that thing at one time or another." Emily took Henry's arm as they walked up onto the porch. "Knock plenty loud, Henry. She might be napping."

But Henry didn't even touch the screen door before Frank was there to let them in.

"Howdy, folks, come on in and set a spell."

They piled into the kitchen and draped coats over the backs of chairs, then lined their boots up near the front door. As they shed outer layers, Angie eased into the kitchen and watched.

"I haven't seen such a ruckus in a month of Sundays," she said.

Margaret was afraid they'd upset the old

59

woman, but she smiled. "And I'm so glad. It's been too long since people piled up in this house. Probably not since Liza passed, God rest her soul."

Margaret wondered if she should say she was sorry, but Liza had been gone a while now. She settled for putting her warm dish on the table in front of Angie.

"We brought you some chicken pie."

"Oh, I do enjoy chicken pie, and so does Frank." Angie gave Frank such a warm look, Margaret almost felt uncomfortable.

"There's bread and pound cake, too." She rushed the words to hide her embarrassment.

"How nice. Frank, what if we put some of that Hershey's syrup on the cake for dessert this evening?"

Frank rubbed his hands together. "I always have enjoyed something sweet of an evening." He winked and Angie swatted his arm.

"Come on into the parlor," she said. "We can sit and visit."

Once everyone settled and they had finished thoroughly discussing the weather, Frank leaned forward and braced his hands on his knees.

"Guess I might know something that'll be news to you'uns," he said.

Emily leaned forward with a smile. "Is it good news?"

"I think so." He looked at Angie. "Shall I tell them?"

Angie waved a hand at nothing. "Oh, go ahead. People will talk no matter what you do. Might as well make sure they've got the story right."

Frank grinned. "I've asked Angie here to be my bride." He reached out and placed a hand over hers where it rested on the arm of her chair. "And she said, 'yes.' "

Emily clapped her hands. "Oh, that is good news. Frank Post, it's about time you got married."

He chuckled. "I reckon it's past time, but better late than never."

Margaret felt something akin to distaste. They were so old. What could possibly be the point of getting married? They probably wouldn't even live much longer. Not that she'd say any of that out loud, but really, it was kind of embarrassing to see two wrinkled ninety-year-olds making puppy-dog eyes at each other.

She snuck a peek at Henry. He looked about to laugh, but was holding it in. She caught his eye, and amusement passed between them. He really was kind of appealing when he wasn't busy being mad.

61

They stayed a little longer before heading home. Frank pulled Henry aside on the porch while the ladies said their good-byes. Back in the car Henry seemed pensive, but Margaret was pretty well ready to write him off as moody, so she paid him little mind.

"What do you think about Frank and Angie getting married?" Margaret asked Emily.

"Well, now, I think it's a hoot. You're never too old for love."

Margaret gave Emily a dubious look. "Seriously? I mean, I guess there's nothing wrong with it, but it seems kind of silly."

"Silly? I don't know that I'd call it that." Emily smiled. "I might call it hopeful or optimistic. I might even call it brave."

"Brave? What's brave about getting married?"

Emily laughed. "Oh, my dear, it's the bravest thing two people can do at any age. To pledge yourself to someone forever — no matter what comes — that takes nerve. I suppose the Lord made us to have all the fluttery, falling-in-love feelings because He knew we'd never hitch up otherwise."

Mayfair jumped in. "They're too old to have children, aren't they?"

Emily laughed again, and Margaret joined in, although she flushed a little when she saw Henry grinning behind the steering wheel.

"Yes, they're well past that age, but they may not be past, well," she glanced around the car. "Other things."

Margaret's blush deepened, and she faced forward, trying to avoid everyone's eyes, most particularly Henry's. She'd read about the sexual revolution, birth control, and feminism, but she didn't want any part of it. She wanted to simplify her life, not complicate it. And she certainly didn't want to think about those things when two people old enough to be her great-grandparents were involved.

"Grandma, when are you thinking of getting a cow?"

Margaret could have hugged Henry for the sudden change in conversation.

"Oh, I'm in no hurry. I'll need someone to milk her every day, so I'll have to sort that out first. I could manage most days, but mornings can be hard on these old joints of mine."

"I can do it," Henry offered.

"Henry, I still have hopes of you finishing college. You have only a year and a half to go. But maybe you could take it over while you're at home."

"I could learn," Margaret offered. "Is it hard?"

Henry snorted. "It is if you're prissy about it."

"Who says I'm prissy?"

Henry darted a glance at her. "I'm just saying you've got to let the cow know who's in charge. Be ready to throw an elbow or block her when she tries to put a foot in the bucket."

Margaret rolled her eyes. He was just trying to intimidate her. "Guess my teacher had better be pretty good, then."

Henry puffed his chest out a little.

"Miss Emily, think you could teach me?"

"Oh, a hard worker like you would be a natural." Emily patted her on the shoulder.

Margaret was pleased to see Henry deflate.

"And you've always been good with animals. Not sentimental, either. I think slaughtering the hog last fall was harder on me than it was on you, and you're the one who fed that critter most days."

"Well, it made me a little sad, but I do like bacon. I just reminded myself that was his purpose every time I went out there to feed him."

Emily turned to Mayfair. "Child, you think you might like some fresh milk and homemade butter?" Mayfair nodded, eyes shining. "Just like Heidi — except she drank goat milk and ate toasted cheese. Do you think we could make cheese?"

Emily laughed. "That's a tall order, but we could give it a try." She slapped her knee. "Well, then, I think between the four of us we might manage a cow. Henry, you and I will go to the stockyards next week and see what we can find."

5

At home that evening, Henry considered what it was Frank asked him as they were leaving. Frank didn't have any family left, and he told Henry he'd always thought Casewell would stand up with him if he ever got married. But since Casewell was gone, he wondered if Henry might do the honors.

Henry sat out on the porch, feet up on the railing, breath clouding the air as he pondered the question. He liked Frank, had known the old man since he could remember. Somehow Frank and his dad seemed to have a special bond. Henry remembered his father saying Frank saved his life once, but Henry always assumed it was an exaggeration. Still, who knew? Maybe the old guy really had saved him. Probably kept him from getting kicked in the head by a cow or something. He couldn't picture Dad doing anything really dangerous.

He thought back to what seemed more and more like a narrow escape the night before. Now that was danger — and excitement. He might have felt a measure of peace on his grandmother's farm today, but it would get boring if every day were like that. Now, running moonshine could get a man's blood up, even if there were only a handful of folks still making the stuff now that store-bought liquor was readily available. Even so, there were still those who preferred quality, homemade hooch. He clasped his hands behind his head. And Charlie said if Henry wanted to go in with him, they could expand their line of merchandise and make some real money. Whatever that meant. Henry just wanted to show his family he could support them.

Oh, well. He'd stand up with Frank. It's what men did — stand up for each other. He'd be moving on to bigger and better things soon enough, might as well help out a friend of his father's along the way.

Decision made, Henry dropped his feet from the railing, stood, and stretched. He was about to head in when his mother stepped out onto the porch. She sat down in a rocker and pulled her coat more snugly around her shoulders.

"Can I talk to you a minute, son?"

Henry slumped back into his chair. "Sure, Mom. Whatcha need?"

She clenched the fabric of her coat and released it. "I'm a little bit worried about you, Henry."

Henry rolled his eyes and slouched lower. "The sheriff stopped by."

Henry froze and his stomach twisted. He'd pretty well forgotten about the sheriff.

"Seems he had some questions about you and those Simmons boys. I guess maybe one of them got into some trouble?"

"Yeah, that's what he said."

"Did you know anything about it?"

"Look, Mom, like I told the sheriff, I don't know anything. Why everyone has to make a big deal about me hanging out with some old friends is beyond me. Seriously, can't a guy spend some time with his pals without getting the third degree?"

Perla sat up straighter, and her hands stilled. "Young man, I'll thank you to keep a civil tongue in your head. Of course I'm going to be concerned when the sheriff comes around asking after you." Tears welled in her eyes. "You and Sadie are all I have left." She stood and reached for the screen door. "Just don't do anything foolish."

Alone again, Henry felt like a rat. He wished he could talk this out with his father.

Dad always knew how to put things in perspective, how to make sense of whatever Henry was going through. He headed for his room. Mom might not like what he was doing, but he was doing it for her. Surely that made it okay.

The next morning Margaret answered Emily's phone. Angie Talbot was on the line, sounding annoyed.

"Well, hey, Angie, are you looking for Emily?"

"No, I'm looking for Frank, and I can't find him anywhere." Margaret thought she could almost hear the tap, tap of Angie's foot. "He's usually here of a morning, but today I haven't seen hide nor hair of him." Her voice dropped low. "You don't think he's got another girl, do you?"

Margaret stifled a laugh. "No, ma'am. Maybe he had an errand to run."

"He always tells me if he's going to be late." Angie huffed. "This is just not like him." Her voice changed again. This time she sounded on the verge of tears. "What should I do?"

"Let me get Emily for you."

Ten minutes later Emily hung up the phone and told Margaret they were going over to see Angie. Mayfair was along again, so all three got into the car, and Margaret drove them to Angie's rambling house.

"She sounded awfully upset," Margaret said. "Do you think something's wrong with Frank? Should we call the sheriff?"

"Not yet," Emily said. "I think I may know what's going on, but just keep driving, and we'll see what's what in short order."

When they got to the house, they headed inside and found Frank trying to soothe an agitated Angie.

"Hey, there," he greeted them. "Might not be the best time for a visit."

Emily bustled in and coaxed Angie onto the sofa alongside Mayfair and got her calmed down.

"She called us worried about you," explained Margaret. "She was so upset, Emily thought we'd better come on over."

Frank sighed and rubbed his hand over his eyes, then motioned toward the kitchen. Emily joined them.

"I've got her settled down in there telling Mayfair how to make homemade soap. She's in quite a dither this morning. Frank, do you need to tell us anything?"

"Guessed it, have you? Well, I don't suppose I could have kept it a secret forever. It's part of the reason I want to marry her." He held up a hand. "Just part, mind you. I love her something fierce."

Margaret felt confused. Clearly something was wrong with Angie, but at the same time here was a man professing his love. She'd never encountered anything quite like it.

"She's slipping, isn't she?" Emily squeezed Frank's arm.

"I'm afraid so." He hung his head. "I told myself it was just the forgetfulness that comes with old age for a long time, but I'm afraid it's worse than that. Might even be that Alzheimer's."

"Oh, Frank. I'm so sorry." Emily patted his arm. "What can we do?"

"Well, I've been trying to keep folks from knowing. She'd hate it if anyone felt sorry for her or treated her different. But it's getting harder." He ran a hand through his snowy white hair, standing it on end.

"Times like this morning. I told her over and over I'd be late today. Got her to repeat it back to me so many times I thought she might get aggravated and take a swing at me. But then she goes and forgets. It's like the morning dew. As soon as the sun touches it — poof." He touched his gnarled fingertips together and flung them apart. "Gone."

"If you need to go someplace, maybe Margaret or I could come sit with Angie, remind

71

her where you are until you get back."

"It'd be a help. I don't much go anywhere without her, but every once in a while something comes up."

Margaret watched the old man's shoulders sag and thought for the first time that he really did look old. She couldn't believe he was planning to marry someone who was losing her mind. She felt rude asking, but couldn't help herself.

"Why are you marrying her if she's only going to get worse?" She wanted to take the words back once Frank settled his gaze on her, but instead she dug deeper. "I mean, from what I hear about that disease, she'll get to where she doesn't even know you."

"I'll know her," Frank said, sadness weighting his eyes. "No matter what, I'll always know her."

Margaret felt tears gather behind her eyes, but she willed them away. This was silly. If some foolish old man wanted to saddle himself with a crazy old woman, who was she to care one way or another? The Christian thing to do was to come sit with Angie once in a while and remind her what her own name was. If Frank wanted to throw away what little time he had left, it was no business of hers.

Emily wrapped an arm around Frank's

waist and squeezed. "You're a good man, Frank Post."

"Not really," he said. "Just selfish." He leaned over to squeeze Emily in return and then straightened his shirt front. "I thank you for coming over to check on Angie and for offering to sit with her if need be. It surely is a comfort to have good neighbors."

"Don't think a thing of it," Emily said.

Margaret followed Emily back into the sitting room, where she was surprised to see Angie and Mayfair sitting and whispering with their heads touching. Mayfair didn't like to be touched by just anyone. They were completely absorbed in their conversation and didn't seem to hear the others enter the room.

"Mayfair, I think it's time to head home," Margaret said.

Mayfair finished what she was saying to Angie and lifted her head to look at her sister. "Okay." Her eyes looked a little glassy.

Margaret felt the oddest wave of possessiveness wash over her. What had Angie done to deserve her sister's close attention? She suddenly wanted to take Mayfair by the hand and not stop until they were safe in their bedroom at home with the door locked.

As they drove back to Emily's, Mayfair

seemed even quieter than usual. Margaret glanced in the rearview mirror and saw that her sister had her head back and her eyes closed.

"You okay, sweetie?"

No response. Margaret pulled over and turned around for a better look. Mayfair's skin was beaded with sweat. Margaret touched her, and Mayfair jerked away, shaking.

"Sweetheart, I want you to eat this."

Margaret fumbled with the candy wrapper. Her fingers couldn't seem to get it undone, but finally the candy popped out. Mayfair grumbled but let Margaret place the sweet in her mouth.

"Suck on it. Get all that good sugar going. Isn't it yummy?"

Mayfair opened her eyes. "I don't feel good."

"I know. The candy will make you feel better. Here, eat another one as soon as you finish that."

Mayfair sighed and took the second peppermint.

"As soon as you finish them both, you can take a nap, and then we'll get you a snack back at Emily's. Okay?"

Mayfair nodded and obediently sucked on the candy. Her color was better, and the sweat had dried, but she looked dazed.

Margaret turned back to the front and restarted the car. As she pulled out, Emily reached over to pat her knee.

"You're a good big sister. She's lucky to have you."

"Thanks for saying so, but I wonder what made her sugar drop. She had her shot and a good breakfast right on time. That shouldn't have happened." Margaret glanced in the rearview mirror again, thinking she was the lucky one and maybe Frank wasn't such a fool after all.

Henry stalked through the living room where Mom sat watching the evening news, Dad's spot next to her hopelessly empty. He could feel her eyes following him, but he kept moving. He opened the front door and clicked it closed behind him. The disapproval was tangible. He thought he could see it like fog rolling in. But he'd made up his mind, and his mother would just have to get used to his new role as provider. He got in his dad's ramshackle truck and headed for the Simmons place.

Clint met him on the front porch, which was propped up at one corner by a broken crate. "Hear the sheriff's been out to see you."

"Yeah. Didn't tell him anything."

Clint squinted at Henry, working his jaw under a scraggly, graying beard. He spit a stream of tobacco juice into the yard. "You sure about that?"

"You accusing me of something?" He didn't know why it mattered, but he wanted the moonshiner to respect him.

Clint flicked an eyebrow and worked his jaw some more. "I reckon not. I reckon if you'd said anything, Pendleton would've been out here by now."

Henry stepped onto the porch and looked the old man in the eye, trying to keep the shiver of fear at bay. "Reckon you can trust me enough to give me some paying work?"

Clint looked thoughtful, laughed, and then slapped Henry — hard — on the back.

"Come on into the house. Charlie's awful pitiful since they took that bullet out of his leg."

Inside, the house was dark and hazy, a combination of wood-smoke leaking from a badly drawing chimney and cigarette smoke from Charlie. Henry smothered a cough.

"Hey, there, Henry-boy," Charlie slurred. It was clear he'd been imbibing in the family recipe. "Come on over here and have a drink with me." He waved broad and loose. "Purely medicinal for me, but you go on and get drunk if you want to."

Henry picked up a pint jar that looked none too clean, and Charlie sloshed some moonshine in it. Henry figured the alcohol would kill anything in the glass. He took a swallow and wrestled it down, working hard not to gasp at the fire.

"Don't be hitting that stuff too hard there, Henry," Clint said. "Might be I have a job for you tonight."

Henry put some swagger in his voice. "What would that be?"

"Since Charlie got shot in his gas-pedal leg, I'm short a driver. Need a delivery made over toward Blanding. Think you could handle it?"

"Reckon I could. When you need it done?"

"Tonight. But Pendleton's supposed to have some extra deputies out after the other night's altercation. You got nerve enough to drive through a checkpoint?"

Henry took another slug of moonshine and found it went down a little easier. "No problem."

Clint grinned. "There's a hundred bucks in it for you." He paused. "Just remember, you'll be owing me for anything you lose between here and Blanding."

Henry swallowed hard. His throat felt tight. He coughed and spit. "Since I won't lose anything, that won't be a problem."

Clint laughed, but it didn't sound pleasant. He slapped Henry on the back again and hollered for Harold. Charlie's younger brother appeared from a back room. "Load the goods in Henry's truck. Throw some hay and those old burlap sacks in there to cover it up. Henry, here, is feeling lucky."

Ten minutes later Henry walked out to his truck, feeling anything but lucky.

Henry didn't see the sheriff's car parked on a side road in the dark, but whoever was inside saw him approaching and flashed the blue lights. For a minute, Henry felt as though the cab of the truck had emptied of oxygen. Then he took a ragged breath and eased to a stop just shy of the dirt drive where the cruiser sat. Sheriff Pendleton got out and walked over to the driver's side window, which Henry rolled down as cold air poured over him.

"Howdy, Henry. Thought that must be you driving Casewell's old truck."

"Yeah, Dad gave it to me a while back." Henry suddenly felt as if his father might be there in the truck with him. How many times had they ridden, side-by-side, on this bench seat? It was an uncomfortable sensation.

"Glad to see you're not with any of those Simmons boys. I heard a rumor they might try and take over one of the Waites' runs to Blanding. Thought I might see one of 'em come through here this evening. Not near the demand for moonshine there used to be, but some of the old folks still have a taste for it. Especially that stuff Clint Simmons makes. He seems to have a steady following."

"Ain't seen anyone on the road much," Henry said. He was grateful for the winter jacket that hid where he must have sweated through his denim shirt by now.

"Where you headed?"

Henry's brain felt scrambled. If he said Blanding it might make Sheriff Pendleton suspicious, and there wasn't really anywhere else he could be headed on this road. He remembered his fiddle case sitting in the floorboards.

"Thought I'd see if I could find a little music — join in with my fiddle," he said, indicating the instrument with a tilt of his head. The feeling his father was there washed over him again, and his face felt hot, his eyes gritty. He gripped the steering wheel hard and ducked his head. He was tougher than this.

But the show of emotion seemed to set

the sheriff back a bit. He bowed his head and slapped the door of the truck once, twice. "This must be a hard time for you, Henry. I hope you know how sorry I am about your dad."

"Yes, sir." It was all Henry could manage.

"Still, you might look for another road to drive down if you want to avoid trouble. Like I told you before, I'd hate to find you tangled up in the Simmons business. A little moonshine I can overlook, but seems they might be branching out into . . ." He paused. "Meaner stuff."

"I appreciate that. Guess I won't stay out too late. Mom will be worried if I'm gone overlong."

Sheriff Pendleton looked Henry in the eye and then glanced at the bed of the truck. "You hauling hay for someone?"

"Grandma's looking to get a milk cow." The words were there almost before Henry thought them. He held his breath, astonished at his own quick thinking.

"That so? Seems like she used to win ribbons for her butter at the county fair. Tell her if she has extra I'd be glad to pay a fair price for it."

"I'll let her know," Henry said. He shifted the truck into gear and began to ease away.

"And, Henry."

He looked back at the sheriff, who stood with thumbs hooked in his belt. "Yes, sir?"

"You be careful now."

Henry pulled away, using every ounce of restraint he had to keep from pressing the gas pedal to the floor. He tried to whistle, but it was shrill and off key, sharp against the emptiness of the cab. He wondered what the sheriff meant about the Simmonses getting into "meaner stuff." He tried to shake the whole thing off and noticed the sense he'd had of his father being present was gone now. And he found the absence worse than seeing blue lights flashing in the rearview mirror.

6

Margaret had the day off, and she wasn't quite sure what to do with it. Typically, she went to Emily's on Saturday, Monday, and Thursday, although sometimes she went other days, as well. Emily paid her by the week and had initially protested when Margaret came extra, but eventually seemed to understand that Margaret was happier on the farm than at home. The extra days became "visiting" days, and Mayfair came along after school and on the weekends.

But this afternoon both girls were at home. Mayfair curled in the window seat, reading, and Margaret sat at the desk they shared, a book of poetry by William Butler Yeats open to "The Wild Swans at Coole." Dad was still at work, and Mom had gone to her bridge club, where she would drink too much and come home weepy. But for the moment, all was peace.

"Mayfair, let's do something together this

afternoon." She turned around and leaned over the back of her chair. "What do you feel like doing?"

Mayfair read to the end of the sentence or maybe the paragraph, placed a slip of paper in her book, and closed its covers before turning her attention to her sister. "I'd like to go see Aunt Angie."

Margaret smiled at Mayfair's use of "aunt." Lots of folks called Angie that as a way of showing respect, but Margaret had gotten out of the habit once she was eighteen or so.

"Sounds good. The sun's out, and it's a beautiful day for a drive in the country."

Mayfair smiled and hopped off the window seat to get her shoes from the closet tucked under the eaves. Margaret trailed behind her. Somehow she felt light today, as if good things might happen. She hummed as she prepared to head out and tried to think if there was anything they could take to Angie. Her mother didn't believe anyone should eat sweets — least of all her diabetic daughter — so there were no cake or cookies to take along. She remembered the two jars of grape jelly Emily had sent home with them last fall when they helped make it. Only one jar had been opened. Margaret fetched the second pint jar, tied one of

Mayfair's hair ribbons around it, and tucked it into the pocket of her winter coat.

Frank answered the door at Angie's house. He ushered the girls in with a finger to his lips. "Angie's having her afternoon constitutional, but she'll be up any minute, and I know she'll be glad to see you."

"Frank Post, I hear you whispering in there. You bring whoever that is on into the parlor."

Frank grinned. "Guess she's up. You girls shed your coats and come on into the house."

Angie was settling into a wing-backed armchair in the front room. She smoothed her skirt over her knees and motioned for the sisters to sit on the sofa. "Girls, I'm so glad to see you. Did Emily come with you?"

"No, ma'am. We'll see her again tomorrow."

"I was hoping she'd stop by and save me the trouble of calling on her."

"Do you want me to take her a message?" Margaret asked.

"Oh no. I'll get Frank to haul me over there or maybe invite her to the house for some pound cake. I wanted to let her know how sorry I am about that call I made the other day." Angie tapped her fingers against the arm of the chair. "It was the oddest thing. My mind was muddled so I couldn't keep track of anything, but I'm clear as a bell now, and I wanted her to know it won't happen again."

"I'm sure she didn't mind a bit," Margaret said.

"Nonetheless, I'd like to clarify things. I apologize for dragging you girls out, as well. It was unconscionable, and I'm ashamed of myself."

"It's all right, Aunt Angie." Mayfair moved to Angie and knelt at her feet. "It won't ever happen again, and that's the main thing."

Angie ran a hand over Mayfair's soft hair. Margaret tried not to be jealous of her sister's rich brown hair that hung in silken waves past her shoulders. She was surprised Mayfair let Angie pet her that way.

"Thank you, child. I know you're right."

Mayfair settled there and leaned against Angie's knee as they talked about the weather and how nice it would be if Emily really did get a cow. Angie talked about churning butter in a stone crock with a round dasher — up and down for what seemed like ages. Margaret enjoyed hearing about how things used to be done and wished she could learn. Who knew? Once Emily got a cow, maybe she would learn, though hopefully things were a bit more modern now.

When the visit drew to a close, Angie excused herself and disappeared into her bedroom. Frank walked the girls to the door and helped them on with their coats.

"I don't understand it," he said. "I was sure there was nothing to be done for — well, for the way Angie's mind was slipping." He shook his head. "But here lately, she's sharp as she ever was, maybe sharper. I just can't explain it, but I surely am grateful."

"Do you think it'll last?" Margaret asked.

"I hope so. But I'm not taking it for granted, just in case it doesn't."

The girls set out in the gathering dusk, driving in silence for a good while. Margaret glanced at her watch. It was time for Mayfair to eat and have her evening insulin shot.

"She really is better now."

"Who?" Margaret was surprised. Mayfair didn't often begin a conversation.

"Aunt Angie. Her mind is better."

"How do you know?"

Mayfair squinted up at the stars popping out one by one. She was silent so long Margaret thought the conversation might be over.

"I can just feel it. It's like when you work a puzzle and someone tries to put in the wrong piece. You can tell something's funny, and when you take that piece out and find the one that fits there . . ." Margaret was driving with one hand. Mayfair reached over to intertwine her fingers with her sister's. "Well, it feels right."

Margaret didn't understand what Mayfair was talking about, but she was grateful for this moment of "rightness." She noticed the warmth of her sister's hand, saw the brilliance of the stars, and listened to the insulating hum of the little car. Soon enough, they'd be home again, a place where so little ever felt right.

Henry stuffed the wad of cash in his pocket. He thought it would feel good to earn so much money with so little trouble. Well, some trouble, but sweating it out while the sheriff leaned in his window wasn't exactly digging ditches. But somehow the money felt soiled, ill-gotten. He shoved it deeper into his pocket without counting it. It wasn't so much that he trusted Clint Simmons as it was he wouldn't challenge him even if the amount was off.

Driving home in the dark, he realized the hay was still in the bed of his truck. He wondered if he was supposed to return it. Shoot, maybe he'd take it to his grandmother for this cow she wanted to get. And maybe she'd let him help pay for the animal. He'd be glad to use this money muddying his conscience to buy a cow. Might make him feel better about the whole thing.

With that thought in mind, Henry let his shoulders relax. He realized he was exhausted. Weariness settled over him, and he was grateful to finally get home and slip inside to his room. He hoped he wasn't disturbing his mother. He hoped she'd gone on to bed and was sleeping peacefully. But something inside told him she was likely lying awake worrying about him. He hardened his heart. Things changed when Dad died, and they'd both have to get used to it.

The next morning Henry woke from a fitful sleep. As tired as he'd been, he expected to sleep heavily, but indefinable dreams had kept him tossing and turning, and he rose feeling like he'd aged ten years.

"Henry, your grandmother called a little bit ago." Mom sipped coffee and eyed him as if trying to come up with a plan of attack. "She said something about going to the stockyards today."

"Yeah. I said I'd take her to find a milk cow."

Mom's face registered surprise. "Oh? You did? That's nice. Although I'm not sure she can handle a cow on her own."

Henry bristled. "She's got me. And Margaret is going to help. Don't treat her like she's old and feeble."

"That's not what I meant. I'm glad she'll have help, but what about when you go back to school?"

Henry poured coffee into a thick mug and sloshed some out onto the counter. He cursed softly and saw his mother stiffen out of the corner of his eye. He debated repeating the curse word louder but stirred a heaping spoonful of sugar into his coffee instead. "I may not go back to school. With Dad gone and Sadie off doing her own thing in Ohio, I figure you need me. Grandma, too."

This time his mother's feelings were clear in her posture. She sat up ramrod straight, her chin lifted, and her blue eyes steely. "You've decided that for sure?"

Henry set his jaw and met his mother's eyes. "Pretty sure."

"Well, then, I guess your grandmother is in luck." She got up from the table where she'd been eating toast and jelly, walked to the sink to deposit her coffee mug with a clatter, and left the room.

Henry watched her go wondering what he would do for breakfast. He thought she'd be making it when he got up. He opened a cupboard and took down a box of Corn Flakes. If he could fend for himself at school, surely he could at home. Warring emotions rose in his chest, but Henry battled them down. The best thing would be to not let himself feel much of anything. He poured cereal in a bowl and added milk. It didn't matter, he told himself. Nothing really mattered but that he fill his father's shoes, one way or another.

"Henry, I have to confess I'm a little bit excited at the prospect of getting a cow." Grandma fluttered around her living room, gathering up a head scarf and overshoes. She settled on the sofa and began donning the layers she thought she'd need for their trip to the stockyards. Henry grinned in spite of his dark mood. He liked to see his grandmother fluttering around. He'd have to keep an eye on her today.

Once they arrived at the stockyards, Henry felt happily distant from his night of delivering illegal liquor. The warehouse-sized barn was a maze of cattle, pigs, horses, sheep, and other animals, with more holding pens in the fields out back. He breathed in the earthy, pungent aroma. It smelled like warm animal hides, manure, and grain, with a faint hint of popcorn from the concession booth out front. It was oddly appealing.

Henry admired a brood sow with a litter of twelve and saw a fine Angus bull that he thought would be a good cross for some Hereford cattle. He imagined which stock he'd pick out for his own farm one day.

Grandma Emily trotted down the sawdust-covered aisle straight to the milk cows. There were several on offer, and at first glance Henry couldn't see any real deficiencies with any of them. On the end, there was a smaller brown Guernsey that caught his eye and apparently appealed to his grandmother, as well. She stood at the rail and reached in to pat the cow on the neck. The animal turned soulful eyes on them, and Henry suspected his grandmother had just fallen in love.

A man and a child stood nearby, watching them.

"She's an easy milker," the man said. "Gentle as they come. Stacy here can lead her around by a ribbon tied to her halter."

"She your cow?" Henry asked.

"Yup, she's four, ripe with her second calf.

She ought to freshen around April. I always did like to birth spring calves."

"How come you're letting her go?"

"Her first calf has come up into about the best milk cow I've ever seen. We hate to let Bertie go, but we don't need two cows, and we do need the cash." He patted the cow on her haunch. "It'd set my mind at ease if I knew she was going to some good folks."

"Oh, we'd take good care of her," Grandma said.

"Mind if I take a closer look?" Henry asked.

The man unhooked the gate, and Henry stepped inside the pen. Bertie shifted slightly to make room and looked at him over her shoulder.

"She ever kick or step in the bucket?"

"Nary a time." The man grinned. "She's practically a pet."

Henry ran his hands over the cow's sides, feeling the swell of the calf. He crouched down and felt her udder — no lumps, cuts, or scars.

"See that? She'll let you handle her even without feed. Gentle as can be."

"Seems like a good 'un," Henry agreed. "How's her production?"

"More than enough for my family of five plus some to sell to the neighbors. Good butterfat, too."

Emily clapped her hands. "I'm so looking forward to making butter again."

"Well, calves from Guernseys don't sell like Holsteins, but then again, Holsteins can be a little more difficult, and they produce way more milk than we could ever use." Henry smiled at the man and child. "If we can afford her, I think Bertie may have just found a new home."

An hour later Emily completed the purchase of Bertie and arranged to have her delivered Monday morning.

"You think you can have the cowshed fit for her by then?" she asked Henry.

"Yes, ma'am."

Henry tried not to let his enthusiasm show too much, but he was itching to get back to the farm and make a few adjustments to the shed. It was little more than a roof held up by three walls with the fourth side open. There was a manger with a stanchion in one corner for holding the cow while she was milked, though it seemed like Bertie wouldn't need it. Henry wanted to put up a partial wall on the fourth side of the shed to give the cow — and whoever was milking her — added protection from the elements. A corner of the tin roof also needed to be tacked down, and he would spread fresh straw on the dirt floor. And they'd need supplies. . . .

"Henry?" His grandmother tugged at his sleeve as they walked toward his truck. "Henry, are you listening?"

"Sorry, what did you say?"

"I said we need to swing by Southern States to pick up some supplies." She ticked items off on her fingers. "I'd like a new bucket — one with a lid, some sweet feed, better get a tin of bag balm, and whatever medicines we might need. Have you learned that sort of thing yet at college?"

"Sure thing. Plus I helped in the dairy once a week, so I have a pretty good idea."

"Excellent." Emily beamed. "I'm so lucky to have you along." She hugged Henry tight, and even though he felt self-conscious about the men at the stockyards seeing such a show of affection, he allowed it.

7

Margaret gave Mayfair her morning shot before they sat down to breakfast Saturday. They were both looking forward to heading out to Emily's and hurried to finish eating. Lenore entered the room as Mayfair spooned up her last bite of oatmeal.

"Mayfair, you need to stay at home today. It's enough that Margaret hires herself out to do menial labor. I want something better for one of you."

Mayfair hung her head but didn't protest. Margaret shifted slightly so that she was between her mother and sister. A week earlier their mother claimed Mayfair wasn't fit for anything better than cleaning. What wild idea did she have today?

"She likes to come. Emily doesn't expect her to work and neither do I. She's just good company."

"I don't care." Lenore squinted at her eldest daughter, as though trying to make her out through a dirty window. "It's high time I started teaching her the finer things in life. I'm tempted to ship her off to a girls' school, where she can learn proper etiquette and how to present herself in the best society, but for now I'll handle her education."

Margaret looked at her younger sister, whose normally pale cheeks were positively ashen. She took her hand and squeezed it.

"This will be fun, sweetie. Mom is a very elegant lady, and you can learn a lot from her." Margaret's words sounded hollow in her own ears, but her mother smiled. Margaret hoped Mayfair was fooled, too.

"Thank you, dear. Now you run along. Mayfair and I are going to have a wonderful day."

Margaret released her sister's hand and walked out the door feeling as though she were leaving a mouse with a bored cat.

"Emily, do you think you'd ever want someone to live in with you?" Margaret dusted the family room while Emily sat rocking and reading *Good Housekeeping*. There was a picture of Mary Tyler Moore on the cover. Margaret wondered how she got her hair to look so perfect.

"Oh, maybe one of these days. I think having you is enough for the time being." She dropped the magazine in her lap. "Sometimes you need a moment all to yourself. When John first died, I didn't think I could stand being alone, but eventually I came to appreciate it." She sighed. "And losing a child — well, that leaves you with a whole other feeling of being alone." She closed her eyes for a moment, then looked back at Margaret. "I remind myself that we're never truly alone. God is always and ever with us."

Margaret nodded and went to put the can of furniture polish away. She supposed what Emily said was true, but there were times when she felt not just alone, but abandoned. Times when she worried what the future could possibly hold for her sister. Times when other people were around but seemed disconnected. Times like now.

"Henry's here," Emily called out. "The cow can't be far behind."

Swiping her hands against her rust-colored pants, Margaret hurried into the family room. Henry stood with his coat unfastened and gloves in his hand. In that moment Margaret was struck by how good-looking he was. He wasn't traditionally handsome — not like Robert Redford, say — but he was handsome in the way a man is when he's pleased with the world and his place in it. Margaret didn't think she'd ever seen Henry like that before.

"Jerry from the stockyard will be here any minute. I saw him coming, but he's taking it slow over the dirt road with Bertie in the back."

Margaret giggled. "Bertie?"

Henry grinned back. "I know. You'd expect Daisy or Buttercup or something like that. But Bertie it is, and I think it's stuck by now."

Margaret wished Mayfair were with them. She loved animals and would have enjoyed being here to greet Bertie. There was a clanking sound outside, and Henry hurried to help unload the cow. Emily and Margaret bundled up to go out and welcome the newest resident to the farm.

Henry and Jerry had Bertie in the side yard, leading her by a rope attached to her halter.

"Halter comes with her," Jerry said. "Owner wanted to throw it in since she's used to that particular one. You reckon you can take it from here?"

"Yup. Thanks for bringing her out," Henry said, shaking the man's hand.

Margaret eyed the cow. "She's awfully big."

Henry laughed. "She's a Guernsey, one of the smaller breeds. Course, she's pregnant."

"Oh, my goodness. Did you mean to buy a pregnant cow?"

Henry rolled his eyes. "I thought you wanted to live the farm life. Sounds like you don't know anything about it."

Margaret bristled but had to admit that she didn't even know enough to defend herself.

"You pretty much keep a milk cow pregnant, dear." Emily patted her on the arm. "That's why they keep giving milk." She turned her attention to Henry. "When is she due?"

"April," Henry said, leading her to the shed. The cow followed along like a faithful dog. She already seemed attached to Henry.

"Well, then, we'll need to dry her around the middle of February. That doesn't give us long to get good at this." She seemed to be including Margaret in the "us," which made her glad, even though she still felt like Henry and Emily were speaking a foreign language.

Emily eyed Margaret and lowered her voice before speaking. "Six to eight weeks before the calf comes you stop milking the cow. That lets all that energy go to the calf instead of our refrigerator. Don't worry.

You'll get the hang of all this."

Margaret glanced toward the cow just as she turned her head and looked back at them with long-lashed, velvety eyes. She thought the cow had things figured out better than she did. A nice place to live, people to take care of her, and clear expectations. Bertie knew exactly what to do. Eat, sleep, give milk, and have a calf every year. Margaret wished with all her heart that someone would spell out that clearly what she was meant to do.

"Time for her morning milking," Henry said, grabbing the new bucket. "Want to help?" he asked, disappearing around the half wall he'd built earlier.

Learning to milk a cow. Now that was something she could get her head around. "I'm coming," she said, swiping at her nose, which had begun to run in the cold.

Inside the shed Henry poured a can full of sweet feed into the manger, and when Bertie put her head between two upright pieces of wood, he snugged the slats in so she couldn't move.

"You have to hold her there?" Margaret asked. "I thought she'd want to be milked."

"She does. And she's so gentle, we probably could milk her with the halter tied to a post, but until she's used to us, the stanchion is a good idea."

Henry walked Margaret through the steps to ensure no dirt or bacteria got into the milk, then sent a couple of squirts onto the ground before placing the bucket under Bertie's udder.

"Here, you try," he said, offering Margaret the stool. "She needs to get used to all of us."

She sat and tentatively squeezed a teat. Nothing happened.

"Like this," Henry said, demonstrating with his hand in the air.

Margaret tried again and got a tiny trickle. Bertie shifted and tried to look over her shoulder.

"It's all right, girl." Henry patted the cow on the rump and crouched down next to Margaret. He motioned for her to grasp a teat, then wrapped his hand around hers to show her how it felt. Margaret nearly leapt from the stool. The unexpected sensation of Henry's rough fingers against the back of her hand was shocking. She'd held hands with boys before, but this was much different. Henry was all business, but at the same time he was tender — probably on account of the cow. Margaret shivered and tried to tell herself it was the cold.

"Think you've got it?" Henry released her

and stood back.

Margaret took a breath and mimicked the motion he'd shown her, even as the back of her hand continued to tingle. Milk came out in a smooth stream.

"Great job."

The praise made her flush, and she kept her face toward the cow's flank. "See how much you can do before your hands get tired."

Margaret shot him a look over her shoulder. Was that criticism? Or concern? She focused on milking, trying to shut worries about what Henry Phillips thought of her out of her mind. After a few minutes her hands did get tired, but there was a good bit of milk in the bucket.

"I guess my hands aren't used to this. Is that enough?"

"Enough for what?" Henry chuckled. "It's not about getting enough. It's about emptying the udder. It's important to strip her dry each time you milk."

He nudged Margaret, and she stood up from the stool. He sat and began to milk at twice the speed she had. In hardly any time he'd stripped the two teats closest to him and began working on the other two. Margaret flexed her hands and realized her forearms were burning from the exertion.

Emily popped her head around the corner and watched. "John had the most beautiful hands and arms," she said. "Milking all his life, plus all the other farmwork. Well, it did wonders for him."

Margaret felt strange hearing Emily share what sounded like a pretty intimate detail about her husband. She stole a glance at Henry's hands — strong and tanned, even in winter. The sensation of those fingers against the backs of hers returned, and she shoved her fists into the pockets of her coat. She was beginning to think farming might be what she was made to do, and not just because it would annoy her mother. She needed to focus on learning as much as she could about running a farm, not the inexplicable feelings stirred by a young man with wavy hair that fell into his eyes as he milked.

Henry tucked his head into Bertie's flank and breathed in the warm scents of cow, milk, hay, and grain. Grandma and Margaret were talking, and their voices supplied a soft counterpoint to the hiss of milk in the bucket. Bertie munched her grain and seemed perfectly content in her new home. And in that moment, Henry was content, too.

Why couldn't contentment like this stay? He watched the creamy milk climb the side of the pail, and a poem he read once came to mind. He couldn't remember it all, but he did remember the last two lines. *So dawn goes down to day. Nothing gold can stay.*

"What did you say?"

"Huh?" Henry jerked, and Bertie lifted one foot, then settled it again.

Margaret was suddenly very close. "I thought I heard you quoting poetry." She blushed. "Sorry, that sounds silly. It's just that I like poetry, and I could have sworn you just quoted Robert Frost."

"I guess maybe I did," Henry admitted. He stripped the last bit of milk from Bertie's udder and clicked the lid in place on the bucket. He handed it to Margaret. "You can take that on in the house. I'll take Bertie into the feedlot."

" 'Nothing Gold Can Stay,' " Margaret said. "That's the name of the poem."

"Yeah, I heard it somewhere, maybe in English class. It kind of stuck with me."

"That's one of my favorites." Margaret looked at him like she was really seeing him, and he felt a little uneasy under her scrutiny.

"You know how to skim that milk once you get inside?"

"I'll show her," Grandma chimed in.

"Come along, we'll let the cream rise and have butter before the day is out."

Margaret followed Emily toward the house, but halfway there Henry saw her stop and look back toward the cowshed. He acted like he was giving his full attention to releasing Bertie from her stanchion and attaching a lead to her halter. But he saw the look on Margaret's face. Confusion? Sadness? Whatever it was, it tugged at his heart. He turned his back and whispered soothing words to the cow. When he turned again, Margaret was gone.

Margaret arrived home to find her father ensconced in what her mother referred to as the "rumpus room" watching *The Mary Tyler Moore Show*. It must have been a funny skit, based on the tinny laughter pouring out of the speakers. Margaret moved through the house, finding no evidence of either her mother or Mayfair. She noticed her parents' door was closed. Probably Mom was in there lying down with a cool cloth on her forehead. That seemed to be her remedy for just about everything.

Margaret climbed the stairs to her bedroom, assuming that's where Mayfair must be. She hoped the day hadn't been too awful. She was eager to tell her all about

Bertie. The door of their room stood ajar, but the lights were out. Margaret moved to her bedside table and clicked on the lamp. She jumped when she saw Mayfair squinting and blinking at her from the far side of the bed. She was jammed in the corner where the bed met the wall, her knees pulled up under her chin, and her cheeks streaked from crying.

The urge to scoop her sister into her arms was almost more than Margaret could bear, but she knew it would be overwhelming, so she sat on the bed and placed one hand on her sister's knee.

"Tough day?"

Mayfair nodded and heaved a stilted sigh. "I don't think Mommy is very happy with me."

Margaret bit her tongue against ugly words. "There's a lot in this world Mom isn't happy with. You can't let that worry you."

"But she could be happy." Mayfair spoke like it was the simplest thing.

"Maybe. Maybe she doesn't want to be."

Mayfair sat up and grabbed Margaret's hand. "Yes, that's it exactly. Why would someone want to be unhappy?"

Margaret squeezed her sister's hand. "I don't know. Maybe it's easier. Maybe happiness seems like something that could disappear at any moment. Maybe it seems safer to say no to happiness than to have happiness say no to you."

She released Mayfair's hand and moved to her dresser. She began to brush her hair with vigorous strokes. One hundred times each night. If she kept it up, maybe her hair would get smoother, fuller, more lustrous. That's what her mother said she needed to do. She figured it was worth a shot. Maybe then boys would give her and her freckles a second look. Maybe then one boy in particular . . . she stopped and hung her head.

Mayfair reached for the brush and began to run it through Margaret's hair, slow and easy. Margaret felt frustration she didn't even realize she carried slide away. The rhythm of the brush across her scalp soothed her and sent tingles over her skin. Almost like Henry's touch had. She let herself remember how his hand felt over hers.

After a few moments, Margaret took the brush and invited Mayfair to sit on the bench. Mayfair not only didn't mind having her hair brushed, she seemed to really enjoy it. The younger girl smiled and slid onto the seat. Margaret ran the brush through the silken strands. Mayfair's hair wasn't just pretty, it never seemed to tangle.

"Shall I braid it?"

"Yes, please."

Margaret parted her sister's hair and wove braids over each ear. She tied them off with pink ribbons.

"There, now wash your face, get into your pajamas, and we'll read out loud until time for bed."

Mayfair stood, the sorrow Margaret had seen when she turned on the light dissipated now. Her sister smiled, grabbed Margaret in the briefest hug, and tiptoed down the stairs to the bathroom.

Yes, thought Margaret, watching her go, best not to wake Mother.

8

Henry hadn't meant to end up at the Simmonses' place again this evening. Sadie called from Ohio, and after she talked to Mom, she asked for him and lectured him about going back to school and not shaming their father. He felt heat rise in him just remembering. She'd always been kind of bossy, and while he'd mostly ignored her when it suited him, today she'd gotten under his skin. Dad hadn't even been her real father. He felt guilty as soon as that thought crossed his mind. He grabbed his fiddle and got into the truck, meaning to drive around but found his way to the Simmonses almost without thinking.

Charlie was still supposed to be laid up, but someone had made him a crutch, and he was hobbling around the house, dropping ashes from his cigarette. Henry remembered being in school with him before he dropped out. Seems like he'd been really good in science. Henry started to ask him about it and then thought better.

"You did a fine job there the other night," Clint said. "I heard the sheriff pulled you over and you talked your way out of it."

Henry puffed his chest out. "Yup. Wasn't nothin' to it."

"Reckon you could do it again? I hear the sheriff's been watching that stretch of road regular."

Henry felt a tingle of warning, but there was no way he could back down in front of these guys. He decided to hedge his bets. "Might be hard to slip through there again this soon. Sheriff might wonder why I was headed out that way again."

"What if you was in a different car?"

Henry's eyebrows rose. "All I have is the truck."

"Might let you drive the Barracuda if you think you've got the guts for it."

Henry swallowed hard and tried to think. The only thing that might be worse than getting caught with Simmonses' moonshine would be doing damage to Clint's 1968 Plymouth Barracuda. He shrugged. "That might work. Wouldn't want to risk your car, though."

"Charlie'll ride along. He can't drive, but he can keep an eye on you." Clint pulled out a cigarette and lit it with a silver Zippo. He clicked the lighter shut. "I reckon you know enough to make sure nothing happens to the car or the 'shine."

Henry swallowed and nodded once. He wondered if Clint would care if anything happened to Charlie. He sure as heck didn't care if anything happened to him.

"I'm even thinking to give you a raise in spite of your not providing your own transportation. Guess you could say it's one of those perks of employment." Clint smiled, as though he liked the sound of that. "I'm gonna give you a hundred fifty if you get back here with the car and my boy all in one piece. How long you reckon it'd take you to make that much using your college education?" He pronounced the last word "ed-u-kay-shun."

Henry didn't think Clint expected an answer, but he pondered the question, anyway. Farming cost money before you ever made anything at it. Of course, if he started out working for his grandmother and gradually took things over . . . He shook his head. Nope, this was easy money. He was in.

"You got the keys?" he asked Clint.

"Whoa there. Harold's loading the car. Remember, the back will ride low with all that liquor in there. Take 'er easy over the rough spots."

Henry wanted to roll his eyes. He'd take her however he could get her.

"Come on in here and eat a bite while you wait. Tough to run 'shine on an empty stomach."

Henry followed the older man into the kitchen, where a woman in a stained housedress stood at the stove. He pictured his own mother in her spotless slacks and blouse. She typically wore an apron in the kitchen, but Clint's woman wiped her hands on her skirt.

"You 'bout ready over there, woman?"

"Hang on. I'm taking the last of it out of the skillet now."

Henry wondered if she was the only one who got away with talking back to Clint. He wanted to ask her name and if she was Clint's wife and mother to Harold and Charlie, but he didn't think conversation — or curiosity — would be welcome.

She slid a platter piled high with fried meat and boiled potatoes onto the table, then opened a bag of Wonder Bread and set it down next to the platter. Clint gestured toward the table where Charlie was already seated and heaping his plate.

"Sit. Eat. You've got work to do."

Henry took a seat, and the woman plopped a mostly clean plate down in front of him, along with a fork. He figured he'd better eat or else he'd offend Clint and maybe his woman, too. Henry eyed her as she stirred something in the skillet — gravy, he guessed. Then again, maybe she didn't care. She looked kind of pale and gaunt, sickly. If she was, he hoped it wasn't catching. He stuck his fork in a piece of meat, since there didn't seem to be any serving utensils. After adding a couple of potatoes and a slice of bread, the woman offered him a bowl of gravy, along with a weary smile.

Henry added gravy and took a bite. Squirrel. Well, he'd eaten most every squirrel he ever shot, and this wasn't half bad. A little tough. Probably Clint's woman didn't parboil her squirrel like Grandma did. But still it was tasty. He finished what was on his plate and hoped that would satisfy his host.

"Got your fill?" Clint spoke as Harold banged open the back door.

"Aw, did you save me any?" he whined.

"Son, I ain't left you to starve yet. Your ma made aplenty. Now sit down and shut up."

Harold grabbed a squirrel leg and was eating before his rear hit the chair. Henry figured manners weren't a priority for the Simmons clan.

Clint turned his attention back to Henry as he fished a key out of his pocket. He dangled it in front of Henry but didn't offer it to him. "Boy, you sure you don't want to back out?"

Henry could see a glimmer in the old man's eyes that he didn't like. Might be Clint would like it if he chickened out. Might be there were worse things than risking his life and freedom to deliver some moonshine.

"My dad raised me to do what I say." He grabbed the key. "And so I will."

Clint laughed and tilted his chair back on two legs. "Well, then get to it."

Charlie jammed his crutch in the back along with his guitar and flopped into the passenger seat. "Bring your fiddle?"

"It's in the truck."

"Get it. There's some decent pickers out there at Jack's place, and it'll give us an excuse if the sheriff gets aholt of us."

Henry grabbed his fiddle and slid in behind the wheel. The engine started with a low rumble that stirred Henry's blood. This was a fine piece of machinery.

"We're gonna make a quick stop along the

way," Charlie said. "Pa thinks you can still make a living running moonshine, but the real money's not in liquor anymore."

Henry glanced at his friend, at least he wanted to think of Charlie as his friend. He didn't feel good about this extra stop, but he pushed down any misgivings, put the car into gear, and eased out onto the dirt road. He was itching to see what the car could do but knew better than to push it while Clint was watching. Once he hit the paved road, he slanted a look at his passenger. "Want to see what she's got?"

Charlie grinned. "Open her up."

Henry did. He didn't see the deputy's car tucked into a side road until after they shot past it. But just that glimpse made everything in him go tight, and he sent up an almost involuntary prayer that the deputy would let them go. His prayer went unanswered.

The flash of red and blue lights filled Henry's vision. He pressed the accelerator and shifted, pushing the car along the pavement, squealing the tires in the curves. The black and white kept coming, but there was no siren. Henry almost wished the deputy would make some noise; the silence seemed to press against his skull. He had a vague impression of Charlie bracing himself against the door and grinning like a crazy man, but he didn't have time to look.

Henry knew there was a side road up ahead that curved through property owned by the Prentices. It had been the main thoroughfare once upon a time, but when the county paved the roads, they straightened them out, and what was generally known as Prentice Road had been abandoned. It was probably grown over by now, but Henry had to get shut of the police car behind him.

"Hang on," he said and opened the Barracuda up as far as he dared.

Charlie gave a Rebel yell, and Henry was grateful to finally have the silence shattered. He downshifted into a turn, and when he whirled out of it braked just enough to take Prentice Road way faster than could be good for either him or the car. Charlie hollered, this time most likely because the rough ride was hard on his leg.

Henry kept the car flying over the rutted, overgrown excuse for a road. He could hear branches scraping down the sides and wondered which would be worse, getting arrested and losing Clint's load of moonshine or wrecking his car.

The road suddenly opened up into pasture on either side and Henry eased the car to a stop. He was panting, though why driving should wind him he didn't know. Charlie held his injured leg and grimaced but didn't speak.

The purr of the idling motor seemed overloud to Henry, but he didn't hear anything else. There was no sign of an approaching car, no flash of lights. He realized his hands were shaking, and he gripped the steering wheel so Charlie wouldn't notice.

"Reckon you outrun him," Charlie said. "It was a doozy of a ride, but it shore did bang my leg around."

"Sorry about that. How mad is your pa gonna be about the scratches?"

"Aw, maybe it ain't too bad. We'll look it over good once we get to Blanding." He pointed at a dilapidated barn just up ahead among some overgrown trees. "And ain't you the lucky one, anyway. You headed straight for the spot we needed to stop. Pull on up there and see if there ain't a sack under that old drum behind the house."

Henry nodded and eased the car down the dirt track, stopping to check under the rusted drum. Sure enough, there was a sack of something under there. He started to look inside, but Charlie hollered at him, and he decided he might be better off not knowing. When they finally eased back out onto pavement, Henry felt like a chicken in the middle of a wide open field with a hawk circling somewhere above.

"What if that deputy's up ahead?"

"Guess you'll have to outrun him again," Charlie said.

Henry didn't ease his grip on the wheel until they pulled into the barn in Blanding where Jack Barnett stored the bootleg liquor he sold out the back door of a rundown dive. Jack himself walked over and knocked on Henry's window with one knuckle. Henry rolled the window down.

"I wasn't sure you boys would make it through. I hear the sheriff's been patrolling every road between here and Wise on the lookout for certain folks known to make questionable deliveries out here."

Charlie opened his door and pulled himself up so he could lean against the car while favoring his bad leg. "Henry, here, outran that fool deputy. Lost him on Prentice Road."

Jack whistled. "Guess this car is as tough as it looks." He glanced at Henry. "And you must be a whole lot tougher than you look."

Henry shoved his door open, forcing Jack to step back, and then walked around the car and unlocked the trunk. Jugs of moonshine nestled there.

"You want these? Or should I take 'em on back to Clint?"

Jack laughed and slapped his leg. "Son, you take those back and your hide won't be worth a plugged nickel." He moved to the rear of the car and grabbed a jug in each hand. "Good show, though."

Henry started grabbing jugs and handing them off to Jack. All he wanted to do was get the car back to Clint and go home.

"You boys got the other, ah, merchandise?" Jack asked.

"You know it," Charlie said, dragging the sack out of the backseat.

Jack rubbed his hands together. "Now we're talking. Hey, I'm headed over to the bar after this. First one's on the house."

"Shoot fire, we ain't going to pass that up," Charlie said. "We aim to play a little, too."

Henry had no desire for a drink, but didn't see a way out of it. And it might be better to let some time pass before heading back the direction they'd just come. "Sure, whatever," he said.

Jack slapped him on the back. "Try not to get too excited, son. Might even be some girls out there this evening."

Girls, thought Henry. Well now, that might not be a bad thing.

■ ■ ■ ■

Margaret put a plate of scrambled eggs with toast in front of her mother and added some coffee to the china cup she always used. Lenore made a face and nudged the plate away.

"I don't see how I could possibly eat anything this morning." She closed her eyes and pressed her fingers to her forehead. Without opening her eyes she told Margaret to add some sugar to her coffee, then picked up the toast and nibbled one edge. "Your father and I have come to a decision."

Margaret stiffened. Her father had left the driveway of their cookie-cutter, two-story an hour earlier without mentioning anything. But then, he probably wouldn't.

"Oh?" She tried to sound noncommittal.

"Yes, it's simply ridiculous that you hire yourself out to do the common work of a maid. You should either be going to school or seriously considering marriage." Lenore's eyes were open now, and Margaret could see how bloodshot they were. "And since marriage doesn't seem likely at this point — especially with your complexion — you have a choice. Quit working for that Phillips woman and start courses at the community college, or find your own living situation."

Margaret stood as though turned to stone. She thought of the woman who turned into a pillar of salt in the Bible. What did she do? Look back at something terrible? Maybe something as terrible as her mother.

"But what about Mayfair?"

Lenore made a face as though her coffee were too bitter. "You've been babying her long enough. It's time she learned to stand on her own. With you at school I'll be able to give her my full attention."

"Have you told her?"

"I don't need to explain myself to my daughter." She placed both hands on the table and pushed to stand. She leaned there a moment, as though finding her equilibrium. "To either of my daughters. I'll expect your answer by the end of the week." She took her coffee cup and toast, leaving the room and her dirty plate behind.

Henry woke with a throbbing head and a mouth that felt like it was stuffed with cotton. He rolled over and realized he was lying in a pile of hay. It had crept under his collar and his neck itched something fierce. He scratched, but it only made things worse.

Moaning softly, he tried to sit up, though his head clearly weighed about twenty pounds. He opened his eyes as though he was afraid of what he might see. And once he got them open he did experience something between fear and dismay.

Sunlight filtered in through cracks in the walls of Jack Barnett's barn. It would have been pretty if it hadn't been shining on the Barracuda sitting in the middle of the barn with long scratches down the sides. Leaves were stuck under one windshield wiper, and mud spattered the car from front to back. Probably hiding more scratches.

Henry groaned and rubbed his temples. The noise he made must have been louder than he realized because there was an answering sound. Not a groan or a moan, more of a sigh — a distinctly feminine sigh. He turned slowly to his left and saw a woman nestled in the hay with a wool blanket pulled up around her. She shifted and stretched and opened her eyes. When she saw Henry, a slow smile spread across her face.

"Morning, lover."

Henry felt rooted to the spot. He remembered drinking too much and playing his fiddle like a man possessed. He remembered girls without near enough on for the late January weather. He remembered dancing — not something he'd ever thought he was any good at, but last night . . . Oh no. He remembered singing along with "My Eyes Adored You" while clinging to the woman in the hay beside him.

"Mornin'," he croaked. "Uh . . ."

"It's Barbara, darlin'. I don't guess we were properly introduced." She snaked her arm out from under the blanket, which fell back to expose her bare shoulder. She smiled at him in a way that made him feel like she knew him a whole lot better than he knew her.

"Uh, Henry," he said, taking her hand.

He tried to look at her without being obvious. He had a feeling she was older than he was. She had blond hair, but he could see that it was dark at her part. Smudged blue eye shadow made her eyes look bruised. Come to think of it, they looked sad, too. Henry kind of wanted to comfort her, but felt sorely in need of soothing himself.

"Don't worry none," she said, sitting up and fishing a tight sweater out from under the blanket. She pulled it on over her head. "It ain't like we're married now."

"I didn't —"

"Course, you didn't. That's the way these things usually go."

She kept stirring around in the hay and

came out with a pair of bell bottom jeans that she tugged under the blanket and wiggled into. Henry's stomach continued to knot, and although he wanted to throw up, he was pretty sure he wouldn't feel any better if he did. She stood and walked over to a pair of platform boots. He watched her hop on one foot and then the other as she pulled them on. He realized their breath was puffing in the cold air inside the barn.

"Where's your coat?"

She gave him a hard look. "Back in the bar. Don't reckon either one of us was feeling the cold much last night." She hefted the blanket and draped it around her shoulders. "Reckon this'll do for now."

Henry scrambled to his feet, wincing at the sudden movement.

"Can I take you home?"

Barbara looked him up and down real slow. "Well, ain't you sweet." She laughed. "I can walk it. Got a place across the creek with my sister. Ain't nothing but a footbridge between here and there. Don't you worry about me none." She snugged the blanket a bit tighter and headed for the door. Halfway there she turned around and looked at Henry again. "Just so you know, you was real nice to me. Can't always say that come morning."

Henry wanted to ask what she meant, but she was gone by the time he'd formulated a question. He buried his face in his hands. In exactly what way had he been nice to that girl?

Something thumped over at the car, and Henry jerked his head up — regrettably. He hobbled over to the Barracuda and peered inside. Charlie was laid out in the backseat sleeping. He must have kicked the door trying to get comfortable. Henry felt his pockets and found the key. He pushed open the wide double doors at the rear of the barn, slid behind the wheel, and started the engine. Charlie jerked to a seated position, looking like someone had stepped on his grave.

Charlie cursed and Henry felt a grim satisfaction. He was glad someone else felt as bad as he did.

"Where'd my girl go?" Charlie asked.

"What girl?" Henry eased the car out and drove around the barn to the road. He turned back toward the road home.

"Linda. Sister to that girl you were with. They might not have been the best-looking women I've ever seen, but they was willing, and that makes up for a lot."

Henry grimaced. What had he done? "I think they both went home."

"Huh. I might've been willing to slip mine a few extra bucks this morning." He giggled — a ridiculous sound. "She surely earned it. Ow! My leg's on fire this morning."

"You probably slept on it wrong," Henry said. He was dreading their arrival at Clint's house, but he didn't know what else to do but go back.

"Well, I did at least one thing right." Charlie slumped against the side window and stretched his leg along the seat. "Man, Pa is gonna skin you when he sees this car."

Henry felt that didn't deserve a response. And anyway, as bad as his head hurt, being killed by Clint Simmons might be a relief. He tried to laugh, but if anything, his mouth was dryer than before. A creek ran alongside the road. He pulled over, and Charlie cracked one eye, then grunted and settled back to sleep. Henry got out and crouched beside the stream to splash icy water on his face. It hurt, but the aftershock somehow made him feel a little clearer. He scooped up a handful of water and slurped it. Now that felt good.

Slinging droplets from his numbed fingers, Henry considered the crystal water. It was beautiful. He bet there would be moss and ferns come summer. Mayfair would appreciate how pretty this was. A smooth white stone gleamed in the shallows. He reached for it, gritting his teeth against the cold sinking into his bones. The force of the water tumbled it once, twice before he snatched it into the frigid air. He held it up and saw how it sparkled in the sun — pure and clean.

A memory of trout fishing with Dad when he was eight or nine flickered in his tired brain. They'd hiked to a remote stream, carrying their poles and other gear. Dad trusted him with the wicker creel. He remembered how it bounced against his leg as he walked. He hadn't much known what he was doing, but Dad had been patient and eventually he hooked a rainbow trout. It broke the surface, splashing water like a spray of diamonds in the sunshine. He'd nestled the trout along with two Dad caught into moss lining the bottom of the creel. That night Mom rolled the fish in cornmeal and fried it for supper. He remembered the look Dad gave him — like they were two men who had, together, conquered the wilderness.

Henry hung his head, letting misery wash over him. Dad was dead, and he'd made a mess of things with that girl last night. He listened to the music of the stream, wishing he could go back in time to that other stream and the sunshine and his father. He tucked the stone in his pocket. For once, he wouldn't blame Margaret for judging him harshly.

"Good thing she can't see me," he said as he got back in the car.

Charlie grunted and then snored. Henry had an urge to shove him out and leave him on the side of the road, but that probably wouldn't help his case with Clint. He started the car and realized it had begun to snow. There really hadn't been any snow since before Christmas. Now huge fluffy flakes drifted down, skimmed across the windshield, and whirled away. It should have been beautiful, but at the moment Henry didn't feel he deserved any kind of beauty.

9

"Child, what is gnawing at you?"

Margaret looked up from the ironing to see Emily standing in the doorway, hands propped on her hips.

"Nothing."

"Well, that just isn't so. I've never seen anyone press napkins quite so thoroughly."

Margaret dialed the heat setting back and stood the iron on the end of the ironing board. She snapped a crisp napkin in the air and folded it as though she was going to be judged on how perfectly the corners met.

"I'm just careful about things."

Emily walked over and took the napkin from Margaret and then led her to the sofa. "If you want to tell me what's troubling you, I'd be glad to listen. Goodness knows, I tamped things down enough times in my life to know how it can fester."

Margaret thumped down on the sofa and buried her face in her hands. She could stand up to meanness or indifference, but kindness undid her completely. "Mom says I have to quit my job and go to school or move out." She lifted her face. "Or I could get married, but that's not likely."

"Is she dissatisfied with your working conditions?"

"Oh no, Emily." Margaret grabbed the older woman's arm. "She thinks this kind of work is beneath her daughter. Somehow she thinks it reflects badly on her."

"What kind of work does she want you to do?" Emily placed her hand over Margaret's and patted. "I've often wondered myself at your being satisfied with something that challenges you so little."

"Mom wants me to do something that puts me in the way of marrying a doctor or a lawyer." Margaret flopped back against the sofa cushions. "She doesn't think women are supposed to *do* anything other than look good and be a credit to their parents."

"Well, then, that leaves things wide open, doesn't it?"

Margaret didn't understand. "What do you mean?"

"Lenore has offered you the chance to go to school and study whatever you want or to step out into the world on your own."

Emily clapped her hands. "Oh, the possibilities. And you're such a smart girl."

"Well, maybe, but what about Mayfair? If I leave or spend most of my time in school, no one will be around to protect her, to make sure she gets her insulin shots on time, and that she always has candy in her pocket just in case. Mom is determined to transform her into some sort of debutante."

Emily sighed and clasped her hands, looking thoughtful. "What if you took her with you?"

"I don't think Mom will let me."

"Maybe. Maybe not. Let's take this one step at a time. If Mayfair weren't in the picture, what would you want to do?"

Margaret tilted her head and squinched her eyes. "Honestly? I'd like to keep working for you and maybe help do more farming. You have chickens and now the cow, and we can put in a big garden in the spring. I'd like to make butter and can vegetables. Maybe raise and butcher another hog." She sat forward and used her hands to illustrate her words. "We could cure hams and bacon, if we had a smokehouse. Being on the farm — it just makes me feel alive and useful. I can see what I've accomplished when I look at a clean bathroom or gather the eggs I use to make a cake." She glanced at Emily and subsided back against the cushions again. "Of course, what you do with the farm is up to you."

Emily smiled and patted Margaret's knee. "I'm not opposed to doing a bit more farming, although I'm not sure about that smokehouse. But is that preparing for your future?"

"I'd save every penny I could, and one day I'd buy a little farm of my own, and Mayfair would come live with me. Maybe we'll have sheep and sell the wool or make things out of it and sell blankets or socks or something."

"No husband or children?"

"It might be nice, but I'm not counting on it."

"Well, I have an idea, but I need to ponder and pray a bit before we discuss it. Go on and finish the ironing, and I might have news for you come lunchtime."

Emily stood and disappeared into her bedroom. Margaret sat a moment, not sure what to think. Would Emily let her come live here? But if she did, Mayfair would be defenseless. How could she abandon her sister? Still, if it would somehow work out, the life she'd just described sounded like heaven. For just a moment, she let herself picture living on a farm, raising a garden, caring for animals, watching over Mayfair. They'd be their own little nation of two — independent and utterly free. Margaret stood abruptly and turned the heat up on the iron again. She glanced out the window at the falling snow and considered that daydreams were little more than snowflakes — lovely, but hopelessly fragile.

By the time Henry pulled up in front of the Simmonses' place, there was about an inch of snow on the ground and more coming down. He saw Clint at the end of the porch messing with something. The old man barely flicked a glance their way as they parked and got out of the car. Charlie half fell out of the backseat and hopped over to the porch. He must have lost his crutch somewhere in the night. Henry joined him, feeling he was about to face a firing squad.

"You boys took your sweet time making that delivery," Clint said.

Henry realized the older man was skinning out a red fox. The animal's pelt looked bright and thick. He'd get some good money for it.

Charlie struggled up the steps and flopped down on a cane-bottom chair. "We stayed for the entertainment."

"Thought you might've." Clint made a

final cut, separating the skin from the carcass. He wiped the blade of his knife on a pant leg. "Either that or you run off with my car and my money."

"We ain't that dumb, Pa," Charlie said, digging in his pocket for a wad of bills. He handed it to his father.

Clint grunted and laid the fox skin out on the porch boards so he could take the money. Henry felt an irrational urge to stroke the glossy fur. He shoved his hands in his coat pockets.

"Mighty fine pelt you've got there," Henry said. "You trap her?"

"Shot her. She's been at the chickens the last couple a nights." Clint stopped counting bills long enough to look at Henry. "Only thing I hate worse than a liar is a thief. Course that 'un," he pointed at the carcass with his chin, "is about to repay me for them chickens."

He finished counting and looked from his son to Henry. "Seems you boys are short." Clint thumbed through the bills again. "I figure there oughta be another fifty dollars in here. Don't suppose ole Jack shorted you?"

"He might've, Pa." Charlie kicked his chair back on two legs and looked unconcerned.

Henry had been afraid of what Clint would do when he saw the car, but this was a new fear coiling in his belly. He knew men had been gunned down for less than fifty dollars. He eyed the rifle leaning against the edge of the porch.

Clint's hand shot out and knocked the chair from under Charlie. "You want to try again, boy?"

Charlie yelped and lay still, grimacing and holding his hurt leg. "Could be I give some money to them girls last night."

Henry blanched. They'd been paid?

"Boy, if you ain't the dumbest cuss I ever knew." Clint whirled on Henry. "And you. Why'd you let him do a fool thing like that?"

"I didn't know." Henry held his hands out in front of him as though trying to fend off what he was hearing. "I was drinking and . . . I didn't know."

"Guess you thought she was after you for your good looks and winsome ways," Clint said with a sneer. "You got a lot to learn, and this here is lesson number one. I'm taking the fifty dollars outta your pay."

Henry tried to swallow but couldn't work up any spit. He guessed he was getting off easy, and after what he'd done the night before, he deserved much, much worse. But Clint wasn't finished.

"And I reckon you owe me another eighty for what you done to my car." He spit and peeled a twenty off the dirty roll of bills in his hand. He wadded it up and threw it at Henry's feet. "You want to drive for me again, maybe you'll be more careful."

Henry picked the money up and stuck it in his pocket. He wasn't sure he wanted to drive for Clint again, but at the same time he didn't want the moonshiner to think he'd lost his nerve. He nodded once. "Yes, sir."

Clint cackled and kicked Charlie's good leg when he'd finally managed to disentangle himself from the chair and sit up. Charlie grimaced, but didn't make a sound.

"You hear that boy? He called me 'sir.' Might be you could learn a thing or two from this one." He turned back to Henry. "Now git on home. I'll send word next time I need you."

Henry got his fiddle from the Barracuda and tried not to run to his truck. He climbed in, hoping the thing would start in the cold. He felt so desperate he actually whispered a prayer, asking God to get him out of there. The often temperamental truck started on the first try, and Henry drove home, taking care on the now slippery roads. He thought to thank God for the help, but when he considered what he'd been up to lately, he decided the truck starting was coincidence. No way would God want to help him now.

Margaret stirred some chicken soup on the stove and then reached bowls down from the cabinet, along with a box of oyster crackers. She'd used Emily's recipe, and the soup smelled wonderful — with lots of carrots, celery, egg noodles, and a chicken that had gotten too old to lay. Emily said it was best to stew a chicken that old, so they'd settled on making soup.

Emily bustled into the kitchen and poured iced tea into two glasses as they settled at the dinette with their lunch. They sat and bowed their heads.

"Father, bless this food for the nourishment of our bodies and bless the hands that prepared it. We thank thee for thy bountiful blessings. In Jesus' name, amen."

Margaret wondered if God was actually listening to Emily. She hadn't talked to Him much herself. Her mother took them to church most Sundays — the big Methodist church in town. It was the perfect opportunity for Lenore to wear her best clothes and gossip with her friends. Or people she pretended were her friends. Margaret had never gotten much out of it.

Maybe she should try going to Laurel Mountain Church with Emily.

Emily's spoon clicked against her bowl, and she reached for her tea. "Margaret, I think I may have a solution to your problem."

Margaret stirred her soup. "That would be nice, but please don't tell me I should take this opportunity to go to school and broaden my horizons or something like that. I may end up doing it, but it's just not what I want right now."

"My dear, if you truly want to learn how to run a farm, and you aren't afraid of some hard work, I might have a place for you to live."

Margaret dropped her spoon and clasped her hands in her lap to keep them from shaking. "With you?"

"Not exactly." Emily's eyes twinkled. "John's mother used to live in that little house to the east over the next rise. He kept it up while he was still alive, and as far as I know Casewell . . ." she hesitated, a cloud in her eyes. "Casewell kept an eye on it ever since. But now. Well, there's no one to look after the place."

"The little gray house?"

"Yes. There's not much to it, and I haven't been in it for years, but we can go over there

138

after lunch and see what you think."

Margaret knew what she thought. She thought it was a miracle. Now, if only she could figure out how to bring Mayfair with her.

They finished eating, although Margaret had to force the soup down, she was so excited. Then there was the tidying up, and then, since it was snowing, Margaret had to wait while Emily got on her coat, hat, scarf, boots, and mittens. Finally, they climbed into Margaret's Volkswagen Beetle and drove the short distance to the house.

Even with the new snow blanketing the roof, the house looked a bit bleak. Its windows were blank, and it seemed . . . lonesome. Margaret thought she and the house might be a good match.

Emily pulled a key out of her pocket and handed it over. "You do the honors."

Margaret inserted the key and jiggled until it turned. She opened the door into a sort of combination kitchen and dining area. It was small with linoleum on the floor and Formica on the counters. Floral-sprigged wallpaper peeled off the walls in places, and there was a dinette table with four chairs that seemed to take up too much room. Emily flipped a switch, and the overhead light blinked on with a buzz. A layer of dust lay over everything, and cobwebs draped the corners, but it wasn't anything a thorough cleaning couldn't fix.

"Looks like Casewell hadn't been here in a while." Emily brushed her mittened hand through the dust on a counter. "I doubt he even noticed the wallpaper. But a little dirt never hurt anyone."

Margaret moved through the room and saw there was a sitting room behind it and two bedrooms to the side, with a cramped bathroom in between. The sitting room had a few pieces of furniture draped with sheets. She could see a twin bed in the first bedroom and nothing but a wardrobe in the second. Everything needed a fresh coat of paint, at the very least.

"We'll have to find you some more furniture, but this should get you started." Emily stood in the doorway between the kitchen and sitting room. She turned a slow circle. "So what do you think?"

"It's perfect." Margaret pushed down a wave of emotion. "But I don't know if I can afford to pay the rent."

"Well, I assumed that might be an issue. I was thinking if you were willing to keep it clean and maybe fix it up a bit, that could serve as your rent." She walked over and looked out one of the naked windows.

"Goodness knows it needs a little life in it, and while I'm not sure I want a roommate, I would very much like a neighbor. We'll give it six months and then see. Could be you won't like it."

Margaret clasped her hands in front of her and squeezed. It was all she could do not to gather cleaning supplies and start in right this minute. "I think I'll like it very much."

"Wonderful." Emily clapped her hands. "You discuss it with your family this evening, and we'll come up with a plan to get you moved in here."

As they drove back to the house, Margaret thought there would be little "discussion" about her moving out. Her mother would probably be relieved, and her father wouldn't notice. The only thing that gave her pause was Mayfair. She needed to come up with a plan to rescue her sister.

10

Henry went to his grandmother's house. Mom would worry when he didn't come home, but he had the feeling she'd know what he'd been up to just by looking at him. He'd disappointed her enough lately. Grandma Emily, though, wouldn't push. He hoped Margaret wasn't there. He should have paid more attention to her schedule.

Henry wanted to stride in the front door like he owned the place, but instead found himself creeping in like a skunk-sprayed dog. He took off his coat and hung it on one of the hooks behind the back door, then kicked off his boots. He flopped on the sofa and tilted his head back. He remembered how, as a kid, he would kick his feet up on the back of the couch and hang his head down over the edge. It somehow made the world look like an entirely different and more mysterious place — sitting upside down.

But now maybe that was the problem. His world was a different place — completely upside down since Dad died. It dawned on him that the house was quiet. No one was home.

"Grandma?"

No answer. He closed his eyes. Where could she be? He should probably get up and look for her. She was getting old. Something might have happened. But he felt weighted down on the sofa.

The sound of people coming in the door awakened Henry, and he jerked upright from where he had slumped over. For a moment, he flashed back to childhood and being too sick to go to school. Grandma would settle him on the sofa with Sprite and saltine crackers, and they would watch game shows. He wished, for a moment, that he could go back to those days.

"I can't thank you enough, Emily. This is a perfect solution."

Margaret spoke as she came in the door unwinding her scarf. Her freckled cheeks had pinked in the cold, and snowflakes sparkled in her hair. She looked happy, and Henry thought it suited her.

"Margaret, the Lord has a plan even when we don't." Emily glanced toward the sofa. "Why, Henry, when did you pop up?"

Henry stood and cleared his throat, running a hand through his hair. "Just got here a little bit ago. I, uh, thought I'd better check on Bertie. See if I could help with the evening milking."

"Well, that's a ways off yet, but you can help us churn the butter from this morning, and we'll give you supper if you want it."

"I guess that'd be all right."

Margaret's expression dimmed a notch, and Henry wondered if she didn't want him around. But Emily was his grandmother. Margaret had less right to be here than he did. She'd just have to lump it.

"Come on then. Margaret, you skim the cream, and I'll fetch the churn."

Margaret moved into the kitchen past Henry. He thought she might say, "Hey," but she pretty much ignored him. He followed along behind the women and leaned on the counter while they bustled about.

"Where were you two?" He didn't much care, but it seemed like the obvious question.

"Over at your great-grandmother's house. Margaret is going to live there."

Henry jerked like he'd been stung. "What do you mean?"

"The little gray house. It's been sitting empty for years, and with your father gone,

144

someone needs to take care of it. Margaret needs a place of her own, and she'll be doing me a favor by keeping it up." Emily stood from where she was rummaging in a cupboard, a glass churn with its crank dasher in her hands. "And it'll be nice to have a neighbor."

"I could've taken care of it." He felt a wave of annoyance that bordered on anger.

Emily put the churn down and patted his arm. "I know, but I'm holding out hope you'll go back to school yet." She slanted a look at him. "If you're going to inherit this farm, you'll need that agriculture degree to keep it up to date."

"Inherit?"

"I've been thinking I'd leave this place to you for a while now. Might even hand it over to you early — once you earn that degree. It'd be a fine place to raise a family."

"You'd really do that?"

"I long to do that," Grandma said and patted his cheek.

His earlier annoyance gave way to something that almost felt like hope. He guessed Margaret could keep the gray house up for now. He'd want to live in the main house, anyway. Might be nice to have Margaret on hand to keep up with the housework and such. Lost in thought, he

145

almost missed it when Margaret spoke.

"I'm hoping I can find a way for Mayfair to come with me."

Henry thought of Mayfair there, moving through the little house, and it somehow made everything seem even better. "What would stop her?"

"My mother. She wants to turn her into a debutante or something."

Henry snorted. "Mayfair? But she's . . . she's not a debutante. Do we even have those in West Virginia?"

"I'm afraid so. Mom failed to transform me into a copy of herself, so now it's Mayfair's turn."

Margaret ladled the last bit of cream into the churn and then attached the top with its paddles. She handed the contraption to Henry.

"You remember how that works, don't you?" Grandma asked.

Henry rolled his eyes and began to turn the crank. "It isn't complicated." He worked the cream, trying to think how he could get Mayfair into the little house with Margaret. By the time solids had begun to form in the buttermilk, he thought he might have an idea.

Margaret, who had been doing something in another room, came back into the kitchen to check his progress.

"So, is it just about appearances with your mom?" Henry asked.

Margaret registered surprise. "Yes, that's pretty much all that matters to her."

"So we have to make her think it's somehow better for her reputation to let Mayfair live with you."

"I suppose." Margaret got out a bowl and a wooden paddle to work the butter.

"So what if you play up how much better and easier her life will be without the two of you around? She could have parties, invite people over, and never have to worry about an inconvenient kid being there."

"Mayfair usually stays out of the way and isn't any trouble. She's so quiet and shy she practically hides anyway."

"When will your mom have people over again?"

"She's hosting her bridge club tomorrow."

Henry strained the buttermilk from the churn and dumped the butter solids into Margaret's bowl. "So make sure Mayfair is inconvenient this time. Make your mom *want* to get rid of her."

Margaret began to work the butter, her brow knit. Henry left her to ponder his idea, but he thought it was pretty good. Actually made him feel kind of useful.

■ ■ ■ ■

Margaret pushed the butter against the side of the bowl over and over again, watching moisture bead up and run out. The glossy yellow surface made her think of spring and daffodils. She couldn't quite remember, but she thought there might be daffodils around the front steps of the gray house. She wanted Mayfair to be there when spring came, so they could watch for the flowers together.

Henry didn't half know what he was talking about, and at first his efforts to jump into something that was really none of his business irked Margaret. But the more she thought about what he said, the more it seemed like it might work. Just maybe not the way he was thinking.

If Mayfair was visible on Friday in all her awkward shyness, Mom would be annoyed and embarrassed. Lenore was such a social butterfly, and Mayfair was the polar opposite. Of course, there was a chance it would backfire and make her more determined to transform her daughter, but if Margaret was there to suggest removing Mayfair in the heat of the moment, it just might work.

The downside, of course, was that Mayfair would be miserable. But surely being uncomfortable for an afternoon would be worth it to leave that house and live with Margaret on the farm. She salted the butter, worked that in, and decided the plan was worth a shot. She'd tell her mother about moving out right before the first guest was set to arrive. And then the show would begin.

Margaret and her mother spoke very little, which wasn't unusual. Margaret helped get the house ready for the bridge party the way she always did, cleaning and doing most of the cooking. She figured the only reason her mother would be sorry to see her go was the loss of free labor.

The first guest was supposed to arrive at three in the afternoon. At two forty-five Margaret found her mother sitting at her dressing table applying lipstick — some hideous Moroccan Melon color. She paused when she saw her elder daughter.

"Can I help you?"

"I've decided to move out. Emily has offered me the house that John Phillips' mother used to live in."

Lenore carefully replaced the cover on her tube of lipstick and mashed her lips

149

together, opening them with a pop. "Is that so? I suppose you think life is going to be just wonderful when you have bills and responsibilities and no one to fall back on."

Margaret itched to say that at any rate life would be pleasanter, but she bit her tongue and measured her words carefully. "I didn't expect you to be supportive, but I knew you were expecting a decision."

Lenore stood, bumping her stool back with her legs. "Fine. I expect you to go then. No lingering, no dragging your feet. And just so you know, I don't appreciate having this sprung on me right before my friends arrive."

Margaret bit her lip to hide a smile. Displeasing her mother shouldn't satisfy her, but she couldn't help it. Especially since Mom would be using this tidbit of news to get sympathy from her friends when she complained about how underappreciated she was.

Lenore swished past Margaret, nose in the air. "Put the hors d'oeuvres out on the buffet."

"Oh, Mayfair is doing that."

"Mayfair? I thought she'd be tucked away somewhere."

"I knew you wanted her to work on her social skills, so I told her she needed to help this afternoon. You know, circulate and charm people."

Lenore sniffed and resumed her forward progress. "Well, that, at least, is considerate of you."

This time Margaret did smile.

In the living room the first guest had arrived. Melba Prince was the doyenne of the bridge ladies, and Margaret knew she was at the top of the list of people her mother wanted to impress. Melba perched on the sofa with Mayfair at the far end looking as though she wanted to disappear into the cushions. Her head was down, and she was tightly gripping the arm of the sofa.

Melba sprang to her feet. "I've been, ah, conversing with your, ah, lovely daughter."

"Mayfair," Lenore snapped. "Sit up, for heaven's sake." She shook her head and laughed in a way that struck Margaret as nervous. "She's a bit shy. We're working on that."

"Shy, indeed." Melba leaned closer. "A bit old for that, isn't she?"

Sparks fired in Lenore's eyes. "Yes, I suppose so. But you know how it is with young people these days." She tried to laugh, but it sounded forced, and Melba didn't join in.

Other ladies began to arrive, and Lenore tried to get Mayfair to pass refreshments.

But after she spilled Tab on two ladies and dumped a tray of cheese and crackers in Melba's lap, Lenore banished her with barely disguised rage. Mayfair fled the room, silent tears streaming down her face. Margaret noted that her mother's treatment of her youngest child seemed to have done as much damage as Mayfair's utter lack of social skills. Ladies put their heads together, and Margaret reveled in the damage the afternoon had done to her mother's reputation. She took over for Mayfair and tried not to enjoy her mother's clear discomfort.

When the last guest finally left, and Lenore went to lie down with a cool cloth and what appeared to be a tumbler of vodka, Margaret finally had time to check on Mayfair. She was curled in the middle of Margaret's bed, sleeping, but it was clear she had cried a while before sleep overtook her. Margaret felt terrible but told herself it would all be worth it if Mayfair got to come to the gray house with her.

She sat on the edge of the bed and jiggled the mattress. "Mayfair." She spoke softly, and her sister's eyelids fluttered open.

"Oh, Margaret, why didn't you stop it?"

Margaret's stomach clenched. "I'm sorry I didn't. I was hoping to upset Mother enough that she'd let you move to the little house on Emily's farm with me." She tried to smile. "And I think it might have worked. I'll go talk to her in a little bit, and we'll find out."

"I want to go with you, but it's not right to hurt Mom."

"She's hurt us often enough."

"That doesn't make it right."

Margaret wrestled with the feeling that Mayfair had a good point. But didn't the ends justify the means? "Sometimes there's no other way."

"There's always another way." Mayfair sat up and put her arms around Margaret's neck, a rare gesture. Margaret felt tears rise at her sister's touch. She told herself it was just the sweetness of the hug. But something deep down was bending inside her, and she was glad Mayfair pulled away before it broke.

11

Henry finally went home late in the afternoon the following day after sleeping on his grandmother's couch. He wondered how the bridge party was going for Margaret and Mayfair. He hoped they'd get what they wanted from Lenore. He hoped he'd get to see them around the farm more, even uptight Margaret. She was kind of growing on him. He paused as he mounted the porch steps. It seemed strange, this thinking about and maybe even caring about someone else. He wasn't sure he wanted to do that, since losing people hurt so very much.

Stepping through the front door, Henry breathed in the rich aroma of roasting meat. He felt his stomach rumble and realized he was ravenous.

His mother poked her head out of the kitchen and smiled. "Your grandmother called to let me know you were likely on your way. Supper will be ready shortly."

Henry nodded, not sure what else to do. He thought Mom would be full of questions, but she seemed to be blithely going about the business of her day. He shucked his outerwear and padded to the bathroom in sock feet. He washed his hands and face and tried to make sense of his mother's attitude. Maybe she didn't care. Or maybe she'd given up. Either way, he felt uneasy. And a little ashamed.

"Soup's on," Mom called. Henry's stomach growled in answer.

He walked into the kitchen and sat at the table. A pot roast with potatoes and carrots took center stage. A bowl of lima beans with bits of bacon and a basket of angel biscuits steamed next to the platter. His mother added a pitcher of iced tea and sat down opposite him.

"I thought you might be hungry, and I was in the mood to cook," she said. "Would you bless the meal?"

Henry froze. His father had always been the one to return the blessing. He was both troubled and pleased that his mother would ask him to say grace. He bowed his head and squeezed his hands together under the table.

"Dear Lord, thank you for this food and

for the hands that prepared it." He hesitated. There should be more than that, but he didn't know what. Dad always found plenty to say, sometimes too much as the food cooled and hunger grew. "Thank you for keeping me — us — safe. And, uh, watch over Margaret and Mayfair." Another moment of silence hung over the table. "In Jesus' name, amen."

"Thank you, son." His mother patted his arm and began dishing up the food. After they ate a moment in silence, she cleared her throat. "Can I ask you a favor, Henry?"

Henry swallowed the bite he was chewing. He had a feeling he might not like the favor. "Sure."

"If you're going to be gone . . ." She seemed to be searching for the right word. ". . . for very long — more than a day, say — can you let me know?"

"I was just —"

Mom held her hand up like a stop sign. "I'm not asking where you were or where you will be in the future. I'd appreciate knowing whether to expect you, or if I should call the sheriff because you're missing."

Henry paled at the mention of the sheriff. It could be bad if his mother called to report him missing. Maybe he should be a little more forthcoming. He speared a potato and examined it. "I guess I can do that."

His mother smiled, and he thought her shoulders dropped a notch. "I appreciate that, Henry. I really and truly do."

Henry had a sudden urge to tell her about churning butter and helping to come up with a plan to get Lenore Hoffman to let Mayfair move in with Margaret. But then he thought about Barbara shimmying into her jeans in the hay the other morning and found he really had nothing to say after all.

Margaret knocked on the bedroom door and then pushed it open without waiting for a response. Her mother made a noise from where she lay on her bed, a damp washcloth draped over her eyes.

"How are you feeling?" Margaret asked.

Lenore dropped the cloth from her face and glared. She turned the cloth over to the cool side and replaced it. "This was the worst day of my life, and it's your sister's fault."

Margaret bit back a smile. "Really? They seemed to like the food."

"But they didn't like wearing it. Mayfair is a walking disaster. It's going to take even more effort than I realized to whip her into shape. I'm exhausted just thinking about it.

I'm not even sure any respectable girls' school will take her."

Margaret felt blood rush to her cheeks, but she suppressed the urge to lash out, taking a calming breath instead. "She could always come live with me for a while. Maybe Emily could teach her a few things. Get her to the point where she'd be ready for something more."

"Emily Phillips." Margaret thought she saw her mother's lip curl. "What does she know that I can't teach that child?"

"Nothing," Margaret said quickly. "But why should you waste your time when Emily would do it without even realizing? It would save you so much time, and Mayfair would be out of your hair until she was closer to what you want."

Her mother moved the cloth and looked at Margaret. Really looked at her. For a moment, Margaret feared her mother might see her for once, but the moment passed.

"You have a point. When are you moving out there?"

"I thought I'd get started tomorrow."

Her mother flicked her hand in a dismissive gesture. "Fine. Take her with you. We'll try it for a month or two and see if there's any improvement. God knows I could use the rest. From both of you." She replaced the cloth, and Margaret assumed she'd been dismissed. It wasn't how she wanted her relationship with her mother to be, but it's how it was. She was just glad she could take Mayfair with her when she left.

The next day Henry strained the morning's milk into a pitcher in his grandmother's kitchen as he watched Margaret drive by in her Volkswagen.

"Grandma, where's Margaret going?"

"I think she planned to drop some things off at the house before coming in today. I should probably just let her stay over there all day. Goodness knows, there's work to be done."

"Anything she might need a hand with?"

Emily walked over and gave Henry a long look. "You know, I'll bet there is. She's a dab hand at cleaning, but if there are any repairs, she might need a man."

"Maybe I'll go on over there," he said, setting the milk bucket down and moving the pitcher to the refrigerator.

"I think that's a grand idea. Tell her to stay until lunchtime, then we'll take stock of what else needs doing."

Henry almost smiled. Margaret wasn't exactly a barrel of monkeys, but at least he didn't have to worry about getting arrested when he was with her. And he wanted to know if she'd managed to pry Mayfair from her mother's clutches.

Henry approached the little house at a jog as Margaret came out the front door.

"Hey," he called out. "Wait. Grandma says for you to stay over here and do whatever you need to until lunchtime."

"Oh. But it's laundry day."

Henry shrugged. "I'm just telling you what she said. Plus, I'm here to help." He suddenly felt self-conscious. "You know. If anything needs nailing together or . . . whatever."

Margaret looked him up and down as though trying to decide if he was capable of helping. He straightened his shoulders and looked down his nose at her. If she didn't want him, he wouldn't stay. He could always go see if Clint had a job.

"Okay."

"What?" Henry felt like he'd lost his place.

"Okay. If you want to help I guess I'd appreciate it. C'mon. Mayfair's at school, and a second pair of hands would be welcome."

Henry trotted into the kitchen behind her. "So it worked."

"What worked?"

"The plan to rescue your sister from the

wicked stepmother. Mother. Whatever."

Margaret bristled. "She's not wicked. Just . . . misguided."

Henry held up his hands. "Hey, no offense. Just trying to make a joke." He examined Margaret's face. "A bad one, I guess. Sorry."

"Well, if we're going to work on this place, let's get to it." Margaret clapped her hands. "The heat seems to be working. That's good. But I don't think there's any hot water. Can you look into that?"

Henry had been hoping for something more along the lines of fixing a loose shutter or hammering down some shingles, but he guessed he could figure out hot water.

"What are you going to do?"

"First I'll clean this place top to bottom. Then I'll start trying to get the old wallpaper down and maybe find some paint." Margaret held her hand up, ticking items off on her fingers. "Then I'll figure out where the furniture will go and what we're going to need to add to it. I also need to take stock of what's in the kitchen and what's missing —"

Henry laughed. "Okay, okay. I'll check on the water."

He tried the faucet in the kitchen — just cold. He went into the bathroom and tried the faucet there to the same end. The water heater sat behind the bathroom door, and he eyed it, hoping it didn't need replacing. That would be a bear of a job, not to mention expensive. He peered out and saw that Margaret was absorbed with wiping down the walls, floor to ceiling. He rolled his eyes. Cleaning walls — women.

He pushed the door halfway to and took a closer look at the water heater. It was gas, which was good. They had free gas out here. He got down on his hands and knees and removed the access panel for the pilot. Well, there you go. It was out. Of course his dad wouldn't have left the pilot burning in an unoccupied house. He smiled. It was nice to think about Dad taking care of this place. He rummaged in a cupboard and found a box of safety matches. He made the proper adjustments and lit the pilot, then adjusted the temperature control dial.

Dusting his hands, he sat on the toilet and felt satisfied with himself. That was easy enough. He should probably go out and see what else he could do, but it wouldn't hurt to let Margaret think this had taken more than a few minutes. He whistled softly and examined the caulking around the tub. Probably needed redoing. He'd pick some up next time he was in town. He thought about his father moving around this little room, around this little house. He imagined for a moment that he could put his feet down in the same places, touch the same things. It was comforting.

"How's it going?" Margaret stood in the doorway, eyebrows raised, looking a question at him.

He jumped up. "Oh, I think that'll do it. I was just giving it a minute to warm up."

"Oh. Good. Maybe you could come move some furniture while you wait."

"Sure." Henry followed her out into the sitting room. The walls were cleaner but still shabby. What they needed was paint.

For the next hour Margaret bossed Henry as he shifted the sofa, moved the dinette into the sitting room and then back into the kitchen, and moved all the bedroom furniture into just one of the two rooms. Margaret said it was so they could paint the other room before buying another bed, but Henry halfway thought it was just to aggravate him. Even so, he found he didn't really mind. He kind of liked being there with Margaret. It felt domestic. It was the first time he'd really felt relaxed since — well, since Dad died.

"Oh, my goodness." Margaret's hand flew to her mouth. "It's almost noon, and I haven't even thought what we'll eat. I meant to get back over to Emily's in time to make lunch."

Henry stretched his back out. "I don't guess it'll matter if lunch is a little late. Although I feel like I could eat my weight in hamburgers right about now."

Margaret rolled her eyes and they hurried into coats and boots and then drove back over to the main house. They walked in to find Emily bustling about the kitchen.

"I decided it was high time I cooked for you, Margaret," she said. "Consider it a housewarming gift."

Henry could see that Margaret was upset. She hung her head, then looked up and smiled as though she'd made up her mind about something. It made her look kind of pretty. Henry felt a stirring of emotion, but he brushed it aside.

"Thank you, Emily. You're far too good to me."

"Pishposh. You need someone to fuss over you a bit."

Emily slid oven mitts on her hands and pulled a tuna noodle casserole from the oven. "I put almonds on top," she said.

She placed the dish next to a tossed salad and a basket of rolls. "Wash up and let's eat."

Henry watched the women as they ate. He knew both of them carried something hard. His grandmother had lost her son and her husband before that. Margaret was leaving home and felt she had to rescue her sister from her own mother. How did they carry on the way they did? How did they know what to do next? How did they look forward without bending under the weight of what was past? How would he? He suddenly felt overwhelmed.

Pushing his plate away, Henry stood, knocking his chair back with a loud scraping sound. "I've got some things to take care of."

His grandmother looked surprised. "Why, Henry, you've hardly finished your lunch. Don't you want some cookies?"

"I'm not a kid." He felt bad as soon as the words left his mouth and tried to soften his tone. "Thanks for lunch. Don't forget to milk Bertie this evening."

He started for the door, grabbing his jacket and shrugging into it as he went. Hand on the knob he, felt more than saw Margaret behind him.

"I appreciate your help today," she said. "I hope —"

He turned without releasing his grip on the doorknob. "What do you hope, Margaret?" He really, truly wanted to know.

Margaret looked surprised. She twisted a strand of hair around her finger. "I hope you don't mind our moving into the house. I wondered if you might feel sentimental about it."

Henry felt his throat tighten. He gripped the doorknob tighter. "I guess I felt a little funny about it at first, but now . . ." He opened the door. "I guess I'm mostly glad." He slipped through the door and eased it shut before Margaret could speak again.

What was that about, Margaret wondered? She walked slowly back into the kitchen and began clearing the table.

"Is he gone?" Emily asked.

"Yes." Margaret set dishes in the sink and began running hot water over them.

"He's still struggling in so many ways. I wish I knew what to do to help him."

"I think, maybe . . ." Margaret stopped, hands unmoving in the sudsy water. "I don't know, but I think being here on the farm with us helps a little bit."

Emily smiled. "I know it helps me. Some days I wake up and think about all I've lost and wonder how I'm going to get out of bed and face it. Then I remember Bertie needs to be milked, and you girls are moving in next door, and Henry is even sadder than I am, and somehow I feel like I have a purpose." She smoothed a wrinkled hand over the tabletop. "Casewell made this table. He made it so we could gather around it to share food and love in equal measure. I don't suppose he meant to limit who would sit here."

Margaret turned back to washing the dishes so Emily wouldn't see the tears in her eyes. She'd never done anything to deserve Emily's love, and sometimes she was tempted to push it away for fear it wouldn't last. But right now, with Henry's words and his grandmother's fresh in her mind, she allowed herself to feel like maybe, just maybe, she belonged.

What was wrong with him? Henry drove aimlessly, trying to sort himself out. He'd enjoyed helping Margaret fix up the house this morning. And it was nice to sit down to a meal with people to keep him company. So why didn't he stay?

Henry felt fear bubble up in his belly but couldn't explain its source. He wanted to strike out, to do some damage, but he doubted it would make him feel any better. He wanted to pull over to the side of the road and cry, but no way was he going to do that. He turned toward the Simmons farm. Maybe he could do another run. He needed something to keep him busy. He might even get caught, might have to talk his way out of another tight spot. It would be exciting.

When he pulled up in the yard, Clint and Harold stood on the front porch, rifles slung over their shoulders. Henry walked toward them, trying to leave his slurry of emotion behind in the truck.

"Howdy, Henry. We're fixin' to do some hunting. You'd better come along," Clint said. "I've got a hankering for a piece of deer backstrap."

Hunting sounded okay. Henry hadn't been hunting since he and his dad got a deer over Thanksgiving, but he wasn't prepared. "Don't have my rifle," he said.

"Use Charlie's. He still ain't fit to hunt with that busted leg."

Harold disappeared inside the house and came back out with a .30–30 Winchester and handed it over. Henry took it and sighted through the scope at the barn. He'd be willing to bet it hadn't been zeroed in or even cleaned for that matter. He guessed he'd do well just to carry it and not take a chance on firing at anything. He pulled the worn leather sling over his shoulder and gave Clint a nod.

"You Phillips boys always did have lucky timing," Clint said and started out toward the back pasture.

Henry wondered what he meant by that, but didn't think it was worth asking. He trudged along beside Harold, who had never been much of a talker. Suited him. He felt his earlier confusion give way as the quiet of the woods and the companionship of men filled his spirit. Clint might have a mean streak, but he was a sure woodsman, moving with an almost feline grace that belied his age. And Henry knew he was a crack shot. This was better than sitting around a table listening to women gossip any day. He inhaled a lungful of crisp air and let it slip out again. Peace began to settle around him, making him think it was just the company of other men he missed.

After walking twenty minutes or so, Clint pointed out a tree stand and waved Henry up into it. He didn't much like hunting from stands but doubted Clint wanted to hear that, so he clambered up and tried to make himself comfortable on the rickety platform. Clint pointed Harold off in one direction, and he circled the other. It was clear they meant to run any deer back this way past the stand. They were leaving it up to him to do the killing. Henry felt a stab of pride at that. He'd show 'em.

He sat and tried to appreciate the fresh beauty of the late January day. Although it was still cold and a skiff of snow lay on the ground, the sun had come out, and Henry felt its warming rays. He leaned back against the trunk of the tree and wished he'd had time for a practice shot. It would be nice to know which direction the rifle was off. And surely Charlie's rifle would be off.

The silence of the woods, the warmth of the sun, and the emotions he'd been battling worked on Henry, and he dozed a little. He jerked upright, feeling disoriented and thinking it was never a good idea to nap in a tree. He rubbed his eyes and looked around when he heard something coming his way. Either a man or a deer was running through the trees in his direction. He pulled up the rifle, made sure the safety was off, and waited until he saw movement, wanting to be absolutely certain it was a deer before he pulled the trigger.

There. The deer bounded through the woods, but its flight had gone from an all-out run to more of a hopping lope. It might even slow to a walk in a minute. Henry sighted through the scope and waited for the right moment, aiming for the chest and praying the rifle wasn't too bad off. He eased his finger onto the trigger, pulled, and nothing. Misfire. Clint would be mad.

Henry's only thought was to eject the bad shell and chamber another before the deer got out of range. Even as he ejected the shell, he remembered his dad telling him to always wait at least thirty seconds in case of a hang fire. He looked in the direction of the falling shell and saw it tumble past the edge of the tree stand right before it exploded.

12

Henry woke and thought he must have drifted off in the tree stand again. Clint would skin him alive if he missed getting a deer. He moved and heard the rustling of leaves. He realized he lay sprawled on the ground. He started to sit up, and pain shot through him. Groaning, he tried to take stock of what was happening.

Hang fire. The bullet he ejected had fired outside of the gun. Fear shot through him. How badly was he hurt? He tried to pinpoint the pain. His head throbbed, and his left arm — no, hand — felt like fire. He touched his face with his right hand. It came away sticky, warm, and wet. That wasn't good.

Clint appeared in his line of vision and squatted down next to him.

"Boy, you get so excited you couldn't stay in the stand?"

"Hang fire," Henry mumbled. He worked

his jaw, but that hurt, too.

"Huh. Guess you'll know not to eject a shell right off next time."

Henry wanted to tell him he knew better this time, but he'd clearly been stupid and talking hurt too bad.

"I reckon you'll live," Clint said and put an arm under Henry's shoulders to hoist him up to a sitting position. As soon as his head was up, he wanted to lay it back down, but instead he gritted his teeth and looked at his left hand. It was bleeding, and there was a bit of shrapnel stuck in the back of it. He felt the world begin to close in and fought to stay upright. He would not pass out in front of Clint and Harold.

Clint chuckled. "Reckon you might not be as pretty as you once was, though." He pulled a mostly clean bandana out of his back pocket and handed it to Henry. "That cut on your jaw is bleeding pretty good. Reckon it might just about match the one your daddy had."

Henry clenched his sore jaw. He'd forgotten his father's scar. Dad had worn a beard off and on, and he was kind of surprised Clint knew about it. He wondered how his dad got that cut. He wondered what else he'd never have a chance to ask Dad about, and a sudden, deep longing for his father

173

sliced through him sharper than any bullet. He bit his tongue to keep from crying.

"Well, get on up. Guess you ain't fit to hunt anymore today. Might get us a squirrel or a rabbit on the way back." He helped Henry to his feet none too gently. "You sure have ruined my chances for getting venison for supper."

Henry shot him a dark look but was just as glad Clint turned the other way. Harold took the Winchester from Henry with a sympathetic glance and led the way back to the house. Henry staggered along behind the pair, hoping he could avoid the ministrations of Clint's woman. He wasn't quite ready to say so out loud, but he wanted his mother.

Perla seemed surprised when she opened the door to Margaret and Mayfair, but she invited them in with a warm smile.

"Emily wanted us to bring you some milk and eggs after Mayfair got home from school," Margaret said, handing the items over.

"I hardly know what to do with all this," Perla said. "I remember how my Aunt Delilah used to make angel cake when she had too many eggs. Of course, that was before she and Robert moved to South Carolina.

Maybe I'll hunt up her recipe."

Margaret stood near the door, Mayfair behind her shoulder, thinking to leave right away. She was eager to get back in time to make supper and return to the gray house with her sister to spend their first night.

"Won't you visit a minute?" Perla asked.

It was on Margaret's lips to say no, but Perla looked lonely, and Margaret knew about lonely, so she forced a smile and stepped inside.

"Come on into the kitchen. I was boiling water for a cup of tea." Perla smiled as she led the way.

The girls slid out of their coats and followed her into the kitchen. The kettle whistled, and Perla fussed about, filling mugs and dunking tea bags. She placed a mug in front of each of them and then uncovered a plate of brownies. Mayfair brightened and helped herself. Margaret swallowed the urge to caution her sister about eating sweets.

Margaret wanted to ask how Perla was doing since Casewell died, but couldn't think how to phrase such a question. Finally she settled on simply asking, "How are you?"

Perla's smile slipped a notch, and she fiddled with her tea bag, finally lifting it from the water and squeezing it against a spoon. "Oh, I'm all right. It's just different with Casewell gone. I never considered that he might . . ."

Margaret filled the gap as Perla trailed off. "I don't guess it's the sort of thing anyone likes to think about." She removed her teabag and stirred some sugar into her mug. "I've never really lost anyone." Now why had she shared that? "My grandparents died when I was a baby, and there really hasn't been anyone else I'm close to." She smiled at her sister. "Except Mayfair."

"I'm so sorry," Perla said.

Margaret wrinkled her brow and took a sip of tea. "Sorry? Why?"

"It's hard to lose someone you love, but I guess it's even harder if you don't have anyone to lose. I miss Casewell every day, but I wouldn't trade a moment of the time I had with him, even if it meant missing the pain."

The conversation made Margaret a little uncomfortable. "But loving someone like that, it just, well, gives them access to . . . to . . ." Margaret wasn't sure what she was trying to say.

"To your heart," Mayfair chimed in, then bit into her brownie with a look of utter contentment.

Perla smiled. "Exactly. I meant to keep

Casewell at a distance when we first met. I wasn't . . . well, I wasn't the sort of woman he should have fallen in love with, but I couldn't help myself." She smiled, and her face almost glowed. "And neither could he."

"How did you meet?"

"In church. The first time I ever saw him was in church." Perla's cheeks pinked. "I saw him look at me, and then my aunt and uncle invited him home to dinner with us, and I hardly knew what to do with myself."

"So it was love at first sight?"

"Was it? Maybe. I don't think I was capable of love just then, but it was something I craved down deep in my soul. I think we all crave that at some point. Maybe that's when we're ripe for meeting someone who can fill us up the way Casewell filled me." Her eyes glistened. She swallowed some tea. "What about you? Is there anyone special in your life?"

Margaret rolled her eyes. "No. And I don't anticipate meeting anyone anytime soon. Seems like romance is for . . ." She started to say fools, but changed her mind. "For other people."

"Oh, I hope not. You're a lovely, competent young woman. You'll be a fine catch for the right man."

Margaret took a brownie and bit into it.

Competent, yeah, that's what boys looked for. She swallowed. "Well, he'll have to come after me, because I don't have time for that kind of nonsense. I have Mayfair to take care of. I guess she's enough."

Perla gave Margaret a look that might have been pity. Which annoyed Margaret. She'd come in here to offer comfort, not receive it.

"Can I go outside?" Mayfair asked.

Margaret glanced at the sun streaming through the windows. It was a gorgeous afternoon, warm with hints of spring coming.

"Sure, I'll be out soon. It's almost time to start supper."

Mayfair grinned, grabbed her coat, and darted out the door like she expected to find a puppy or a playmate.

Perla watched the younger girl go. "You two are good for my mother-in-law. I'm glad she has you."

Margaret sighed. It was nice to know someone appreciated her.

Henry fell out of the truck at the end of the dirt drive leading to his parents' house, landing on his hands and knees. He could swear he'd seen a man disappear up a trail in the woods — a trail he'd walked with

Dad a hundred times. It looked like Dad. He knew it wasn't, but he had to stop, had to check. A white rock caught his eye — quartz — rough and square, unlike the water-worn stone he found in the stream. Dad once said something about how sometimes you could find gold mixed in with quartz — never much, but where there was quartz you should keep an eye out for something even more valuable. He managed to pick up the rock and slip it in his pocket. For some reason it felt important that he take it with him.

"Hey, Henry."

He looked toward the voice, squinting when blood ran into his eye. He staggered to his feet and reapplied Clint's handkerchief to the cut.

"Dad?"

"It's just me. Mayfair."

He saw her then as she stepped away from the shadow of an oak tree. She reached out and almost touched his bloodied hand, her fingers hovering over his battered flesh.

"Does it hurt?"

Henry tried to speak but heard himself whimper instead. He clenched his jaw. He needed to act like a man no matter how bad it hurt.

"Some," he gritted out.

He realized Mayfair was humming — some old hymn, he thought, though he couldn't place it. She looked him in the eye, which surprised him, shy as she was. He noticed gold flecks amongst the brown, and it occurred to him that he didn't hurt near as bad anymore. Probably going into shock, he thought.

Mayfair lightly touched the back of his injured hand, and the bit of metal lodged there fell out. He sighed. It was like finally getting to sit down at the end of a long day. He closed his eyes and didn't open them even when he felt Mayfair brush against the cuts on his face. It reminded him of how it felt when his mother used to lean down to tuck him in at night, her hair tickling his cheek. And then words to the hymn Mayfair was humming began to roll through his mind. *". . . When nothing else could help, love lifted me."*

Henry opened his eyes. "What did you do?"

Mayfair shrugged. "Sometimes I can help. Sometimes the hurt on the outside is easy to fix." She peered at him. "Perla and Margaret can clean you up better than I can. Let's go back to the house. Besides, I'm hungry."

Henry felt different, though he couldn't

put his finger on why. He got into the truck as Mayfair clambered in the other side. He flexed his hand and was surprised that it seemed better. The cuts were still there and plenty of dried blood, but somehow it didn't look as bad as he thought. Maybe Mayfair's getting that bit of metal out had done the trick. Maybe he'd been more scared than hurt. He glanced in the rearview mirror and saw that his face was much the same — a mess, but not quite the mess he'd thought.

Pulling up to the house, Henry considered dropping Mayfair off and heading back to his grandmother's. No need to get his mother worked up over his injuries. But even as he thought about leaving, a desire to let his mother care for him rose up and wouldn't let go. It was silly for someone his age, but he really did want the comfort only his mother could provide.

Mom pushed open the door and waved. Margaret followed and seemed to be getting ready to leave. She called out for Mayfair to come on. Henry was embarrassed for Margaret to see him like this but guessed there wasn't much he could do about it. He stepped out of the truck.

"Why, Henry, what in the world?" His mother hurried over and laid her warm hand against his cold cheek.

"Misfire," he said. "I was hunting."

"Come into the house, I'll get you cleaned up."

Mom hurried inside, but Henry stopped where Margaret stood on the porch.

"Are you all right?" she asked.

The concern in her brown eyes touched a place Henry thought he'd buried when Dad died. He swallowed and nodded. "Yeah. I thought maybe I was hurt pretty bad, but I guess it was just panic or something." He touched the cut along his jaw that now seemed shallower.

Margaret reached out, then withdrew her hand. "I'm glad you're okay." She turned to shoo Mayfair into her Volkswagen and climbed in after her. Henry watched her drive away and felt something stir when she turned to look back and wave one more time. If he didn't know better, he would call it hope.

13

Back at Emily's, Margaret shared what happened to Henry. Emily called to check on her grandson, and Margaret could tell that whatever Perla told her was reassuring.

"Well," Emily said, dropping the handset into place. "Sounds like he's going to sleep it off and be just fine." She pulled Mayfair into a side hug and gave her a brief squeeze. "So how is it that you came riding in with him?"

Mayfair shrugged one shoulder. "I felt like going for a walk. And then Henry came, and he needed help. Sometimes I can help people." She looked at Margaret. "But now I'm really hungry. I ate that brownie, but it wasn't enough."

Margaret looked hard at her sister. She was shaky and sweat dotted her forehead.

"Let me get you some juice."

She hurried into the kitchen and sloshed orange juice into a glass. Mayfair's hand shook as she accepted it. She seemed to have a hard time swallowing, but as the juice disappeared, she steadied, and Margaret felt the panic that always rose up during one of Mayfair's episodes begin to recede.

She wanted to ask Mayfair what she meant about being able to help, but her sister looked so worn out, she decided to leave it till another time.

That evening, Margaret walked in the door of their new home and felt tension slip from her shoulders. The house was quiet. There was no muffled sound of a television in her father's study. No tapping of her mother's heels on the linoleum. Only silence. Only peace. And no worries about what the evening might bring.

Margaret felt like doing something — playing gin rummy or working a puzzle — but it was clear Mayfair could barely keep her eyes open. Margaret tucked her sister in the twin bed in the bedroom and made up the sofa for herself. It was a dark, Naugahyde monstrosity that creaked and squeaked as she settled against the cushions. Maybe she could make a cover for it. It would take a lot of fabric, but might be worth it. There was a slightly musty smell, and she buried her face in the freshly laundered sheet that she'd dried outside in spite of the cold weather. Her mother preferred to use the electric dryer, claiming a clothesline looked trashy, but Margaret preferred to hang sheets out to dry unless it was raining or snowing.

Lying there, staring at the ceiling in the dark, Margaret thought about Perla meeting Casewell for the first time in church. Did they know right away? Or did they have to figure out how much they loved each other? Seemed like love should be obvious. She thought about Henry being injured and Mayfair — what did Mayfair say? That she helped Henry? Margaret wondered if being more social, more hands on like that had somehow triggered low blood sugar. Like the day they visited Angie Talbot.

She turned to face the window and tried not to fret about Mayfair. Instead, she wondered what Henry's mother meant about not being the sort of woman Casewell should have fallen in love with. Did she have some dark secret in her past? Whatever it was, Casewell must have gotten over it. She wondered if it was really worth loving someone that much only to lose them.

She considered Frank and Angie. It was weird, old people getting married when they probably wouldn't even live much longer.

Was that worth it? Why couldn't they just live together? She'd heard people talking about "free love." Although that hardly seemed to apply to two people in their nineties.

She remembered the shiver Henry's touch had sent through her when he was showing her how to milk. She thought about how he looked at her every once in a while, as though he saw something she didn't even know was there. He'd looked at her like that today, and she'd almost reached out to touch him. But she didn't care about Henry Phillips. Not like that.

Margaret tossed and turned until she finally had to get up and readjust the sheets. She moved to the window and leaned against the frame. Moonlight silvered the frosty world outside. That's how she felt — sharp and fragile, solid yet ready to shatter. She thought about how the sun would creep over the horizon in the morning and everything would soften. Maybe that's what love did — softened you. Then again, maybe love was nothing more than the thrill of moonlight sparkling on ice.

Henry woke on the sofa in his mother's house. He smelled bacon and felt hunger rise up in him. His mother had never cooked all that much, often leaving it to Dad. It kind of embarrassed him when he was younger. Most of his friends' mothers did all the cooking, but it was just the way it was, and he hadn't thought about it in a long time. He guessed his mother had no choice but to do the cooking now.

The memory of the accident in the tree stand came over him slowly. He still didn't feel all that certain about the extent of his injuries. He looked at his hand. There were cuts and marks there, but they didn't look fresh, and they hardly hurt at all. How long had he been sleeping?

He remembered Mayfair touching his face and how the burning, aching fire smoldering there eased. He remembered how Margaret almost reached out to touch him — like she wanted to, but something held her back. Probably his fault. He needed to be nicer to her. He was actually beginning to look forward to seeing her.

And then he remembered praying. He surely hadn't prayed much lately. He couldn't remember what he said, exactly, but he knew he closed his eyes and asked for something. Maybe help. Maybe healing. Maybe relief. Or had he just been wishing? Sometimes he didn't really know the difference.

He stood like an old man, expecting everything to hurt, only nothing did. He flexed his injured hand and decided there really wasn't any serious damage there. He walked around the corner to the bathroom and leaned on the sink to examine his face in the mirror. The blood on his shirt was dried and stiff. He examined the left side of his face. It looked like he'd had some bad acne and maybe walked through a briar patch. But again, the cuts were closed over and well on their way to healed. He fingered the long cut along his jaw — still tender. That was the one so like his dad's.

"Henry?" Mom's voice came from the living room, and then her head popped around the doorframe. "Oh, there you are. How are you feeling?"

"Pretty good," he said. "I thought I was hurt worse than this. Guess fear will do that to you, make you think you're hurt bad when you're just roughed up a little."

Mom opened her mouth and then closed it again as if she was going to say something but changed her mind. "You were sleeping so soundly I hated to bother you last night. I'm just glad you seem better this morning. Breakfast's about ready if you feel up to it."

His stomach rumbled as though in answer. "I guess I am," he said with a laugh. "Just let me wash up."

Mom headed back to the kitchen, and Henry ran the water until it got warm. He wet his hands and splashed water on his face. The cuts tingled a little, as though the water were antiseptic. He soaped up and rinsed off, patting his face and hands dry. He winced a little at the cut on his jaw, but nothing else hurt more than a little. He sure was lucky. And hungry. He tucked the towel back over the rod and went to the table.

"Frank and Angie have set the date."

Emily was practically dancing when Margaret and Mayfair came in Sunday morning. They were all going to Emily's church together. Margaret was kind of looking forward to it after too many Sundays in the big fancy church her mother felt suited their "station in life." The idea of a small country church appealed to her immensely.

"When?" she asked, trying not to think it had better be quick before one of them keeled over.

"Valentine's Day. Isn't that romantic? Frank says it'll save him remembering their anniversary, but I think he's a romantic deep down." Emily slipped her feet with their sensible pumps into overshoes as she talked. "Perla is going to make the cake,

189

and you and I are going to do little finger sandwiches and mints and canapés, and I don't know what all. You can help me decide."

Margaret grinned in spite of herself. She wasn't sure how she'd been roped into catering a wedding, but she didn't mind. It might even be fun. If she wasn't going to fall in love and get married, she could at least help take care of those who did.

Mayfair climbed into the back of the Volkswagen, and the three of them drove to church, where Emily knew everyone. She introduced Margaret and Mayfair but seemed to sense that neither girl was entirely comfortable meeting new people and eventually left them with Cathy Stott. Cathy was eager to tell them how her son Travis had become a doctor and had gone in with another man in a practice up near Wheeling. Margaret was glad not to have to make conversation much beyond nodding her head, but she could see where Cathy might wear someone out.

Soon enough the service started, and Margaret found herself enjoying the hymns and the enthusiasm with which the congregation sang them. As the last strains of "In the Garden" faded, the pastor rose and, without any preamble, launched into the Scripture reading.

"Whither shall I go from thy spirit? or whither shall I flee from thy presence? If I ascend up into heaven, thou art there: if I make my bed in hell, behold, thou art there. If I take the wings of the morning, and dwell in the uttermost parts of the sea; Even there shall thy hand lead me, and thy right hand shall hold me."

Margaret realized she was holding her breath. She loved the Psalms with their poetry. Somehow they spoke to her more than any story in Genesis or even the stories about Jesus ever had. She was glad the pastor opened today with pure poetry.

"If I say, Surely the darkness shall cover me; even the night shall be light about me. Yea, the darkness hideth not from thee; but the night shineth as the day: the darkness and the light are both alike to thee."

Pastor Johnston stopped and looked out over the congregation as though giving them time to absorb what he'd said. Margaret thought about the moonlight shining the other night. It hadn't been light exactly, but not dark either. She imagined God seeing dark times like that, outlined in silver, because the darkness was light to Him. She squeezed her hands in her lap and waited for more. Would there be more?

"For thou hast possessed my reins: thou hast covered me in my mother's womb. I will praise thee; for I am fearfully and wonderfully made: marvelous are thy works; and that my soul knoweth right well."

The pastor asked them to bow their heads and he prayed, but Margaret didn't hear what he said. She was thinking of those last words. They sounded like Shakespeare could have written them, but no, here they were in the Bible. *Fearfully and wonderfully made.* Who was? The one who wrote the poem? Or everyone? Surely not her. She had seen herself. She knew herself, and she was a long way from wonderfully made.

The prayer ended and Pastor Johnston began his sermon. It was about how God knew them all, deeply and personally. Knew them better than they knew themselves, and He loved them anyway. Not because they were wonderful, but because they were His and He knew the potential that lay in each and every heart. The pastor claimed that what God wanted from them was that they live up to that potential. Even in small ways.

Margaret shook her head. She doubted she had much potential, she doubted God had planned much for her, but she realized that she wanted to live up to whatever small thing He intended. She promised herself that she would figure out what it was. Taking care of Mayfair, helping Emily, learning to farm, whatever it was, she was going to give it her all. Margaret felt lighter as the service ended. For the first time in a very long time she felt like she might have some purpose, like God might — eventually — come to be pleased with her, even if her mother never was. She smiled. And it felt good.

14

Henry grabbed the phone on the second ring. Clint's drawl wasn't the most welcome sound. Henry had begun to have second thoughts about his chosen method for providing for his family but doubted Clint would care.

"Boy, ain't seen you around lately. You been avoiding me? Or maybe you're still laid up from your carelessness."

Henry ran his fingertips over the scar on his chin. More than a week after the accident he was nearly as good as new with only a few fading marks. Except for this scar — that one seemed like it would stay after all. "I've been busy," he said.

"I need you to make a run for me tonight. Got a new buyer, so this one oughta be easy. Sheriff won't be lying in wait for you."

"Guess I thought Charlie would be up and about by now. Maybe you don't need me anymore." Even the hint of disagreeing with

Clint made Henry's palms sweat.

"Charlie's doing the run to Jack's place. You'll be solo this time. You be here at six." Clint hung up, and Henry guessed he'd better go.

Over the past week, he'd been hanging around the house, helping his mom pack up some of his dad's stuff, and he'd been at his grandmother's a good bit, doing the milking, helping Margaret fix up her house, and not saying much. He liked that no one seemed to expect too much of him — maybe because of his injury. They accepted whatever he was willing to do and mostly left him alone. Well, except Margaret. She got kind of bossy sometimes, but he didn't mind that as much as he used to. Somehow he thought Clint would be more demanding.

Maybe what he needed was someone who expected something of him. He took a shower and put on decent clothes. Maybe Clint would send him someplace interesting, with music and girls. He'd take his fiddle, but this time he wouldn't drink. If he was going to get tangled up with anyone, he wanted it to be a conscious decision. He'd be making good money, regardless. Especially since Charlie wouldn't be along to mess things up. Maybe this was a blessing. The cut on his jaw tingled, and he rubbed it. Yeah, a blessing.

As soon as Clint saw Henry, he began giving him a hard time about his nearly healed wounds.

"You using some kind of miracle salve?" he asked, grabbing Henry's hand and turning it over to examine the new pink skin. Then he grabbed Henry's chin, and Henry jerked away.

"Just healed fast. That's all."

Clint looked at him sideways. "Maybe. And maybe you had some special doctoring. I hear that youngest Hoffman girl might be some kind of healer."

Henry felt a bolt of fear run through him. He'd just as soon Clint didn't know Mayfair existed.

"Way I hear it, she set Angie Talbot's mind to rights. Ain't no medicine can do that."

"That's pure gossip," Henry scoffed. He knew Clint's woman went to see the Talbots from time to time, and anyway, Wise was the kind of place where everyone knew everyone else's business.

"Maybe. 'Course seems like gossip almost always has a seed of truth buried in there somewhere." He peered at Henry's face again. "Might be that girl could do my old woman some good. She's got the female complaint."

"I don't see how she could help." Henry wanted more than anything to steer the conversation in another direction. "How about this run you want me to make? Time's a wastin'."

"In a hurry, are ya? Well, this one should be easy."

The new run turned out to be a simple drop-off. In a cemetery — no music, no girls — just an envelope of cash hidden in a tombstone. Clint gave him directions to an old graveyard adjacent to a Baptist church up north. It was dark when Henry arrived. A poor excuse for a moon lit his way. He was supposed to find a large stone that stood a good four feet tall with the name Bert Williamson inscribed on it.

Apparently Bert had been known for his moonshine when he was still living, and some of his kin, who kept up his business for a time, felt it was appropriate to honor him by giving him a hollow marker. A section at the top lifted away, and several gallons of liquor could be stored inside. The Williamsons had given up running moonshine a decade or so ago, but they still facilitated its delivery. And Charlie had arranged for the Simmons family to be the county's new supplier. Henry found that a bit odd. Seemed most moonshiners were running out of business, not finding new customers. And Charlie had never struck him as much of an entrepreneur. Oh, well, it meant money in his pocket, and that was the main thing.

Henry got out of the truck and stumbled over a footstone. He muffled a mild curse. He didn't think anyone was around, but making a lot of noise didn't seem like a good idea. He planned to find the stone and then go back to the truck for the liquor. Being in a cemetery after sunset made him feel funny. He wasn't afraid. It just felt like a place he wasn't meant to be. He stood and scanned the markers. There, one stuck up well above the others. That had to be it.

He wound his way over to the stone and found the removable section. Easy. He hurried back to the truck. Best to get this over with and head home. He was steps away from the stash of moonshine when someone said, "Howdy."

Henry yelped and grabbed at his chest.

"Oh, hey there, didn't mean to scare you," the voice continued.

A man stepped away from the front of the church, and Henry could finally see him against the dimming sky.

"You gave me a start," he said.

"Guess you didn't expect anyone to be here this time of day."

Henry could feel the tension stretching his shoulders tight. Who was this guy? And what was he doing out here? Could he be Clint's new customer? Sweat popped out under his arms, even though it was cold.

"This is my church," the man said, nodding toward the building. "I like to come out here of an evening sometimes. Spend a little time with God."

"Oh yeah. That's good." Henry waited for the man to ask what he was doing there.

"It is good. Jesus knew how important it was to spend time alone with His father. I think folks tend to overlook how important one-on-one time with God is." He stepped forward and stuck out a hand. "Raymond Sawyer. Call me Ray. I'm the pastor here."

Henry took the man's hand in the dark of the cemetery and was surprised at how warm it felt. "Nice to meet you."

"Likewise. You in a hurry?"

"No, I guess not," Henry said. His head told him to get out of there as fast as he could, but there was something about this man that appealed to him, maybe even reminded him of Dad. He wanted to keep talking.

"Come on inside. I want to show you something."

Henry followed Ray through the front door of the church. It was only a little warmer inside and smelled kind of musty with a hint of lemon furniture polish. Ray flicked on a light above the podium up front. The church was pretty simple — some rows of pews, a dais with the podium, and some chairs to one side that looked like they might be for a choir. A bare wooden cross hung on the wall above the dais. The single light caused it to cast dramatic shadows. Henry felt an urge to cross himself like he'd seen a Catholic buddy do at college.

Ray led the way up to the podium, where an immense Bible lay. He flipped to the front cover and then turned a few of the parchment pages until he came to some handwritten entries.

"Here you go — everyone who's been married, born, or died in this church since 1798."

Henry stepped up and began to turn the pages. The names went on and on. Babies being born, people getting married, old folks — sometimes not so old — dying. It was impressive. Sometimes the script was fancy; sometimes it was a barely legible scrawl. An entire community, a whole other world recorded at his fingertips. He stepped back and looked at Ray.

"It's great, but why show me?"

"You were out there in the cemetery. I figure you were looking for family. Searching for your history or some such."

"Uh, yeah. It's getting pretty dark, though. Guess I'll have to come back another time." Henry glanced at the book, looking for a name to throw out if Ray asked whose history he was after.

"Of course, there's a whole lot of history in here that goes even further back. Maybe goes back so far that you and me are kin."

Henry tried to hide his confusion. What was this guy talking about?

Ray flipped forward in the Bible and then brightened, like he'd found an unexpected surprise. "Like this here," he said. "Sometimes the good Lord whispers in my ear, and right now He says what you're looking for is more likely here than out there." He tapped the open book, then nodded toward the cemetery.

Henry wanted to walk out and be done with this crazy pastor, but he couldn't resist looking where the man's finger pointed. It was Genesis 25:34. He read the verse out loud. "Then Jacob gave Esau bread and pottage of lentils: and he did eat and drink, and rose up, and went his way: thus Esau despised his birthright."

He knit his brow and looked at Ray. "What's that mean?"

Ray shrugged. "It means ole Esau there thought his stomach mattered more than where he came from and where he was going. Come on back Sunday, and maybe I'll have a sermon on it. Now, I'd best be getting on home, and probably the same goes for you."

"Yeah, guess I'd better."

The two men walked out and Ray set off whistling down the road. Henry hopped in his truck and drove over a ridge out of sight. He sat there for fifteen minutes, then circled back and stashed the liquor inside the Williamson stone in the cemetery. One of the jugs seemed significantly lighter than the rest and Henry was tempted to check it out, but he was in too much of a hurry. He wanted nothing more than to get on home, wanted nothing more than to forget the crazy preacher who spoke in riddles.

"Frank and Angie have decided to tie the knot right there in the parlor of her house on Valentine's Day." Emily handed Margaret another stack of towels as she cleaned out the linen closet, sorting, organizing, and deciding what needed to be thrown away. "I guess we'll need enough food to feed fifty or so. It won't be a big do, but there are quite a few folks who want to wish them well."

Margaret smiled. Now that she'd gotten used to the idea, she was kind of excited about the wedding and the reception to follow. It would be nice to celebrate something, and goodness knows, she wouldn't be celebrating Valentine's Day otherwise. She even had a dress picked out to wear. Her mother had insisted on buying it last spring, even though Margaret thought it was too fancy. She'd brought it out to the little house on a whim, and now she was glad.

"If Henry's the best man, who'll be the bridesmaid?" Margaret pictured one of the older ladies of the community in some flouncy chiffon number and had to grin.

"I think she asked Perla."

Now *that* Margaret could picture. Perla might not be exactly young, but she was a beautiful woman with her still mostly blond hair and petite frame. Margaret considered her own figure. Big-boned, her mother said, as if that sounded any better. One of her girlfriends in school said she was just curvy, but when someone like Twiggy was the benchmark, it was hard to be curvy. She sighed and sorted through her stack of towels, setting the worn ones aside.

"These would make a nice rag rug for the bathroom," she said to the back of Emily's head, where she was rooting in the bottom of the closet.

Emily looked over her shoulder. "That's a wonderful idea. That can be our next project once the wedding is done." She dusted her hands and stood. "Now, I'll let you organize the nicer things while I go find the recipes I want to use. You have a better head for organization than I do."

Margaret began tucking towels, sheets, and other household items back into the closet. Fantastic. She wasn't thin or pretty or popular, but she had a head for organization. What man wouldn't want to snap her up?

Henry tried to stand still while his mother hemmed a pair of suit pants that belonged to his father. Initially, he balked at the idea of wearing Dad's suit, but then he thought about how his father was Frank's first choice for a best man, and the idea began to grow on him. It was like his father would be there in a way.

"Think I should throw Frank a bachelor's party?"

His mom removed some pins from her mouth and looked up. "I know this wedding is a bit out of the ordinary, but I don't see any reason to make fun of Frank."

Henry bristled. "I'm not making fun. He's pretty sharp. He might like to go out. I sure know some places I could take him."

Mom bowed her head, inserted one more pin, then stood and fisted her hands on her hips. "There. Take those off and stop talking nonsense. I hate to think of you knowing about such places."

"How do you know what kind of places I'm talking about? Might be I was going to take him to a church dinner." Henry stripped down to his shorts and shoved the pants at his mother. "You always want to think the worst."

"You've given me cause to think the worst of late. The sheriff stopped by again. He seems to think you might be doing some questionable work for that Simmons clan."

"What did Pendleton say?" Henry thought he'd feel tougher if he were wearing pants.

"Sheriff Pendleton, if you please. Show some respect. He was just checking up on you. He and your father were friends, and he's concerned that you're falling in with the wrong crowd." She folded the pants in her hands. "As am I."

"No one needs to check up on me, and why is it that all of a sudden everyone knows what Dad would have wanted? He should have stuck around and let me know himself."

Henry saw his mother's face fall and wished he could snatch his words out of the air. Knowing he couldn't, his instinct was to storm out and pretend he hadn't behaved like a child throwing a tantrum. Instead, he flexed his fingers and reached out to lay a hand on his mother's arm.

"I'm sorry. It's just that sometimes I feel . . ." Tears clogged his throat, and he cleared it. "I feel like he left me, left us, I guess. And it makes me mad."

Mom stepped closer and slipped an arm around his waist. "I know. Sometimes I feel the same way, that it was selfish of him to up and die. He should have loved me more than heaven." She smiled and a tear trickled down to fall on the pants she held. "But one of the things that made your father such a wonderful man was that he didn't love anyone or anything more than he loved God. He's probably having a good laugh over something with Jesus right now." She squeezed Henry. "And picturing that helps me let go. Maybe you need to find a way to let go, too."

Henry nodded, squeezed his mom back, and headed for his room, where he dressed before walking out to Dad's workshop. The stool he'd damaged the day of the funeral still sat on the bench, a layer of dust coating it. He ran a hand over the marred surface, then grabbed a hammer and knocked it to pieces. He shoved the bits of wood into the stove, found some old newspaper, shoved that in, and struck a match.

As the flames began to lick the pieces of wood, he felt a moment of satisfaction. He was taking charge, taking over, letting go, like his mother suggested. But as a leg began to blacken, regret pierced him, and he grabbed a dowel off the workbench to try to fish the leg out. He finally snagged it and flipped it onto the floor. Then he stomped on it until the embers died. Breathing heavily, he stooped to pick up the leg and yelped when it was still hot enough to burn him. He juggled it onto the workbench.

Henry stood looking at the stick of wood charred on one end. Why did he do that? Why did he do anything? Suggesting a bachelor's party for a ninety-year-old and destroying his dad's handiwork? He felt like there was something buried deep inside that was worming its way out. He was a little bit afraid of what it might be.

The hammer and chisel Henry used sat on the workbench. He picked them up, found a soft rag, and wiped them down. He returned them to their places and then began dusting the workbench and taking stock of what supplies were on hand. He found a pretty piece of birds-eye maple and turned it over and over in his hands. Dad was probably saving this for something special. Maybe he'd make a new stool out of it. Maybe he'd use the charred leg and rebuild something — a wedding gift. He ran a hand over his father's tools and began to work.

The wedding didn't take long. Angie had said she didn't want a bunch of hoorah, just a chance to speak the words that had been on her heart most of her life. Henry stood next to Frank, feeling small inside his father's suit, and his mother stood next to Angie, looking perfect.

Henry glanced over at Margaret, who sat with hands clasped looking happy — a good look for her. She had on some burgundy-colored dress with puffy sleeves and a neckline that showed off her, well, Henry turned his attention elsewhere.

After the brief ceremony, Reverend

Ashworth said a prayer and invited them all to join in the reception. Henry had asked Charlie to come play guitar along with his fiddle, and they offered up some lively entertainment for the guests. Charlie had been uneasy at first, saying he didn't expect that crowd would be excited to see him, but once the music got going, he relaxed and fit right in, even if he was sober.

Eventually they took a break, and Henry spotted Margaret standing with Mayfair in a corner of the kitchen. He guessed Mayfair wouldn't much like this crowd. He grabbed two cups of punch and headed their way.

"You two thirsty?" He stood so he blocked most of the crowd, and he could see Mayfair relax. She took the cup and smiled, which was all the reward he needed.

"It was a nice ceremony," Margaret said.

"Yeah. You, uh, look nice." He wanted to say more, to tell Margaret that he'd come to admire her in a lot of ways but couldn't quite think how to put it into words without sounding corny.

Margaret blushed under his gaze and lifted her drink too quickly, spilling a little on the front of her dress. Henry grabbed his handkerchief and dabbed at it before he thought about what he was doing. Margaret went from pink to scarlet and grabbed the cloth from him.

"I can do it."

"Sorry." Henry felt heat climbing up his neck, too. He couldn't think what to do or say when a child cried out in the other room.

Conversation stopped except for one old woman who clearly couldn't hear anything but her own voice. Henry stepped away from the girls to investigate, pushing into the sitting room. A little girl sobbed, holding her hand while her mother tried to look at it.

"Can I help?" Henry asked.

"I don't know what's the matter. She was over there near the window when she suddenly screamed bloody murder. Now she won't let me look at her hand." The mother was clearly embarrassed and exasperated.

Henry knelt down and wiped the child's tears with his thumb. "Can I take a look?"

Lower lip quivering, the little girl slowly extended her hand. There was a red welt that looked like a bee sting to Henry.

"She must have run up on a leftover wasp or something. They get warm inside and think it's spring."

"We can put baking soda on it." Margaret stood behind Henry, leaning forward to see the child's hand better. He turned his head at the sound of her voice and found himself looking right at the neckline he'd noticed earlier. He whipped his head back around.

"Sounds like a good idea. How's that sound to you?" he asked the child.

She shook her head and jerked away from Henry. He thought she looked really flushed and seemed to be sweating all of a sudden. Her cries became whimpers, and she coughed, then gasped. She seemed to be choking, but that didn't make sense.

Margaret appeared with a bowl in her hand, which she shoved at Henry. He took it as Margaret grabbed the little girl and looked at her closely. The fingers on her injured hand were already swollen, and the welt looked vicious.

"Is she allergic to bees?"

The mother's eyes widened. "I don't think so. But then again, I don't know that she's been stung before. What should we do?"

"We need to get her to the hospital. Henry, you drive." Margaret's mouth was set in a grim line and fear shot through Henry. "What's her name?"

"Amanda."

He handed the bowl back to Margaret and scooped the child into his arms, but she stiffened and seemed to fight for air. He started for the door and found Mayfair was there ahead of him. She held out her hand, and he skidded to a stop almost against his will.

Margaret nearly bumped into Henry when he stopped near the front door. She peered around him and saw Mayfair put her hand on the little girl's chest. Amanda relaxed, then took a deep breath and resumed crying, though more softly. She buried her face in Henry's shoulder and began hiccupping.

"Is she okay?" The mother was at Henry's shoulder, tugging at his arm.

"I think maybe she is." He let the child slip into her mother's arms.

"Dab some of that baking soda on there. I think that's all we'll need," the woman said.

Margaret obeyed, but the child's hand was no longer swollen, and the site of the sting was just a raised red spot.

"I think it was a false alarm, folks." Henry kind of waved at everyone who had gathered around. "She seems to be okay now."

People began moving away, resuming conversations and nibbling on the food Emily and Margaret had prepared. Frank stepped up to the little group gathered around Amanda. He started to put a hand on Mayfair's shoulder, then withdrew it.

"That was mighty interesting. Seems I've

seen miracles like that once or twice before."

"What are you talking about?" Margaret felt protectiveness swell in her breast. What was Frank suggesting?

"That child was in trouble, and then Mayfair there, well, she seemed to take the trouble away."

"Nonsense," said Margaret, moving to stand as close to her sister as possible.

"She needed help," Mayfair whispered, then added, "I'm tired."

"I guess it's about time we went home, anyhow. It was nice being part of your wedding day, Mr. Post."

Margaret asked Henry if he'd get their coats. She was afraid to leave Mayfair for even a moment. She laid a hand on her sister's shoulder and watched Henry as he went to the bedroom to dig jackets out of the pile on the bed. He'd been remarkably levelheaded with the child, and she appreciated the way he seemed to want to look after Mayfair. Plus, he looked downright dashing in a suit and tie.

"I smell popcorn."

Mayfair's voice was so small and soft Margaret barely heard it. She leaned in close. "What's that, sweetie?"

"Popcorn," Mayfair said. Then her eyes rolled, and she collapsed onto the floor like a puppet with its string severed.

Margaret dropped to her knees next to her sister as she jerked and her whole body seemed to clench. Henry was suddenly there stuffing a jacket under Mayfair's head. He shoved a chair back out of the way and grabbed Margaret's hand. She felt herself squeezing hard and supposed she should be self-conscious, but was too grateful to worry.

"She needs sugar," Margaret said.

Mayfair stopped jerking, and Margaret released Henry's hand so she could lift her sister's shoulders and hold the cup of punch someone pressed into her hand. Mayfair turned her head, but Margaret followed and managed to get her to swallow some of the sweet liquid. Her eyelids fluttered, and her hazel eyes almost seemed to glow as she gazed up at her sister.

"I'm so tired," she said. "Can we go home?"

Margaret scooped her sister into her arms, staggering a little under the weight. "Oh yes. We're going home now."

"I'll take you," Henry said.

Margaret thought to protest but realized she was shaking. It would be good to let someone else drive. "Thank you."

Guests gathered around, looking worried, so Margaret pasted a smile on her face. "I think she's okay, just a little diabetic episode. Nothing to worry about." She wondered if she was trying to reassure them or herself.

Angie appeared at her elbow with a plate. "Take some cake home with you. I'm sure she'll be fine and might like a bite later on."

Henry eased Mayfair from Margaret's arms, much to her relief. Margaret took the plate from the old woman's hand and tried to take comfort in her words. But the worried look on Angie's face didn't do much to set her mind at ease.

Margaret scrambled into the backseat of the little car, and Henry settled Mayfair in the front. Margaret sat forward, her hand on her sister's shoulder. Mayfair dozed off before they were halfway home.

Henry pulled up at the gray house and shut off the engine. He looked at Mayfair, her long lashes resting against pale cheeks.

"I hate to wake her."

"Me too. Let's sit a minute," Margaret said.

They sat in silence for several beats as Mayfair slept peacefully.

"Did she save that little girl?" Henry turned in the seat and whispered to Margaret. "Did she — heal her?"

Margaret shook her head and squeezed

her hands together. "I don't know. There have been times . . ." She let her gaze drop to Mayfair's dreaming face.

"What?"

Margaret looked him in the eye. "I think I had appendicitis. Mother said I was bellyaching and refused to take me to the doctor. It's the sickest I've ever been in my life and the pain . . ." She laid a hand on her abdomen. "Well, I thought I was going to die. I kind of hoped I would and quick, too. Then Mayfair came to me where I was lying in bed and laid her head on my belly." Margaret shifted her gaze so that she was staring out the windshield. "It was like butterfly wings brushing me inside and out. And then I was well."

"Just like that?" Henry sounded skeptical.

"Just like that." Margaret looked at him again. "And then there was Angie's memory, and I'm thinking she might have had something to do with your hand, and now this child. Mayfair talks about how she can 'help' people."

Henry kneaded his hand like maybe it ached. "Butterfly wings . . . yeah."

"And each time she does whatever she does her blood sugar takes a nosedive. I'm wondering if that's what caused the episode today. That was the worst ever." Margaret

216

brushed a strand of hair from her sister's cheek, causing her to shift and sigh.

"Let's get her inside," Henry said. "We can figure this out later."

Margaret agreed and gave silent thanks that she didn't have to do this alone. At least not today. But who knew what tomorrow would bring?

15

Margaret tucked Mayfair into bed, even though she was probably too old for it. But Mayfair seemed exhausted and didn't protest changing into a nightgown and crawling between the sheets in the middle of the afternoon. Almost immediately her breathing evened out and her face relaxed. She looked to be utterly at peace, and Margaret almost envied her.

Henry was clattering around making coffee in the kitchen when she came out. She was surprised for a moment and then realized that of course he'd know his way around the place. She slid into a kitchen chair and traced patterns across the Formica tabletop. Henry sat opposite her and looked like he wanted to say something. She had the strangest feeling he was about to take her hand when the door opened with a whoosh of cold air.

"I came as soon as I could get away," Emily said, removing a scarf from her head. "Oh, that coffee smells wonderful."

"I'll pour you a cup," Henry said, jumping to his feet. "I'll pour us all a cup."

Emily slid into his vacant chair with a sigh and grasped Margaret's hand the way Henry didn't. Margaret felt a stab of disappointment but quickly brushed it aside.

"How's Mayfair?"

"Sleeping. Tired. I think she's fine. I just wish I knew what happened."

"Has anything like this happened before?" Emily released Margaret's hand and accepted a cup of coffee from Henry.

"Not that I know of."

"Well, it looked an awful lot like the seizures my cousin Freda used to have. She was an epileptic. I was terrified of her when I was a child and didn't understand what was happening."

"But do people suddenly get epilepsy? Out of the blue like that?" Margaret tried not to wring her hands. "How serious is it?"

"I don't really know much about it, and I'm certainly not saying that's what she has. But I think we should take her to a doctor just in case."

As they talked, Henry leaned against the counter, added milk to his coffee, walked to the window where he pushed the curtains back, then returned to the counter.

"Henry, light somewhere," Emily said.

He looked startled and moved to take the third chair at the table. Then he stopped and seemed to rethink it.

"You know, I think I'll go check on Bertie, maybe gather the eggs if that needs doing."

Emily made a shooing motion with her hands. "Yes, yes. Go do the chores."

Henry shrugged into his jacket and headed out the door with a look of relief on his face.

"Just like a man," Emily laughed. "They can always find something to do outside when there are problems inside."

Margaret tried to smile, but she was scared for Mayfair. Emily patted her hand again. "Perla's coming over in a little while. We're going to watch over the two of you in shifts until we're sure Mayfair's all right. Unless your mother is coming over?" She raised an expectant eyebrow.

Margaret was relieved to have help but wished Emily hadn't brought up her mother. She had no intention of calling her parents. Her mother would either tell her to handle it herself or turn Mayfair's illness into a personal crisis. She wanted someone to help her be responsible for her sister, and she'd much rather have the Phillipses' family than her own.

"I'll be glad to see Perla," she said, dodging Emily's hint.

Emily sighed and patted Margaret's hand, as though she understood. "All right then, let's pass the time with a few hands of gin rummy." Her eyes twinkled. "We don't have to play for money, but we can if you want to."

Margaret smiled, in spite of herself. Emily was the last person to gamble.

Henry finished mucking out Bertie's stall and forked some fresh hay in. He wanted it all done before Margaret fetched the cow that evening. He liked the work, found it soothing after the strangeness of the day. He flexed the hand that had been injured when he misfired. Good as new. Had Mayfair healed it? Maybe. He guessed if she did, that was a good thing.

A scuffing sound brought Henry around to the front of the shed. Clint leaned there, his beard looking wilder than usual. He spit tobacco juice on the ground, and Henry almost spoke up. He didn't want the cow byre soiled like that.

"Where'd you come from?" he asked.

"Charlie come home from that wedding between the senior citizens. Said there was some sort of hoorah. Sounds to me like that girl's been healing folks again. Like maybe she's touched." He scratched under one arm. "Old woman could use some help like that."

"That's a load of bull." Henry tossed the pitchfork in the corner where it clanked and fell over. He didn't pick it up. "I got work to do."

Clint stood upright. "You got work to do for me is what I came for. Need another load hauled out to Jack in Blanding. His business is doing real good." Clint rubbed his hands together. "I got a load in the car now. Switch it on over to your truck. I figure you go in the afternoon like this and no one will much be looking out." He sneered at Henry. "Especially when they see a fine, upstanding boy like you out and about."

Henry picked up the pitchfork for something to do and looked at the wall as he spoke. "Can't do it today. Too much going on around here. Maybe Charlie can take it for you."

He didn't hear Clint move, just felt the older man grab a handful of shirt collar and jerk him back so that he fell hard in the middle of the shed. He sat, stunned, looking up at Clint, his tobacco-stained beard quivering.

"You hard of hearing, boy? I didn't ask a

question." Clint's hand rested on a knife sheathed on his belt. Henry hadn't noticed that before. "Now get up from there and come load the 'shine before I decide to cut your pay — or something else — in half."

Henry stood, and for a moment he felt like he could muster the strength to tell Clint no. He saw his mother's car go by out on the dirt road, probably on the way to tend Mayfair. He looked at Clint. How was it that he'd been craving this man's approval?

Clint nodded after his mom's car. "Maybe I should step on over there and look in on the ladies. See how that girl's doing. Sounds like working a healing might have took it out of her. It'd be the Christian thing to show my concern."

Climbing to his feet, Henry gave Clint a mean look. He might not have much choice in whether he made this delivery, but he could choose not to play Clint's game.

"I'll run your 'shine, but I won't have you messing with my family," he said.

Clint laughed. And rightly so, thought Henry. He's meaner than six of me.

They transferred the jugs to the bed of Henry's truck, laid a tarp over them, and then threw in a chainsaw and a few sticks of firewood.

"You got that fiddle of yourn?" Clint asked. "Seems that crowd out at Jack's liked your playing the other night. Take it along, and you'll have a good reason for being out that way."

Henry got in his truck and swung by what he now thought of as Margaret's house before he headed out. He let the ladies know he'd be gone for a while but would check back on them before bedtime.

He pulled Margaret aside as he headed back out. "Clint Simmons has been hanging around," he whispered. "Charlie was at the wedding and gave him the idea that Mayfair might be a healer." He darted a look at the bedroom door that was open a crack. Did he see Mayfair moving around? "Anyhow, I told him to get on out of here but wanted you to know just in case."

"He wouldn't do anything, would he?" Margaret asked a little too loud.

"Who wouldn't do anything?" Grandma chimed in.

"Clint Simmons," Margaret said.

Grandma made a dismissive sound. "Oh, I know Clint and Beulah from way back. He's an old goat, but he's harmless enough. And Beulah's a saint for putting up with him all these years." She waved a dismissive hand. "Why would you even mention him?"

"Henry says maybe we should keep an eye out for him." Margaret seemed to have completely missed the fact that he was trying to tell her something in confidence.

"*Pshaw.* You go on about your business, Henry, we'll be fine."

After Henry left and Emily went home, the little house seemed to swell with silence. Margaret hadn't really spent time alone with Perla before. It's not that she didn't want to, she simply wasn't sure how to. Perla always seemed so put together — and so elegant — kind of delicate and dainty. Margaret felt awkward and too tall in comparison.

Margaret looked around the plain room and wished she'd spent more time making it pretty. Maybe some curtains or a cloth for the table. It occurred to her that if her own mother came in, she wouldn't care what she thought, but she wanted Perla to be pleased.

Perla sat at the table and fiddled with a dish towel. "I'm glad you and I have some time to get to know each other." She glanced up at Margaret. "I thought maybe we could talk."

"Well, okay. How about I make some tea?"

"That sounds lovely."

Margaret bustled around the kitchen, filling the kettle, finding two mugs that matched, and digging out a tin of tea. Soon, the two women sat at the table sipping from steaming cups.

"Did you want to talk about anything in particular?" Margaret asked.

Perla glanced toward the bedroom. The door stood partially open, and they could see Mayfair's sleeping form curled in the bed. Margaret stepped over and closed the door in case Perla was worried about her sister hearing.

"Actually, there is." Perla picked up her spoon, then set it down again.

Margaret began to feel uneasy.

"I saw what Mayfair did for that child today. And I saw Henry's hand after she 'helped' him, as she put it. I know what a misfire injury looks like, and his hand . . ." She shook her head. "There's something special about your sister."

"I've always known she's special." Margaret tried not to sound defensive, but she didn't like where this conversation was headed.

Perla gazed into empty space over Margaret's shoulder. "I know how hard it can be to have a knack for something. The kind of knack that sets you apart and makes

226

people look at you differently. I think Mayfair may have a knack for healing people."

"I don't know what you're talking about." Margaret stood and dumped the rest of her tea into the sink. She rinsed the mug, staring out the window at the darkening sky. What business did Perla have coming in here and talking to her like this? And so what if she'd thought the very same thing?

"It's nothing to be ashamed of. Or afraid of." Perla finally looked at Margaret, and she felt, maybe for the first time in her life, that someone was really trying to see beyond her abundance of freckles and outward competence to the girl inside.

"The summer I met Casewell, Wise suffered a terrible drought. Somehow the food I cooked saw us through. I'd always had a way of cooking food so that it lasted longer than it should have — fed more people than made sense. But that summer was the first time I saw that God might have given me that ability for a reason."

"What are you saying?" Margaret turned around and leaned against the sink.

"I'm saying that miracles don't always feel like it at the time. I'm saying that blessings can be difficult, but they are blessings nonetheless."

Margaret shook her head. "I don't understand."

"No, it's the sort of thing you never really understand. I just wanted you — and Mayfair — to know you aren't as alone as you feel."

Margaret wrapped her arms around herself and looked at the floor. "Well, thanks, I guess. I'm not sure Mayfair is a healer or anything, but I appreciate you wanting to help." She looked back up at the older woman and saw not sympathy, but kinship there. "And I appreciate you sharing your story."

Perla nodded once and tapped the table. "Speaking of cooking, what's for supper around here?"

Margaret smiled. "Emily brought egg salad sandwiches from the wedding, and I think there's a good-sized hunk of cake, which I think you might have baked. Guess that means it'll be more than enough?"

Perla smiled back. "That sounds just right."

The run went smoother than Henry anticipated. All the way to Jack's place he kept imagining police cars and deputies hidden down every side road. Any car that pulled out behind him struck a chord of fear. Once he arrived, he caught a glimpse of Barbara inside the makeshift bar but ducked on out before she saw him. He'd thought he might like to play some music, but the itch to slide his bow across the strings faded the longer he was away from Mom, Grandma, and even Mayfair and Margaret.

Guessing his mother might still be with the girls, he drove over to Margaret's house. He hoped they'd have something to eat. He was ravenous.

Henry's tires crunched over remnants of snow in the yard at the gray house. Light poured out the kitchen window, warm and inviting. Henry suddenly felt good. He was glad to be there.

Laughter greeted him when he knocked on the door, then stepped inside. His mother and Margaret were at the table eating wedding cake.

"Oh, Henry, you've caught us having seconds," his mother said.

Margaret grinned — something Henry couldn't recall seeing before. "But when cake lasts like this one does, why not?"

That last statement mystified Henry, but he let it go as his mother pulled out a chair and fetched a plate of sandwiches from the refrigerator.

"Are you hungry? We're just eating leftovers from the wedding, but they're delicious."

"Don't mind if I do," Henry said, plopping down in the chair.

Margaret stood and fetched him a glass of iced tea. His mother added a dish of pickles to the plate of sandwiches. Henry thought he could get used to being waited on like this. He tossed one of the little sandwiches into his mouth and chewed. He tried to speak, but the egg salad muffled his question.

"What was that?" Margaret asked as his mother said, "Don't talk with your mouth full."

The two women looked at each other and smiled. Henry felt left out. He swallowed and cleared his throat. "I said, 'How's Mayfair?' "

"She's sleeping. I think that seizure or whatever it was really wore her out." Margaret looked at the closed bedroom door. "But maybe I should check on her. She ate a bit earlier with her shot, but I'd love to see her eat something more."

She walked over and eased the door open. She peered inside and then eased the door shut again.

"I hate to bother her," she said. "She can

eat in the morning."

Henry released a breath he didn't realize he was holding. What had he been thinking? That Clint might have spirited her away? The old man might be a crook, but he was no kidnapper. He relaxed and ate another sandwich. Maybe things would work out okay after all.

16

The next morning the shrill ring of the phone wakened Henry. He sat up in bed and stretched. He'd probably slept too late anyhow. He heard Mom answer on the second ring. After a moment her voice changed, and she sounded upset. He slipped into yesterday's clothes and padded out into the living room.

Mom stood with her hand over the receiver. "Mayfair's missing," she said. "We need to get over there. Margaret is beside herself."

Henry felt his stomach flip. Swallowing hard, he tried to think of a plausible explanation. Anything but the idea that sprang to mind as soon as Mom spoke.

When they walked into the gray house, Margaret stood in the middle of the kitchen working her hands and shifting from foot to foot. Grandma was already there, looking more worried than he'd ever seen her. Mom moved to put an arm around Margaret and gave her a sympathetic squeeze.

"Any chance she went out with somebody?" Henry asked.

Margaret gave him a withering look.

"Yeah, stupid question. Do you think —"

"What? Do I think what?" Margaret's voice held a tinge of hysteria.

Henry ran a hand through his hair. "Seems like word might be getting around that she's a healer. You don't think, well, that anyone would —"

"Would what? Take her? That's stupid." Margaret stomped her foot. "She isn't a healer. She isn't."

"Stories are getting around about some of the things that have happened — my hand, the little girl with the bee sting." He reached toward Margaret. "I'm not saying she is or isn't, but I can see how people might get that idea. Might put ideas into folks' heads."

Margaret whirled and went into Mayfair's room. "There has to be a clue," she said. "Help me find a clue."

Margaret dropped to her knees and crawled under the bed. "I see something. There's a piece of paper." She emerged with a sheet of lined notebook paper in her shaking hand. "It must have blown off the nightstand when I opened the door."

She sat on the edge of the bed and fumbled at the paper. Mom took it and read it aloud. "Margaret, I need to help someone. I'll be back soon. Love, Mayfair."

Tears welled in Margaret's eyes. She looked utterly defeated. "What do I do?"

Henry squared his shoulders. "You stay here with Mom. I have an idea about where to look."

"You tell me right this minute, Henry Phillips. Is it that Clint person?" Margaret spoke sharply, but she didn't move.

"Just give me until noon."

"We should call the sheriff's office," Mom said.

"They won't do anything. She left a note, and there's no reason to think anything bad has happened. Hang tight." He grasped Margaret by the shoulders and looked straight into those honey flecked eyes. "I'll bring her home. Don't you worry." He grabbed his hat and coat and hurried out to the truck.

Margaret thought she might explode. How could Henry expect her to sit here and wait? How could she do nothing? What if Mayfair had another seizure? It was already past time for her insulin shot. Mayfair was essentially defenseless. It had always been

Margaret's job to care for her little sister. She wanted to cry, scream, and run around the yard in circles. She wanted to pursue Mayfair to the end of the world if need be. Margaret fell into a chair, laid her head in her arms on the tabletop, and cried, not caring that Perla and Emily stood watching her. What she wanted was someone to fix everything. Her sister, her situation, her future, and this stupid feeling she had that Henry Phillips was her last chance for a hero.

The rough dirt road leading to Clint's place showed evidence of recent travel, but Henry couldn't tell if a vehicle had come in, gone out, or both. He eased into the yard, parked, and got out of his truck, checking all around. It would do no good to burst in with accusations. Anyway, if his hunch was right, Mayfair had chosen to come here.

No one came out to greet Henry, which was unusual. It wasn't that the Simmons family was friendly — more like in a hurry to run trespassers off. He stepped up on the crooked porch and pulled open the screen door, which let out a raspy groan.

He rapped on the paneled door and called out, "Hello, the house."

Silence. He knocked again, and the door

jerked open. Charlie stood there looking sullen.

"What you want, man?"

Henry fumbled his words. "Uh, just stopping by to see if, uh . . ." What? To see if a twelve-year-old girl had turned up?

"I expect you're huntin' that girl Pa thinks can heal Ma."

Henry blinked. "Actually, I am."

"Get on in here, then." Charlie jerked his chin toward a door at the end of the front room and disappeared into the kitchen, scratching his nether regions as he went.

Henry heard a man's voice rumble and a woman respond. It didn't sound like Mayfair. Then there was a broken sob, a pause, and next thing Henry knew Clint Simmons jerked the door open and stood there glaring at Henry.

"What are you doing here?"

"I, uh, I stopped by for —" Henry caught a glimpse of the woman he assumed was Clint's wife curled in the bed. She looked wrung out, but there was a peace about her. "Is she sick?"

Clint shoved Henry back toward the sofa. "Seems like I told you she ain't well. Seems like you didn't much care one way or the other. Seems like nobody in this godforsaken town gives two cents for anyone with the name of Simmons."

Henry held up both hands and tried to keep his balance. "I didn't mean anything. Just thought maybe I could help."

Clint sneered. "What do you think you can do?"

Henry was at a loss. He didn't suppose there was much of anything he could do. "Grandma would be glad to come see to her," he blurted.

"Would she now? Might be she thought to help once before." Clint pushed Henry toward the front door. "You ask her how it turned out that time."

Henry held up his hand before Clint could bully him back outside. "All I wanted was to check on Mayfair. I had a notion she might have come here last night."

Clint's shoulders sagged, and he lost his swagger. "She did. Said she might could help." He glanced back over his shoulder. "She's in there now. Guess you'll be taking her on home."

"If she's ready to go. Her sister's awful worried about her."

Clint's eyes lit up a bit. "Run off without permission, did she? She's quiet, but she's got spirit." He smiled. "And the purest heart I've ever seen. Haven't known anyone as through and through good since . . . well, it's been a long time."

Henry saw the door Clint came through open wider, and Mayfair appeared, looking worn out.

"Hey," she said.

"Hey, there. Margaret is sure missing you this morning."

Mayfair made a face. "I knew she wouldn't let me go, so I came on my own."

"It's a far piece to walk," Henry said.

"Mr. Simmons was out driving around. He brought me here."

Clint chimed in. "It was the durndest thing. After I spoke to you, I walked around a little, thinking about days a long time back when I used to hunt your grandpa's land. When I finally got in the truck to go home, I hadn't hardly got to the main road afore I saw that young'un walking along. Picked her up, and she said she'd like to come see Beulah. So I brung her."

Mayfair smiled at Clint, and Henry was stunned to see the crusty fellow look at her with soft eyes and something that could only be described as affection.

"I had a feeling he'd be along. I knew it was my best chance to come see Beulah."

Her smile faded. "But I'm not sure I can help her, after all."

Clint cleared his throat. "Darlin', your

visit has been the best medicine she's had in a long time. And I thank you for it." He turned to Henry. "Now get her on home. I know Beulah would take kindly to seeing her again sometime. If she wants to come."

"Oh, I'll come," Mayfair said. "Probably in three days."

Clint nodded once, glared at Henry, and disappeared back into Beulah's room.

17

Margaret still sat at the table, head resting on her arms, when Henry entered with Mayfair in tow. Emily and Perla hovered nearby, but they had finally given up trying to console her. Oddly enough, she found their quiet presence more comforting than anything they'd said. Margaret raised up when she heard the door open and cried out, leaping to her feet when she saw Mayfair.

"Where in the world have you been? Are you okay? You're overdue for your insulin. Have you eaten?"

Mayfair smiled and slid into the chair Margaret vacated. "I wanted to help Beulah Simmons, but I don't think I did." She sighed. "And I am hungry."

"Who's Beulah Simmons?" Margaret asked as she readied Mayfair's shot and administered it.

Emily jumped in before Henry or Mayfair

could speak. "She's the wife of Clint Simmons and a saint if there ever was one. Clint's a bit of a character. Some folks say he keeps a moonshine still out there in the woods somewhere back of his house, but I wouldn't know about that." She gave Henry a look Margaret couldn't decipher. "He hasn't always lived on the right side of the law, but he would never hurt a child, and like I said, Beulah's practically an angel."

Margaret fired up the gas stove and began laying strips of bacon in a pan. "Why did you go to see her? And why wouldn't you just ask me to take you?"

"She's sick," Mayfair said. "And you wouldn't take me to see a family that runs moonshine."

Margaret froze. "No, I guess I wouldn't. But you still should have told me." She dropped bread in the toaster. "It could have been dangerous. Clint sounds shady. He could have hurt you."

Emily took Margaret's hand and led her to a chair before moving to the stove and taking over breakfast. "Oh, Clint has a heart buried under all those layers of ornery. When he was a young man, he turned his life around for Esther Holt." Emily looked sad. "But then she passed, and I don't think he's over it yet."

"Hey," Henry said, just remembering something. "I told Clint you'd be glad to come see if you could help his wife, but he got mad and said I should ask you about helping once before. What was that about?"

Emily closed her eyes and pressed her hands together like a child praying. "I was there when Esther died."

Everyone stilled and looked at Emily as bacon popped in the silence. She sighed and rubbed her eyes. "Esther was Charlie's mother. She had it in mind to give birth right there at the house, so Clint called me when she went into labor."

Emily blinked her eyes and looked up at the ceiling. "I'd helped with births a few times over the years, but I was no midwife, and I told them so. Still, Esther and I always doted on each other, and she said I was the closest thing she had to a mother since her own died when she was ten. And I was too foolish to consider how horribly wrong things could go with a home birth."

Toast popped up and Emily buttered it absently. Margaret thought maybe the story was finished, but the older woman resumed speaking. "She died while I tried to stop her bleeding and Clint held her in his arms. She insisted I hand her Charlie to hold while I worked on her. I can still see them when I close my eyes. Clint Simmons with his arms wrapped around a dying woman and their child."

Emily braced herself against the cabinet and then straightened up and filled the percolator with water and coffee. "It's the worst thing that's ever happened to me. Worse than losing John or Casewell. At least I didn't feel responsible for their deaths."

"But it wasn't your fault," Margaret cried.

"Oh, honey, it probably wasn't, but I can't help feeling I should have done something different, all the same. I don't blame Clint for holding a grudge."

"But he remarried," Henry said. "He must have gotten over it."

Emily gave a hollow laugh. "You don't get over a thing like that. Ever." She walked over and wrapped an arm around Perla's shoulders. "When you lose a spouse, you carry that pain with you forever, even if you do find someone else to love."

Perla squeezed Emily's arm and took up the story. "I didn't know about Esther, but I can fill you in on Beulah," she said. "She was a couple of years ahead of me in school before we moved to Comstock, and she was, well, not very popular. I guess she was kind of a big girl and quiet, and her father was a bully. When I moved back, she was generally thought of as an old maid. So when Clint Simmons, who was a rapscallion but had been as good as gold to Esther, turned up a widower with a new baby, I think Beulah saw her chance."

Perla stood to fetch down coffee mugs and opened the refrigerator to get out the milk.

"Anyway, she always managed to be where Clint was, and she did everything she could to take care of that baby. I guess Clint finally figured it wouldn't hurt to have a mama for little Charlie." She grasped the coffeepot and looked a question at the three at the table. They all nodded, but no one spoke. Margaret figured they all wanted to hear the rest of the story.

"So they got married, though I don't think there was much love between them. Eventually they had Harold, and I heard Beulah lost some babies — some early on, and at least one was a stillbirth. Clint never did treat her right to my way of thinking, although I haven't seen Beulah in a good ten years, so maybe it got better."

"I reckon not." Henry seemed to speak without thinking. "Well, it doesn't look that way to me, anyhow."

Perla handed around the coffee and milk. A sugar bowl already sat on the table, and Margaret added two heaping teaspoons to her mug and then as much milk as she could without spilling over. Mayfair did the same. She slurped the concoction and thought about Beulah Simmons in a loveless marriage. She glanced at Henry. If you couldn't have what you wanted, she guessed you'd have to settle for what you could get. Still, it seemed like someone's story should have a little happiness in it.

That evening, Henry stopped by to check on Margaret and Mayfair. The girls were in the living room, watching the sunset out the window. Henry settled into an overstuffed chair Grandma insisted she didn't want or need anymore. Silence reigned for a moment, and Henry felt more at peace than he had in a long time. He'd helped return Mayfair home, and Margaret was glad. And strangely enough, he was glad Margaret was glad. He glanced at her. He guessed she really was a lot prettier than he'd thought in the beginning. Her freckles made her kind of special — unique. He started to speak, but Mayfair beat him to it.

"I can't keep her from dying," she said.

"What?" Margaret wrinkled her forehead and took her sister's hand.

"Beulah. She told me to call her that. I can't keep her from dying."

"Of course you can't. A doctor might be able to do something, but it's ridiculous for people to think you can do anything."

"Sometimes I can," Mayfair said with a sigh. "I'm hungry again. Will you make me a grilled cheese sandwich?"

"Sure. Go wash your face and test your sugar level. I'll have it ready in a jiff."

Margaret headed for the kitchen and gave Henry a look he failed to interpret. He followed her and propped himself in a corner to watch her work.

"Are you just going to stand there?" she said none too gently.

"Can't think of anything else that needs doing."

Margaret clattered a skillet onto a burner. "How is it you know those people, anyway?"

"The Simmonses?" Henry shifted. "Well, I went to school with Charlie."

"They don't seem like the kind of people you'd want to associate with." Her shoulders slumped. "Well, except Beulah might be nice. Maybe it's all too much for her since she's sick."

"What's too much for her?"

"Keeping up the house. Keeping those boys in line. The way I look at it, if there's a strong woman running the house, it keeps the whole family strong. Kind of a foundation." She held her hands out as though she were supporting something.

"I never thought of it that way."

"That's what I want." Margaret seemed chattier so long as she focused on preparing food and didn't look at him. "I want to be the rock for my family, the port in the storm, the solid foundation. I like it when people depend on me. Maybe that's why I'm so upset with Mayfair. She's always depended on me, and then she goes off like that, and I don't even understand why."

She ran out of steam. Henry wanted her to keep going. She was interesting to him.

"Go on," he said.

"Oh, I'm just rambling." She melted butter in the skillet and added two sandwiches. "I'm probably too tired to even make sense."

"No, I like what you're saying. I like the idea of the wife and mother being the cornerstone of the family. It sounds right to me." He thought about his own mother. "Maybe I haven't given Mom enough credit. She —" He swallowed hard. "She's handled losing Dad really well. Better than I have. I guess I've kind of taken her for granted."

Margaret flipped the sandwiches and got two more ready to go into the pan. Henry could feel her looking at him out of the corner of her eye. She seemed to get her second wind.

"Guess that's the kind of woman you'll be looking for in life, then." He saw her close her eyes. Was she flirting with him? She put the finished sandwiches on a plate without looking at him.

"You know, I think that's exactly the kind of woman I'm looking for." Henry stepped closer and squeezed Margaret's arm before picking up the plate and carrying it over to share with Mayfair, who appeared from the bathroom as if on cue.

Henry avoided the Simmonses over the next few days. He wasn't sure how Clint would feel about the part he played in recovering Mayfair, and he knew he didn't want to run moonshine anymore. Although it had been profitable, he didn't feel good about the money he earned. And, truth be told, Clint seemed kind of volatile lately.

The morning after Mayfair's return, Henry woke to the smell of pancakes and bacon. He shuffled into the kitchen where his mother was busy at the stove.

"Somehow it seemed like a pancakes morning," she said.

"Suits me." Henry poured himself a cup of coffee and slid into his seat at the table.

"Did you have any plans for today?" His

mother's tone was light, but Henry thought she might be getting at something.

"Not really. Did you have anything in mind?"

"I was hoping you'd help me sort through the rest of your father's things. I haven't had the heart, well, more like the courage, to do it, and I thought there might be some things that would be important to you."

She set a plate heaping with buttered pancakes and bacon in front of Henry, and he waited for the topic of conversation to rob him of his appetite. But it didn't. He picked up the syrup bottle and poured.

"Sure, we can do that."

Fortunately, Dad didn't have too much stuff. They set most of his clothes and shoes aside to give to charity. Henry already had his dad's good navy blue suit and a pair of work boots that were a little loose. There was also a watch and two belt buckles that Henry decided to keep.

"I don't know what to do with his mandolin." Henry's mom cradled the instrument in her arms. "He hadn't played in a while, but it was his treasure."

Henry took the instrument and plucked a string. He regretted not playing with his dad on New Year's Eve. He guessed a lot of people would do things differently if they thought it was their last chance. "Can I have it?"

"Of course you can. I didn't know if you would want it since you play the fiddle."

"Who knows? Maybe I'll learn to play it. Lots of musicians can play more than one instrument. Might even take a music elective at school."

"So you're going back?" Mom looked hopeful.

"Maybe." Henry didn't want to crush her hopes entirely. "Eventually I might."

"That would be good." She reached out and ran a hand over the glossy body of the mandolin. "I can just picture your father looking down from heaven and smiling to see this in your hands."

Henry stiffened. He didn't like it when Mom talked that way. Dad was gone. It wasn't like he was going to catch him peering over the edge of a cloud so he could wave hello. He tried to remind himself that thinking about heaven was comforting to his mother. He wrapped his fingers around the neck of the instrument in the same worn spot he imagined his father's hand had rested. Now this was tangible. This was something he could hold onto and remember, way better than a vague notion of heaven. He guessed it wasn't much, but it was surely better than nothing.

The first night Mayfair was home again Margaret had been tempted to nail the bedroom window shut. But now she was beginning to relax. They were getting back into the rhythm of things, school, going to Emily's, milking the cow, fixing up the house. Then, on the third morning after her return, Mayfair said it was time to go see Beulah.

Margaret wrinkled her nose. "You want to go back there?"

"I told Beulah we'd come back. She needs us."

"Needs us to do what?" Margaret was annoyed. This was not how she wanted to spend the day.

"To care," Mayfair said.

Margaret rolled her eyes. Didn't the woman have family? Surely she had parents, siblings, somebody. Then she thought about her own parents and how the most important people in her life besides Mayfair — Emily, Perla, Henry — were someone else's family.

"Oh, fine. When do you want to go?"

"As soon as I get home from school," Mayfair said, skipping into her bedroom to trade her pajamas for a smock and turtleneck.

That afternoon, Margaret met Mayfair as she stepped off the school bus and bundled her into the car. She tried to work up some enthusiasm for their visit as she drove to the Simmonses'. She couldn't believe she was taking her sister back to what she couldn't help but think of as the lion's den.

18

Beulah's eyes lit up when Margaret and Mayfair slipped into the front room. She sat propped on the sofa with a worn quilt tucked around her knees. Charlie sat with his feet propped on an ottoman watching television. Beulah had a Bible open in her lap.

"I thought today would be the day," Beulah said. "I counted three days and just knew you'd come."

Mayfair fluttered onto the sofa next to the woman who looked older than she probably was. Margaret watched her sister take this strange woman's hand, and something seemed to pass between the two that sent a pang of jealousy through Margaret.

"How are you feeling?" Margaret wanted to take charge, but she wasn't sure how to do it.

"Oh, much better," Beulah said and patted Mayfair's hand. She got a faraway look on her face and echoed herself. "Much better."

Margaret laced her fingers together, released them, and crossed her arms. "Is there anything I can do for you?"

"Oh, well, no. I don't suppose so. I put in a load of laundry a while ago, and I ought to hang it out. But that can wait." A smile creased her lined face. "Just sit and visit with me for the time being."

Margaret shifted from foot to foot. She had nothing to say to this woman. "How about Mayfair visits with you while I hang out that laundry, then I'll come join you?"

Beulah half rose then sank back down. "Oh, I can't let you do that." Her eyes pled with Margaret, but she couldn't tell if the plea was to help or to let it go. She opted to help since sitting in the dingy room while Charlie watched an episode of *Sanford and Son* turned up too loud didn't hold much appeal.

"I'll be done in no time," she said, looking around for the laundry room.

"On the back porch," Beulah said, nodding toward a doorway. "I surely do appreciate it."

"Glad to help." Margaret wound her way through the unkempt house until she found a dented washing machine, emptied its contents into a wicker basket missing one handle, and headed out the back door, where she found a clothesline.

It was a cold morning, but the sun shone bright, and Margaret found she didn't mind hanging out the family's faded sheets and towels. She was glad there weren't any personal items to handle. Touching Clint Simmons's underwear — clean or otherwise — might have been too much.

Pegging the last washcloth, Margaret stood back and admired the linens billowing in a slight breeze. If they stayed long enough, she'd bring them in. She tucked her numb fingers under her arms and went back inside. She had to pass through the kitchen to rejoin Mayfair and Beulah, but the stacks of dirty dishes begged to be washed. And then she thought she might as well wipe down the counters and table. She wished she had a mop for the floor, but settled for wiping up the worst of the sticky spots with an old rag she found under the sink. Then she dried the dishes and tidied the cupboards as she put the dishes away.

"Margaret? Are you in the kitchen?" Beulah sounded worried.

"Yes, ma'am. Just tidying up a bit."

"Come sit with us. There's no call for you to do my housework."

Margaret sighed, hung the dingy dish towel on the stove handle and went into the living room. Beulah motioned toward a rocking chair near the sofa, and Margaret sank into it. Charlie had disappeared, leaving the room blessedly quiet.

"I ought to scold you for cleaning my house, but I guess I'll thank you instead. Heaven knows I wasn't going to get it done, and those boys . . ." She shook her head. "Well, I didn't raise them like I should have."

"I don't mind — honest. Actually, I kind of like setting a place to rights." Margaret blushed. "Not that your place needs —"

"Oh, but it does." Beulah cut her off. "I may be feeling poorly, but I can see fine. Now leave my sorry mess for a minute and tell me about yourself."

She looked so expectant, Margaret wished she had something to tell. "There's not much. I work for Emily Phillips. Mayfair and I just moved into that little gray house on her property. We're pretty happy there, I guess."

Beulah waved a hand in front of her face as though fanning away a fly. "No, no. Tell me about you. What are your dreams, ambitions? Do you have a young man? What will you do with your life?"

The hungry look in Beulah's eyes made Margaret want to take stock of her life and find something interesting to tell the older woman. "Mostly I just want to live on a farm and raise a family."

"I'm glad to hear it. Too many young women these days are all caught up in their rights." She said the word *rights* like it was dirty. "All I ever wanted was a home and a family." She sighed. "But then, nothing ever turns out quite the way you think." Beulah examined Margaret closely. "Do you have a young man in mind to help you make this dream come true?"

An image of Henry flashed through Margaret's mind, but she ignored it. "No. No one in particular. I just might have to take in orphans or something."

Beulah leaned forward and gripped Margaret's knee with surprising strength. "I can see it in your eyes. There is someone. Don't settle for less than your heart's desire." She sagged back against the cushion and pulled her nubby sweater tighter around her shoulders. "Settling can seem like a good idea, but you'd best fight for what you want."

Mayfair reached over and took Beulah's hand. Again, something special seemed to pass between them, and Margaret bit the inside of her cheek. It was only her imagination.

"Sometimes what you want doesn't matter." Margaret was surprised by how angry she sounded. She tried to temper her comment. "What I mean is, you have to do the best you can with what life gives you."

Beulah looked around the dark room. "Settling can be worse than trying for something better and failing. At least then you'd know you tried."

Margaret felt the conversation was drifting into deep waters. "Well, I'll do my best not to settle," she said. "Now, how about I make you a cup of tea?"

"Oh, I meant to offer you some tea," Beulah protested. Then she looked at Mayfair and smiled. "But since I have a feeling you know your way around my kitchen now, why don't you go ahead?"

Margaret stood, glad to escape further conversation, and went into the kitchen to put a pan of water on the gas stove before heading out back to bring in the sheets that were dry. The towels would take a bit longer. Beulah might just have to tend those herself. On the way back in, she saw the bathroom and stopped long enough to clean toothpaste, whiskers, and dried soap off the basin. She guessed it was good they used toothpaste and soap. She glanced at the tub. That would take more time than she had. She pulled a mold-spotted shower curtain closed and reentered the kitchen in time to catch Mayfair pouring hot water over tea bags in three mugs.

"It's good for her to talk to you," Mayfair said.

"Well, I guess I'm glad, then."

Mayfair gave her sister one of her sweetest smiles and carried two mugs into the front room, leaving Margaret to bring her own. They stayed long enough to drink their tea, and then Margaret announced it was time to go. Beulah looked disappointed. Then she brightened.

"But you'll come again," she said.

Mayfair said they would before Margaret could jump in. She wasn't sure this was a friendship she ought to encourage. At least they hadn't seen that awful Clint Simmons. There was something about him that frightened Margaret.

When Charlie showed up at the door, Henry was tempted to leave him out in the cold. But he kept knocking, and Mom let him in.

"Hey, Henry, can I, uh, have a word with you?"

Henry cut his eyes to his mother, who sighed and left the room. "What do you want?" he asked.

"Need you to finish a run to Jack's for me."

Henry thought he might not mind taking his fiddle over there and playing for a while. Some of those boys weren't half bad, and he was itching to play some music. Even if that girl he woke up next to in the barn was around. It had been long enough that she'd know not to expect anything from him. Charlie must have taken his hesitation for indecision.

"You'd better do this, or Pa'll string you up."

Henry thought Charlie sounded a little bit desperate. "Did he send you over here?"

"Sure he did. Said you'd better do this or else."

"Why aren't you doing it? You can drive fine now."

"I'm taking care of another piece of business this evening. I've got the load in the car, it'll just take a minute to shift it over." Charlie started out the door, clearly expecting Henry to follow him.

Henry grinned. It was kind of fun making Charlie sweat. Guess he could use a night out. He hollered in his mother's general direction. "I'm going out. Be back soon."

Load shifted, Henry drove to Jack's place, feeling lighter than he had in a long time. He knew running moonshine wasn't right, but it seemed like he was getting kind of good at it, and it was nice to make some real money. Charlie even paid him up front. He liked being good at something.

When he pulled into the barn at Jack's, Henry got out whistling and began unloading the moonshine. He knew the ropes by now. He looked across the field at the lights from the bar. It looked inviting, the way the light spilled out across the yard. He wasn't going to drink anything, just play a little and get warmed up. Maybe he could get the best of being under Clint's thumb after all.

As Henry started for the house, a figure stepped into the doorway of the barn. His heart double-timed for a minute, and then he realized it was probably just Jack coming up to take inventory.

"I was hoping you'd come again." The voice was soft, feminine, and somehow familiar.

"Who, me?"

"Yeah, you." She stepped forward into the circle of light cast by one dusty bulb hanging from the ceiling. It was Barbara.

"Oh, hey." Henry didn't quite know what to say. He'd convinced himself she would have given up on him by now, but it sounded like she had ideas. How was he going to let her down easy?

"I'd have called you, but I didn't know your number," she said.

Henry kicked at a clump of hay. "Yeah, well, I've been pretty busy. Don't get out this way much. I was going to play a little before heading home." He raised the hand holding his fiddle.

"I'm pregnant."

Henry froze. He watched as her hand strayed to her belly. He looked at her eyes. There was defiance there.

"Are you saying . . . ?"

"I am." The look got harder, like she was daring him to deny it.

Henry ran his fingers through his hair. Lord, what had he done?

"Are you . . . will you . . . what do you want me to do?"

She tossed her head. "I ain't asking you to marry me. I just want you to do right by the baby. Maybe even take it and let your mother raise it once it comes. Where I live ain't fit for a child."

Henry tried to breathe in, but it was a fight. He finally drew a shaky breath and let it out again. "I don't know about that."

She stepped closer and pointed at him. "You can tell your family, or I will. Don't make no difference to me. I want to see this child have a chance."

Henry swallowed and looked at the woman in front of him. Her hair looked oily, and her clothes didn't fit well. She was missing a tooth on the left side of her mouth, but in spite of the flaws, she was pretty. Except for the hardness around her eyes and the way she held her mouth that made Henry feel like he was her last hope in the world. He shifted his gaze to her belly, and she placed both hands there, as though protecting her child from him.

"Okay," he said. "I need some time to think about this, but we can figure something out. How do I get in touch with you?"

"Write your phone number down, and I'll get in touch with you," Barbara said. "I'll give you two days to come up with a plan, and then I'll call you." She looked at the dirt floor, and some of the fire seemed to go out of her. "And don't try to blow me off. I can get Charlie to tell me where you live, and I'm not too proud to show up at your door."

Henry found a paper sack under the seat

in the truck and a stub of pencil his father probably used for woodworking projects. What would Dad think about how his pencil was being used now? Henry wrote his phone number down and handed it to Barbara, who stuck it in her pocket and turned away, then stopped.

"You wouldn't have a few dollars on you?" she asked.

He'd left the night's pay in a can under a loose board in Dad's workshop. He couldn't buy liquor if he didn't have cash. Henry dug into his pocket and came up with three crumpled ones and some change. "It's all I have," he said, holding it out.

She turned slowly and took the money. "I can get men to buy me liquor, but not many of them want to buy me a bottle of milk." She cupped a hand to her belly again. "It don't matter for me, but I'd just as soon feed this little one right."

She moved toward the door and stood there, silhouetted against the light from across the field. "I'll be talking to you, Henry," she said and was gone.

Henry climbed into the truck and rested his head on the steering wheel, all thoughts of music driven from his mind. What in the world was he going to do now?

19

Henry needed advice. He needed his father. He brought his fist down on the dashboard of the old truck and gunned the motor, tires spinning as he pulled away from the barn and the pregnant girl. As a matter of fact, he probably wouldn't be in this predicament if Dad were still around. Henry cursed. He hoped his father was looking down from heaven to see this. Maybe he'd be sorry.

He drove aimlessly, not knowing where he was going. He tried to think through the situation but couldn't come up with a plan. It surprised him when he saw the Talbot sisters' house up ahead. Lights were on in the sitting room, and he whipped into the drive not certain what he planned.

Frank stepped out onto the porch as Henry shoved the truck into Park. The old man raised one hand and then dropped it to his side and leaned against a post holding up the tin roof. Henry spilled out of the truck and tried to walk toward Frank like a man who knew what he was about.

"Howdy, Frank. How you likin' this weather?"

Frank stood upright and considered Henry. "Been a mite warmer of late. Crocuses poking through over there by the steps." He pointed with his chin. "Makes Angie awful glad, and anything that pleases that woman pleases me."

Henry felt his stomach knot tighter. Wouldn't it be nice to have a woman who made him happy? He had Barbara, who was making him miserable, Margaret confusing him, Mom nagging at him, and Grandma, well, he guessed she was usually a comfort. He put one foot up on the edge of the porch and leaned on his knee.

"Marriage suits you, then?"

"Down to my toes." Frank leaned forward and peered into Henry's face. "I'm thinking you didn't come here to ask about my love life, though."

Henry took a deep breath and blew it out slow. "I guess maybe I need some advice."

Frank nodded. "Come on in and sit. Angie's tending to her evening toilette, so we'll have the parlor to ourselves."

Henry smiled at Frank's language. The old man had been a world traveler, but he pronounced the French word with a mountain twang that let Henry know he was making fun a little. He was surprised he could smile.

Inside, the house was warm and the lights not too bright. Henry kind of wished he could just lean back on the sofa and go to sleep. He felt bone weary and wasn't sure he even wanted to talk about his problems right then. But Frank looked at him with an open expression that had him spilling everything out before he even knew what he was going to say.

He told about how he'd been running moonshine, about not wanting to go back to school, and about Barbara. When he finished, he subsided into the sofa. He felt like he was made of lead, and the softness of the cushions pillowed around him.

"Is that all?" Frank asked. Then he grinned at Henry's incredulous look. "It's enough. I just wanted to make sure we have everything out on the table."

Henry thought of Margaret and how he'd been thinking of her differently lately, but he decided that really didn't matter at the moment. Even if he was interested in more than friendship, having gotten another girl pregnant probably wouldn't recommend him to her.

"So how can I help you, son?"

"What would my dad tell me to do?" Henry tried not to let his voice quiver.

Frank leaned back and stared at the ceiling. "He'd tell you to get shut of Clint Simmons and that whole clan. Your father had a bit of history with ole Clint. When Casewell was young and foolish, he stole moonshine from a Simmons still. When I came up on them — I was known to drink in those days — Clint was fixing to cut on your dad. That's were he got the scar on his chin. I talked Clint out of skinning your dad alive, and we all came to a satisfactory understanding."

Henry sat stunned. He couldn't imagine his father ever doing something so . . . wrong. And not a little foolish. He guessed maybe Frank really had saved Dad's life.

Frank looked Henry in the eye. "I suspect Casewell would tell you to go on over there and tell Clint straight to his face that you're done working for him."

Henry started to protest, but Frank held up a hand. "Somehow, after this business with Mayfair, I think that might work out better than you anticipate. As for school, I'm pretty sure he'd tell you to get your hindquarters back in class." Frank squinted at Henry. "But you know that already. As for this business with the young lady, he'd tell you to go talk to your mother."

Henry scrunched his forehead. "What? Why would I do that? She'll probably disown me when she hears this. She's already mad at me."

"Son, your mother is a complex woman with a history all her own. She was your age once, and she may have made some decisions that weren't the best, but she came through them, and I have a feeling she'll be a whole lot more help to you than your father ever would."

Henry flopped his head back on the cushion and noticed a crack in the ceiling. Frank's advice and the revelation about his dad sat in his gut like week-old biscuits. But at the same time, he suspected his father would agree with most of it. Except for talking to his mother. That was ridiculous.

Heaving himself to his feet, Henry stuck out his hand. "I appreciate your listening to me. Seems like I don't have anybody to talk to much these days."

Frank shook Henry's hand. "There's not having anyone to talk to, and then there's not talking to the ones you've got. You make sure you know which is which."

Henry sighed and trudged out the door to his truck. What did he expect? There was no magic wand he could wave to fix everything. No last-minute miracle to save his hide.

When she wasn't in school, Mayfair was with Margaret at Emily's. Even when she wasn't technically working, Margaret liked being at the farmhouse. It felt safer there, like nothing bad could happen. The three of them were sitting at the table sipping hot chocolate on a Saturday morning when Henry stomped in with the milk. He didn't speak and barely looked at the women.

"Good morning, Henry," Emily said.

He grunted and set the milk pail on the counter. "Bertie's got pinkeye."

Emily frowned. "I thought that only came on in the summer. We'd better call Dr. Langley and get him out here to look at her."

Margaret got up to strain the milk. "Seems like less today."

"I told you, Bertie has pinkeye. Cuts down on production." Henry looked like he wanted to dump the milk over Margaret's head.

She raised her eyebrows. "No need to get mad about it. I was just commenting."

"Well, keep your comments to yourself unless they're helpful."

"Henry," Emily chided, putting a hand on his arm. He jerked away.

"Call the vet. I'll be out at the shed." He started toward the door.

"Hey, where's Mayfair?" Margaret looked around, but her sister was no longer in the room.

Henry peered out the window. "Looks like she's in the cowshed. If she messes with Bertie's eye, she can make it worse or even get pinkeye herself." He glared at Margaret. "Why don't you keep better track of her?"

Margaret felt as if she'd been slapped. "I keep up with her just fine. Why don't you stop being such a pain in the rear end?"

Henry looked taken aback, but then he slammed out the door. Margaret grabbed a jacket and followed him.

In the cowshed Mayfair had her arm around Bertie's neck singing " 'A' You're Adorable." Bertie seemed to like it, but Henry grabbed Mayfair's wrist and pulled her away from the animal. Bertie swung her head to look after Mayfair as Margaret stepped closer to see the cow's eyes.

"They look fine to me, Henry. What makes you think she has pinkeye?"

"Because she's holding the left eye closed most of the time, and it's watering. Are you blind?"

271

Margaret took another look. The eye was wide open and clear. She made a sweeping motion to invite Henry to take a closer look. He did and cursed.

"Watch your language," Margaret said.

"I'll say whatever I feel like. You're not the boss of me."

Margaret felt anger rise in her. Henry was being a jerk. He was mistreating Mayfair, alarming Emily for no good reason, and using language none of them needed to hear. She'd had enough.

"Henry Phillips, I am sick and tired of you dragging around like you're the only person in the world who's ever suffered anything. Losing your father is no excuse for acting like an overgrown jerk who only cares about himself. You've been rude to your grandmother, mean to Mayfair, and you've treated me like dirt." She stomped her foot on the hay-strewn ground. "I've had just about enough."

Henry looked surprised, then red began creeping up his neck. He leaned toward Margaret, stuck his finger in her face, and opened his mouth, but before he could speak Mayfair was there. She put a hand on Henry's arm and one on Margaret's. She didn't speak, but Margaret felt there was a voice inside her head whispering *peace.*

Henry lowered his accusing finger, and the red faded from his face. He looked at Mayfair as if she'd just parted the Red Sea. Margaret could swear she saw tears in his eyes, but he turned away. His shoulders slumped.

"Guess I was mistaken. I could have sworn that eye was infected."

"It's good to be cautious," Margaret said. "We can't be too careful with our Bertie."

"Right." He nodded. "Think Grandma's got some more chocolate back there in the kitchen?"

"I'm sure she does." For a moment Margaret had the urge to take Henry's hand and walk with him back to the house, but she caught herself before she did. Had he been reaching for her hand? Or was that her imagination?

She heard a sound behind her — kind of like a kitten mewling — and even as she turned, she saw Mayfair falling.

"Get some juice. Now."

Before she finished speaking, Margaret was on the ground cradling her sister's head as the girl's body stiffened and quivered. Saliva ran from the corner of her mouth, and Margaret wiped it away with her shirt-tail. Henry reappeared with a glass of Tang and helped Margaret get Mayfair to a sitting position. Together they held her while Margaret pressed the glass to her lips. At first she didn't think the child could swallow, and liquid ran down her chin. Mayfair's eyes were fixed and glassy. Panic began to rise in Margaret, but then Mayfair swallowed convulsively, taking juice down and coughing.

"Good girl. Try some more." Margaret could hear the pleading in her own voice.

Mayfair swallowed again, and this time it seemed to help. She relaxed a bit and was able to finish the juice. Henry's eyes met Margaret's over Mayfair's head. The tenderness she saw there let her know he hadn't meant anything he'd said or done that morning. Except maybe what he meant to tell her now. And she was too frightened to interpret exactly what that was.

20

Henry could see his mother sitting on the sofa reading a novel. Talking to her about his problem had been at the bottom of his list, but somehow after seeing Mayfair suffer a seizure and the way Margaret handled it, well, he wanted his family.

She looked up as he came inside and let the book drop. "Henry, Emily called to let me know what happened. Is Mayfair all right?"

"She's better now. But I think Margaret is really worried. She said something about how these seizures or whatever are happening more often."

"Poor child. I tend to think she should be home with her mother, but then I remember what Lenore Hoffman is like." She shook her head. "Sometimes life isn't fair, but God can use everything, if you let Him."

"Everything?" Henry flopped down in a rocking chair and kicked off his boots.

"Absolutely."

"I've got a problem, Mom." Henry ran a hand through his hair until he felt like it must be standing on end.

"I'll help if I can," she said, folding her hands over the book in her lap.

"There's this girl."

His mother smiled and smoothed her skirt over her knees. "It's about time."

"Not like this." Henry hung his head. "I . . . she . . . I don't even remember, and it was only that once . . ."

"What is it, Henry?"

"She's pregnant." He snuck a look at her face. It was definitely a shade paler than it had been.

"Pregnant. Who is she?"

"Her name is Barbara. I don't think you'd know her." He peeked again. Was that relief? Surely not.

"What are you going to do?"

"I don't know." Henry threw his hands up in the air and began jiggling his knee. "I was hoping you could . . . advise me. Frank thought maybe you could."

His mother leaned her head back against the sofa and tapped her folded hands against her mouth. She closed her eyes and seemed lost for a moment.

"What does Barbara want?"

Henry winced. "I guess she wants help. Maybe money to take care of the baby. She didn't say anything about getting married." He jiggled both knees. "I guess she doesn't have anybody to help her, really."

"She didn't say anything about getting rid of the baby?"

Henry's eyes flew to his mother's face. "No. As a matter of fact, she seems anxious to take good care of it."

"Good. I'm glad of that." Mom seemed to fall deep into thought again. "Ask her if she'll come stay here."

"What?" Henry wanted to rub his ears to make sure they were clear.

"She needs help. She needs to eat the right food and drink plenty of milk. She needs someone to make sure that baby is born healthy and into a home where people will love it."

"But, what if she thinks . . . I mean are you saying I should . . . you know . . . marry her?"

"No. I'm not saying that at all. I'm saying there's a young woman out there who's pregnant and scared, and even if you weren't responsible, we'd have a duty to help her as best we could." She looked around the room. "This house is too quiet and too empty with your father gone. If she wants

277

to come here, she's more than welcome."

Henry felt his mouth drop open and snapped it shut. He was too shocked to say much of anything. He stared at his mother as she picked up a notepad and pen from the end table and began making a list. She looked up at him and tapped the pen against her lower lip.

"No matter what has happened between the two of you, I don't think it would be appropriate for you to stay in the same house with Barbara unless . . . well, it wouldn't be right. You call your grandmother, and see if you can stay with her for the time being."

Henry felt his blood run cold. While he was glad his mother wanted to help, he hadn't really thought about other people knowing. But of course they'd know. Grandma and Margaret and Mayfair would all find out in short order. He hung his head. In spite of how Margaret could get on his last nerve, he liked her — more and more lately. And although he'd given up on the idea that she might fit into his future as soon as he found out about Barbara, he'd still rather she didn't know.

And now she'd be sure to encounter the girl who carried his child. Henry wished he could throw up. He wished he could honestly claim the child couldn't be his. He wished he could remember that night, but then again, maybe it was just as well.

He stood. "I'll head on over to Grandma's and talk to her."

Mom smiled. "I'm glad. It's the kind of conversation you should have in person. Are you going to call Barbara from there?"

"No. She said she'll call me. Tomorrow. I don't have her number."

His mother's mouth tightened, but she didn't criticize. "Let me know what she says as soon as you can. I'll need to get ready for her."

Henry started to say maybe she wouldn't want to come, but that was just wishful thinking. She'd be a fool to turn this offer down, and he suspected Barbara was nobody's fool.

Henry thought his grandmother might send him out back to cut a switch. When he told her about Barbara, she crossed her arms and tapped her foot at him. She didn't say anything at first, but the disapproval radiating from her was worse than words. When he ran out of steam, he stood, head hanging, awaiting the verdict.

"Of course you can stay here. But, Henry, this is a terrible trial for your mother, and

I'm so very disappointed in you. Your father — well, no need to rub salt in the wound. I suspect you know what your father would think." She dropped her arms and headed down the hall. "Although maybe not everything he'd be thinking."

When the phone rang the next day, Henry dove for it, speaking almost before the first ring faded away. It was Barbara. Henry explained his mother's offer, adding that he'd be living with his grandmother for the duration of her stay. Barbara hesitated.

"What's the catch?" she asked.

"No catch. My mom seems to want to take care of you."

"Does she think she gets to keep the baby? I haven't decided what to do for sure."

Henry bristled. "Seems to me if that baby's half mine I should have some say, too."

Barbara was silent for a moment. "Yeah, I guess so. We can talk about that later."

"Hey, when is the . . . ah . . . baby supposed to arrive?"

"Not for a while yet. We've got time to figure this out."

Henry wrinkled his brow. Why did he feel Barbara wasn't really including him when she said, "We"? He shook off the feeling.

This was new territory, and he had no idea what to expect.

He arranged to pick Barbara up at Jack's barn. He offered to come to her house, but she said the barn would be better. By nightfall his mother would have a new tenant, and he suspected by lunchtime the following day most of the people in Wise would know why. Including Margaret and Mayfair. He told himself he didn't care, but his stomach hurt and he felt tired to his bones.

When Margaret and Mayfair opened Emily's front door, Henry was already there, and the milking was done. Margaret glanced at the clock. He seemed early. She noticed two of his jackets on the coatrack near the door — his work coat and a nicer one for going to town or church. And there was an extra pair of shoes next to his boots.

"You moving in?" she asked with a laugh.

Henry slurped his coffee and shoved the last bite of a biscuit in his mouth. "Glmph, mmfth humph."

"What did you say?" She hung her own coat next to Henry's. She kind of liked seeing them there, side by side.

Henry swallowed. "I'm, uh, staying here with Grandma for a while."

Margaret felt her cheeks pink and told herself it was the warmth of the house after the coolness outside and not the thought that she'd be seeing even more of Henry. "Really? She'll like that."

"Who will like what?" Emily walked into the room.

"Henry staying with you. Guess he's going to knock me out of a job milking the cow." She wagged a finger at Henry. "I want to milk her at least three times a week. I need to keep in practice."

Henry got to his feet. "Sure. I need to . . . uh, run an errand." He nodded at Margaret, gave his grandmother a borderline guilty look, and bolted for the door.

Margaret looked after him and then turned to Emily. "He's a bit off this morning."

Emily sighed. "Yes, I suppose he would be. Margaret, come sit down a minute."

"I was going to get after cleaning the bathtub."

"That can wait a little. I'd like to tell you something."

Margaret felt dread well up inside her. Was Emily going to ask her to leave the gray house? Did she want to move Henry in there? Is that what all this was leading up to? She pasted a smile on her face and sat, bracing for the worst.

After dropping Barbara off with his mother and suffering the most awkward twenty minutes of his life, Henry drove to the Simmonses like he was trying to see how slow he could go without stalling the truck. He'd taken Frank's advice about talking to his mother, and he guessed that had worked out. Not exactly how he wanted, but at least it wasn't weighing on him like it had been. So maybe confronting Clint would work, too.

Henry knocked on the front door. It was beginning to feel like spring might come after all, but it was still plenty cold standing in the shade of the porch with a March breeze blowing. He stomped his feet and blew into his hands, then knocked again.

Clint opened the door and looked Henry up and down like he was a beggar come for a handout. "What do you want?"

"I need to talk to you a minute."

Clint hung his head and stepped back. "Come on in here. Beulah's resting, so keep it down."

Henry was surprised. He didn't expect Clint to have that kind of consideration for his wife. Maybe the old coot wasn't as mean as he made out. Henry guessed he was about to learn the truth of that.

Clint pulled the bedroom door almost shut and then stood in front of the smoky fireplace with his arms crossed, looking expectant. Henry debated sitting, but figured he'd better stand as long as Clint did. He wasn't sure what to do with his hands, so he shoved them into the pockets of his barn coat and rocked back and forth on his heels.

"I want out," he said.

"Door's right there." Clint had a gleam in his eye.

"Of the moonshine business. I don't want to run 'shine for you anymore."

"I ain't asked you to lately."

"But Charlie —" Henry bit off the words. Clint didn't want to hear logic. "What I mean to say is, I'd be glad if you didn't ask me again."

"All right." Clint reached down a tin of tobacco from the mantel and rolled a cigarette. Hardly anyone rolled their own anymore, but of course Clint would.

"All right?"

"Yeah. You act like you thought I'd make you do it. Course, I find out you told anyone anything that might get me or mine into trouble with the law, I'll skin you alive."

Henry had a picture of a much younger

Clint holding a knife to his father's face. He felt the hair stand up on the back of his neck.

"I guess I know better than to do anything like that."

"Guess you do."

Henry wondered if the discussion was over. "I'll be heading on now," he said.

Clint nodded and turned toward the fireplace. He leaned against the mantel and flicked most of his cigarette into the flames. Henry hesitated for a moment. It was the strangest thing, but Clint actually looked sad. He shook off the image of the man and the smoky fire and headed outside.

Before he reached his truck, Charlie intercepted him.

"What're you and the old man talking about?"

"I quit the moonshine business. Guess I won't be seeing you much anymore."

Charlie pulled at his chin. "He just up and let you quit? I knew he was getting soft. Makes me wonder . . ."

"I'd best be getting on." Henry didn't feel like messing around with Charlie. He seemed to get into trouble every time they were together.

"Hey, did I hear your ma took in that girl from out at Jack's?"

"Where'd you hear that?"

"Word gets around. You know how it is."

"Well, not that it's any business of yours, but yeah." Henry opened the truck door.

"Knocked her up, did ya?" Charlie snickered. "I'd have bet you didn't have it in you."

Henry gripped the door handle harder. Charlie wasn't worth his time or effort. "I guess the main thing is having the guts to do something about it now."

"What? You gonna marry her? That'll be the day." Charlie laughed again, and it didn't sound pleasant.

"Maybe I will." Henry got in the truck, started the engine, and pulled away. He glanced in the rearview mirror, and the look on Charlie's face was worth it. A mixture of shock and . . . what? Fear? Surely not. What did that boy have to be afraid of other than his own father?

21

Margaret laced her fingers together, then alternated the grip. It always seemed funny that when the left thumb was on top, the grip felt natural, but when she switched to the right thumb, everything felt out of kilter. Kind of the way she felt waiting for Emily to say whatever awful thing she had to say. And Margaret had a feeling it was going to be truly awful.

"Margaret, I'm going to tell you this straight out." Emily folded her hands on the kitchen table and leaned forward. "Henry's gotten a girl into trouble, and she's staying with his mother for the time being. Henry will live here while Barbara is with Perla."

Margaret furrowed her brow. "Into trouble? Who's Barbara?"

"She's a girl he met, well, I'm not entirely sure where it was, but it was somewhere he shouldn't have been. And now she's pregnant."

Margaret shot to her feet without knowing she was going to. "Pregnant? She's going to have a baby? Henry's baby?"

Emily reached out a hand and motioned for Margaret to sit. "I know it's a shock. But I'm glad he wants to do right by this girl."

"Do right? Is he going to marry her?" Margaret felt like a swarm of bees was loose inside her skull. She plopped back down for fear she might fall over.

"That I don't know. But he — we — are going to see that this child is taken care of. I guess that baby will be a Phillips, and we're going to make sure it has a family."

Margaret popped up again like a jack-in-the-box. "I'm going to get after that tub. I appreciate you letting me know about . . . everything."

She rushed to the bathroom, plopped down on the toilet lid, and buried her face in her hands. Henry was lost to her. She told herself there had never been a chance. She told herself she didn't really even like him. She told herself it had been nothing more than an idle daydream and he never would have made her happy anyway.

Hot tears spilled onto her fingers, and she wiped her hands on her slacks. She dug out cleaning supplies and a scrub brush. Henry

Phillips wasn't worth caring about. He was a low-down womanizer who didn't care about people. She spilled cleanser into the tub and began scrubbing like she would if she thought she could scrub Emily's words out of her head. Tears mixed with the cleanser, and Margaret vowed to keep lying to herself until it didn't hurt anymore.

Henry didn't know where to go when he left Clint's. He had no desire to go to his mother's, where Barbara would be settling into his bedroom and making it her own. And he didn't want to go to his grandmother's, where Margaret surely knew everything by now. He almost wished he could go back to school.

Instead, he drove to the Talbots'. He guessed it should be the Posts' now that Frank was the man of the house, but it would take the community of Wise a long time to get over using the name that had fit that land for the past hundred years or so.

The late March afternoon had warmed nicely, and Frank and Angie were sitting in a porch swing soaking up the sun. They both waved as he pulled into the yard.

"Howdy, Henry. Come and sit a spell," Frank said.

Henry walked over and sat on the edge of

the porch near the couple. "Fine day for sitting in the sun," he said.

"Fine day for just about anything — or nothing, so long as you can do it with your sweetheart."

Frank wrapped an arm around Angie and kissed her forehead. She swatted at him, but Henry could tell she liked it. He wondered if he'd have anyone to sit in a swing with when he was ninety. If he lived that long.

"You just visiting, or you got something on your mind?"

Henry admired how the old man didn't waste time. Maybe that's how it was when you got old.

"I guess I've got something on my mind," he said.

Angie leaned forward. "Well, spit it out then. Or is it too harsh for my tender ears?"

Henry grinned in spite of himself. "I reckon you can take it, Miss Angie. Has Frank told you about my problem?"

"I should hope he did. There shouldn't be secrets between a man and his wife." She wagged a finger at Henry. "Not that I'd tattle it to a living soul. It's just between us."

"Well, Barbara moved in with Mom today." He flicked a look at the couple. They didn't seem surprised. "And I told Clint I wasn't going to, uh, work for him anymore."

"How'd all that go?" Frank asked.

"I guess it went better than I expected. The thing is, Charlie wondered if I was going to marry Barbara, and, well, now I'm wondering if I should."

Angie crossed her arms, pressed her lips together, and looked at Frank.

"My wife is allowing me to speak, in spite of having an opinion of her own on the matter," Frank said. "Henry, do you want to marry her?"

"Not particularly. But she seems okay, and I'm glad she didn't do anything to, well, to hurt the baby. And I'd sure like to be there to take care of him or her."

Angie made an exasperated sound. "The question is, does she want to marry you? I swear, you men think you can just decide things and women will go right along with it." She leaned toward Henry. "Did you ask her?"

"When she told me she was pregnant she said she didn't want me to marry her; just that she needed someone to help take care of the baby." Henry felt hope rise in him. Maybe he didn't need to marry her, after all. Maybe she'd let his mother adopt the baby.

Angie snorted. Not very ladylike. "That

291

doesn't mean a thing. There's hardly a woman in this world who'd tell a man she wants to marry him before he asks. A lady likes to be asked." She sat back as though resting her case.

"That's true," Frank said. "Found that out the hard way."

Angie swatted him again.

Henry sighed. "I guess I'd better talk to her, then."

"I would if I were you, son," Frank said. "You can burn a lot of years not talking about something."

The next day Mayfair insisted they go back to visit Beulah. Margaret invited Emily to come along, but she wasn't sure of her welcome and said maybe next time. At the Simmonses' house Beulah sat in a dining room chair in the front yard. Spring had begun to show signs of arriving, and the sun was bright, but Beulah sat swaddled in quilts and shawls. She wiggled an arm out to wave the girls over.

"I'm so glad you've come," she said. "I'm feeling much better."

Mayfair's forehead crinkled, and she took the woman's hand. "Are you?"

"I am. If only because of the peace of mind you've given me. Now come inside, and we'll have a nice visit."

Clint stepped out onto the porch and nodded at them but didn't speak. Beulah struggled to stand, and her husband rushed to her side. He slid an arm around her waist and helped her to the house. Mayfair dogged their steps.

Once inside, Margaret wished they'd stayed in the yard. The house was gloomy and had a definite chill. Clint stoked the fire until it blazed bright enough to chase some of the drear away, then left them alone. Mayfair sat close to Beulah while Margaret perched on a cane-bottomed chair. She itched to find a dustrag and a broom.

"I see you over there wishing you could clean my house," Beulah said.

Margaret protested.

"No, it's all right. It needs a good cleaning. I try to get Harold to help out, but I think it hurts his pride to do women's work."

"I'd be more than glad to run a dustrag over a few things," Margaret said. "If it would be a help to you."

Beulah sighed and sagged deeper into the sofa. "Honey, it would. When I'm gone, these boys can wallow in their own filth, but for the time being I'd surely like to see a shine on the end table there."

Margaret was on her feet. "Where are your supplies?"

Beulah directed her, and Margaret felt something like a surge of happiness. It was silly, but she felt that doing a little cleaning was the best comfort she could give. And she was good at it. Mayfair seemed to comfort people by her very presence. Margaret suspected her absence — or at least her fading into the background — was her gift.

She hummed softly as she wiped down the tables and found a dust mop to get at cobwebs in the corners. Clint stuck his head into the room once, paled, and ducked out again. Margaret was glad to know a clean house was a weapon against him. She swept the room out and was debating taking up the braided rug and dragging it out into the yard for a good shake when she finally turned her attention back to Beulah and her sister.

They were sleeping. Mayfair's head on Beulah's shoulder, hands clasped. Margaret smiled. Now that was worn out — sleeping in the midst of her cleaning. She tiptoed over and laid a hand on Beulah's arm.

"Beulah? How about I take this rug out and shake it real good?"

Beulah blinked and opened her eyes as though she was returning from somewhere very far away. "What? The rug? Oh, honey, don't mess with that thing. I'll get the boys to drape it over the fence and whack it a few times."

She stretched her arms and then swiveled her neck. "Lawsy, I must've needed that nap. I feel better than I have in months. Maybe it's the pleasure of a clean room." She smiled and then peered at Mayfair. "This young one must need some rest, too."

"She's been having a hard time with her diabetes lately."

"Sugar? My mother had the sugar. It was awful. She lost most of her toes before the end. This child is too young and too good for such as that."

Margaret touched Mayfair's arm. "Wake up, sweetie. It's time to go."

Mayfair made a sound like a balloon losing the last of its air as her head flopped forward.

Margaret grasped both shoulders and gave her a little shake. "Mayfair? Wake up." Icy fingers wrapped around her heart. "Beulah, do have orange juice or something sweet to drink?"

"I think so."

The older woman struggled to her feet

and shuffled into the kitchen. She returned in what felt like at least a year to Margaret with a glass of juice. Margaret sat on the arm of the sofa and cradled Mayfair against her chest. She gently pried her lips open and poured a little juice in. It ran down Mayfair's chin. She tried again and more juice ran down onto her sister's shirt.

"She has to take it. She just has to take it," Margaret whispered.

"Honey, we need to get her to a doctor."

"If we can get her to take some juice —"

"Margaret. I'll get Clint to take you to the hospital. I saw this with my mother. She needs a doctor."

Margaret held Mayfair, willing her to wake up, to absorb a little of the sugar on her tongue until Clint appeared and scooped the child into his arms. Margaret cried out and then clapped a hand over her mouth. He was only helping. They got in his car and flew to St. Joseph's Hospital.

22

The smell of roast chicken permeated the air even before Henry set foot in his mother's house. He'd missed lunch, and his stomach rumbled. It might be awkward to eat a meal with Barbara and his mom, but based on the aromas coming from the kitchen, he thought maybe he could manage it.

Inside, Barbara laid a third plate and silverware on the table. Mom smiled at him as she spooned mashed potatoes into a bowl.

"I saw you pull up. Seems like you timed things just right."

"I didn't set out to come for supper, but since it's ready . . ."

Mom walked by and bumped him with her hip. "By the time you wash your hands, we'll have this on the table."

Barbara didn't look directly at Henry, moving to the stove to dish up green beans instead. He could smell the bacon grease, and his mouth watered. He hurried to wash his hands.

The three of them sat, and Mom said grace. Henry was grateful she hadn't asked him. He wasn't sure God was on speaking terms with him at the moment. They passed the dishes and ate in silence for a few moments.

"How's your grandmother?" Apparently Mom was going to make conversation.

"She was fine when I left there this morning. I've been over at the Talbot place."

"Oh? Are Frank and Angie settling in well?"

Henry shrugged and swallowed a mouthful of potatoes. "I guess." He made a face. "They're kind of touchy-feely. Like they're flirting with each other."

His mom smiled as if that was the best news she'd heard in a long time. "As it should be." She turned to Barbara. "Frank and Angie are a sweet couple who just got married."

"Even though they're ninety," Henry said under his breath.

"Ninety?" It was the first peep he'd heard from Barbara. "They got married when they were ninety?"

"Or thereabouts," Henry said. "Guess it

took 'em a long time to figure things out."

Mom dabbed at her lips with a napkin. "I think they figured things out quite a few years ago. It just took them until now to do anything about it." She gazed out the window into the distance. "Sometimes you have to wait, so as not to hurt someone you love."

"Ain't that the truth," Barbara said and then looked embarrassed. She took a bite of chicken and looked at her plate.

Mom patted Barbara's arm. "There's something I've been wanting to tell you, and while I thought I'd tell Henry later, he might as well hear it, too."

Henry felt his appetite ebbing. This couldn't be good. He eyed the dried apple pie cooling on the counter. Well, maybe it wouldn't be that bad.

"When I married Henry's father — Casewell — I already had Henry's older sister, Sadie. Henry knows that much." She leveled her gaze at him. "What he doesn't know is that I was never married to Sadie's father."

Henry was washing a bite of bread down with milk, and he snorted the liquid into his nose. He coughed and swiped at his face with his napkin, finally standing and finding a paper towel to blow his nose. He turned around and stared at his mother. He knew Sadie was his half sister, but he'd never thought to ask about her father. He'd just assumed he'd died. Or something.

"I'm sorry, Henry. I should have waited until you swallowed."

"Why? You waited about twenty years, what's another thirty seconds?"

"Come sit down and finish your supper. I know this is a surprise to you, but as you can imagine, my story is likely to be a comfort to Barbara."

Henry staggered over and slid into his chair, all thoughts of pie gone from his head. Barbara held her fork as though she'd forgotten about it. Her eyes were fixed on his mother.

Mom turned her full attention on Barbara. "I made a bad decision because I fancied myself in love. Maybe I was, but it still wasn't right. I don't know how you feel about Henry." She glanced at him. "Or he about you, but I want you to know that God can use anything for His purpose, and good will come of this. I feel very confident about that."

Barbara laid down her fork, and a tear tracked her cheek. "I . . . thank you for telling me. I thought it was only bad girls like me that got into this kind of trouble."

Mom squeezed Barbara's arm. "We're all bad girls. It's just some of us are forgiven. I don't know where you stand with God, but if you ever want to talk about it, I'd be glad to listen."

Barbara nodded her head and crumpled her napkin in her hands. "I don't know why you're being so good to me."

"Because so many people have been good to me throughout my life. And God has been best of all. Now, let's finish up before this food gets cold."

Henry picked up his fork and stuck a bite of chicken in his mouth. He chewed mechanically, staring at his mother. "Does Sadie know?"

"She does. She remembers before Casewell became her father, so I explained it as best I could when she was younger."

"What about Grandma?"

"Yes, and she had qualms about me marrying her boy, but she forgave me."

Of course she did. Frank and Angie probably knew, too. Seemed everybody knew but him. Of course, he could have asked. He hesitated, then blurted his next question.

"What did Dad think?"

"He judged me for it when he first found out, but after we — well, we got to know each other better that summer the drought was so bad, and we overcame a lot together. I think it made our marriage all that more special, having to work so hard to understand each other."

Henry didn't know what shocked him more — that his mother had an illegitimate child before she married or that his father married her in spite of it. "I'd better be getting on back to Grandma's," he said.

His mother gave him a knowing look. "I guess this is a lot to take in. Here, let me give you some pie to share with Emily. You might even talk to her about all this. She's a wise woman."

Henry nodded and waited for the dessert, then drove to Jack's instead of the farm. He wasn't going to drink or talk to girls, he just wanted to get lost playing his fiddle. As he made the turn away from home, he remembered that his whole point in going by the house was to talk to Barbara about whether or not she wanted him to marry her. He wondered why Sadie's father hadn't married his mother, and anger welled up in him. He'd like to tell that jerk a thing or two.

The anger dissipated. Yeah, like maybe his kid would want to tell him a thing or two one day if he didn't marry Barbara. The weight of his situation settled back over him.

Why did his father have to go and die and start this whole mess? He should be halfway through the semester at college and hearing from Dad how proud he was to have a son earning a degree. He should be planning to come home for the summer to work on the farm and help in Dad's woodshop. He should be doing a lot of things. Contemplating marriage to a girl he barely knew wasn't one of them.

The sounds of the hospital filtered into the dim room where Margaret sat holding Mayfair's limp hand. She'd slept a little through the night and thought it must be morning by now but didn't have the energy to try to find out for sure. She'd been sitting there long enough to recognize certain sounds and patterns in the hall. The squeak of a nurse's shoes, the beep of a monitor in the room opposite, the murmur of people talking, as though lowering their voices would stave off illness or even death.

She opened her mouth to speak to Mayfair again, but talking to her hadn't done anything, and she suddenly didn't have the energy to try again. She released her sister's hand just as she heard a new sound outside. It was somehow bigger and brighter than anything she'd heard up to this point. Not the rush and rumble of an emergency, more like the joy of a party. Margaret turned toward the door.

"Here you are. Beulah called to let us know Mayfair was sick." Emily bustled into the room, flipped the curtains all the way back, and snapped on a light. Perla appeared right behind her. "No need to sit here in the dark. It's a beautiful morning. Now tell us how Mayfair is."

Margaret started to speak, but instead of words, a wailing sob burst out of her. Perla stepped forward and wrapped both arms around her shoulders, rocking as Margaret sobbed. She tried to catch her breath. She was astonished by the violence of her tears and her inability to stop them. She gasped and felt her nose running on Perla's sleeve. She was horrified and embarrassed and hated to think of anyone seeing her like this, but she was powerless to stop.

And in that moment Margaret felt something release. She was powerless. There wasn't a thing she could do to fix Mayfair. She couldn't make her parents love her any more than she could make Henry love her. And yet, somehow, here were people who did love her. Two women who were no kin to her had come to her aid. They came to offer what they could, even if it was only a shoulder to cry on.

The crying eased, and Margaret took a deep, stuttering breath. The air was like cool water washing over her heart. She hiccupped, and Emily handed her a tissue as Perla eased her grip. Margaret blew her nose and blinked at the two women.

"I guess you needed that," Emily said.

Margaret managed a weak laugh. "Maybe I did."

Emily looked around the room. "This is the same hospital we brought John to when we found out he had cancer." Her eyes clouded. "I felt like crying, too." She exhaled a huff of air and stood up straighter. "But that was a different day and a different situation."

She smoothed Margaret's hair back from her hot forehead, and Margaret thought she might dissolve beneath the older woman's hand. But there was strength, too. She took another breath, this one steadier than the last.

"She's in a diabetic coma. They've done what they can to bring her sugar levels to normal, but her brain swelled. Is swelling. I'm not sure. Anyway, it's causing the coma, and they" — she choked a little — "they don't know . . . when she'll wake up."

Margaret had started to say "if" but

thought better of it. Perla hugged her again, and Emily moved to the bed where she took Mayfair's hand. She leaned over and spoke into the girl's ear. "We're here to keep your big sister company, Mayfair. You relax and have a nice rest. We'll take good care of the chickens and of Bertie until you feel better."

She stood and stroked Mayfair's arm, then her cheek. Perla pulled a chair closer to the bed so Emily could sit, then sat on the foot of the bed. Margaret took up her sister's other hand again, and the three women sat like that talking about the farm and life and plans for the future for the next hour. Margaret thought that if Mayfair had been awake it would have been one of the happiest hours of her life.

Henry played far into the night, losing himself in the music. Around three or four in the morning he grabbed a nap on a sofa in Jack's back room, then headed for the farm sometime after sunrise. He hoped Grandma assumed he'd spent the night at home in spite of Barbara's being there.

Instead of going into the house when he got to his grandmother's, Henry went out to milk Bertie and feed the chickens. He was surprised to find that no one had

306

gathered the eggs. Mayfair always did that. He collected almost a dozen into his ball cap — they were laying better now that the weather was warming up — and headed for the house, balancing eggs in one hand and carrying a bucket of warm milk in the other.

He kicked at the front door when he got there, trusting his grandmother would hurry over and open it for him. Nothing. He kicked and waited. Still nothing. He finally set the bucket down, opened the door, and managed to get everything inside.

"Grandma," he hollered.

The house was silent. Where could she have gone? He walked into the kitchen trying to avoid knocking off the dirt on his shoes. He got the milk and eggs situated, then checked the house over. No Grandma. And no note or anything else to tell him where she'd gone.

He heard a sound at the front door and went to check it out. Barbara stood there, peering in through the glass.

"Where'd you come from?" Henry asked as he opened the door.

"I walked over. Beulah Simmons called this morning, and I thought — well, it don't matter what I thought. She called to get your mother and grandmother to go to the hospital to sit with that girl."

"What girl?"

"The sister of the girl that works for your grandma."

"Mayfair? What happened?"

Barbara shrugged and took a tentative step toward the sofa as though not sure she'd be allowed to sit. "She's sick, I guess. Perla said she passed out or something, and Clint carried her to the hospital. Your mother left, said she was going to get your grandma and head over there." She fiddled with the zipper on her jacket. "I got kind of nervous over there by myself and figured maybe you'd stayed back. Now seems like you didn't know about it at all. Wonder why that is?"

She looked up through her eyelashes, and Henry felt frustration rise. Why did he have to get mixed up with a girl like this? He truly was a fool.

"I can't babysit you. I need to get over there and find out what happened." He moved toward the door and then stopped. Could he leave Barbara here? Should he take her along? She was his responsibility now — sort of.

"Why don't you call and see what you can find out?"

Henry stopped his dithering. Well, that wasn't a half-bad idea. He found a phone book and dialed his grandmother's black rotary phone. He listened to the whirring and then the ringing. He got connected to the right floor, and a nurse brought his mother to the phone. She filled him in on Mayfair's condition and said he should pray. She didn't ask where he'd been. Henry wished she'd asked him for something, maybe to go out and use the old hand plow to break up the garden for planting. That would be easier than sitting here fearing the worst.

He hung up the phone and turned to Barbara who, he noticed, had dark circles under her eyes. "Mayfair's in a coma from her diabetes. Mom says we should pray." Barbara nodded like he was passing along any other message. "They'll be home by bedtime."

Henry still had his jacket and boots on, so he removed them and then stood, arms akimbo, trying to decide what to do next. He remembered the milk.

"You know how to strain off fresh milk?"

Barbara looked surprised that he was addressing her. "Sure. I used to help my ma before she died."

Henry realized he knew next to nothing about Barbara. He motioned for her to follow him into the kitchen. Maybe it was time he learned something about the mother of his child.

Henry had a hard time getting Barbara to open up about her past, but she did share that her mother died when she was eleven — of cancer — and her father had more or less expected her to take her mother's place. She'd cooked, cleaned, and pretty well raised her two younger siblings. There was also an older sister, Linda, who left home as soon as she could. Henry got the feeling there was something significant Barbara was leaving out, but he didn't press her.

She'd wanted to go to school and learn to teach or maybe be a nurse. She thought she'd like to work with kids some way. Maybe that was why she wanted this baby. She didn't ask Henry any questions in return — almost as though all the curiosity had been drained out of her. Henry decided he might even get to like her, to count her a friend under other circumstances. But as it was, they had skipped right over friendship and moved on to something else.

"I guess your dad wouldn't think much of you having a baby," he said.

"I guess he wouldn't, but I don't aim to tell him."

They were sitting at the kitchen table

drinking coffee that Barbara made. It was good coffee.

Henry felt the moment had come to ask the question that had been weighing on him. He shifted like there was a bit of grit on his chair bothering him. "I know you said you didn't expect it, but what would you say if I told you I was willing to marry you?" Henry took a swig of coffee to wet his suddenly dry throat.

Barbara looked at him over the rim of her cup and seemed to consider. "I guess I'd have to think about it." She put the mug down. "That wasn't exactly what I'd call a declaration of love."

Henry puffed his cheeks. Girls. Why did it always have to be about love? "Loving people sets you up for pain. I'm making a practical suggestion here."

A cloud passed over Barbara's face. Henry guessed maybe she knew a thing or two about pain. They'd both lost a parent, and he guessed life hadn't turned out the way either one of them expected. Maybe they did have a good bit in common after all.

"You've got a point," she said with a gusty sigh. "I don't know about marrying, but I guess it's something I ought to consider. What would your mother say?"

"Mom? I guess she'd be glad to know her

grandbaby wasn't going anywhere. Other than that, I don't know."

"I wonder why she didn't marry the man who . . . well, you know."

Henry appreciated Barbara's attempt at delicacy. "Maybe something happened to him. Maybe he didn't know."

"Maybe he offered, and she turned him down." Barbara seemed to like that idea. "Her life turned out all right."

"I guess so. It probably wasn't easy there at first, though." Henry had never thought about his mother this way. He was beginning to think she was a lot stronger than he'd given her credit for.

"Easy. What's that?" Barbara took their empty mugs to the sink and washed them. "I'll think about it. Now, how about you take me back to your mother's house? Surely they'll be home soon."

23

Margaret looked at the pay phone in the lobby as if it were a loaded gun. She did not want to call her parents. One of the nuns offered to do it for her, but she felt even worse pawning the job off on anyone else. Although it might help if that someone else had a direct line to God. She whispered a prayer just in case and picked up the receiver. Her mother answered on the fourth ring.

"Hoffman residence, this is Lenore speaking."

"Hi, Mom, it's Margaret."

"Yes, what do you need? I have guests."

Margaret swallowed convulsively and tried to think of something sensible to say. "Mayfair's in the hospital. I thought you'd want to know."

There was a shriek and a babbling sound before Margaret's dad came on the line. "What's this about Mayfair?"

"Hey, Dad. She . . . well, it's her diabetes."

"Did she let her sugar drop too low again? Your mother has told her and told her —"

Margaret cut him off. "Yeah, well, it went way too low this time, and she's in a diabetic coma."

Margaret heard her mother's voice in the background asking questions. Her dad put a hand over the receiver and said, "She's in a coma." There was another shriek, and Margaret could hear other voices in the mix.

"Your mother is very upset by this. I don't think you've handled this very well, Margaret."

Margaret fought the urge to hang up the phone. "Sorry, Dad. Are you going to come down here?"

He must have done a better job of covering the mouthpiece this time because Margaret couldn't make out what he was saying. He came back on the line.

"Not right now. Your mother is in no condition. You stay there and keep an eye on things. Call us if there are any changes, and we'll be over in the morning. Your mother is absolutely devastated. We'll see you tomorrow."

There was a click and a buzz. Margaret slowly hung up the phone. They hadn't even asked what room Mayfair was in or what the doctor had to say. Margaret slumped in an uncomfortable plastic chair and wished she were anywhere else in the world.

When Henry pulled up in front of his mother's house, he saw that Mom and Grandma were already there. He glanced at Barbara and wondered if they would think it was inappropriate for them to be together. Like he could do any more damage at this point.

As soon as they got inside he asked, "How's Mayfair?" He really wanted to know, but he also hoped to divert attention away from any questions about Barbara.

Mom rolled her neck and closed her eyes. "Much the same, I'm afraid. They've done what they can to get her sugar where it needs to be, but the swelling in her brain has yet to go down. It's just a matter of waiting at this point."

Barbara ducked down the hallway, and he could hear water running. Grandma patted the sofa cushion next to her, and he obliged her by sitting.

"You been getting to know the mother of your child?"

Henry jerked as if he'd caught himself dozing off. How did she know?

"Yeah, I guess so. She didn't have the easiest time growing up."

"I supposed as much. What do you think of her now?"

Henry scratched his head. "I guess, if the circumstances were different . . ."

"You might like her," his grandmother finished.

"Yeah, maybe I would."

"And now you're thinking about marrying her."

Henry jerked his head up. "What makes you think —"

"I've known you since before you were born. And I like to think we raised you to be the sort of young man who would want to take responsibility in a situation like this."

Henry heard a door close down the hallway and guessed Barbara had gone to bed. In his bedroom. "Well, maybe I should marry her."

Grandma nodded her head and patted his hand. "Maybe you should." She was quiet a moment. "Now, how long has it been since you two were . . . intimate?"

Henry felt heat rise all the way to his hairline. He turned to his mother for help, but she just gave him an expectant look. "Not that long, I guess. Maybe six weeks?"

Both women nodded their heads like they knew something he didn't. Mom spoke first.

"She's showing already."

"Showing more than six weeks, I'd say. Especially if this is her first."

"It might not be the first."

"Even so, she's at least three months along. I'd stake Bertie's next calf on it."

They nodded at each other again.

"What are you saying?" Henry felt like they were speaking a foreign language.

His mom looked him in the eye. "I think she may already have been pregnant when you . . . when you —"

Grandma jumped in. "When you spent the night together. Is there any chance this child could be someone else's?"

Henry thought about Jack's bar and how Charlie said he paid for the girls to go with them. Could it be? And could he be that stupid?

"Well, I guess there might be a possibility . . ."

"Yes, I imagine there is." His mother walked over and pinched the tender spot where his shoulder sloped into his neck. "But that doesn't let you off the hook, young man. Whether you're the father or not, you did something you shouldn't have. And that young woman needs someone to take care of her."

She let go, and Henry resisted the urge to

massage his neck. He flinched when Mom spoke again.

"Barbara is in a difficult place. We're going to continue taking care of her, and I want you to treat her like gold. Don't say anything about this. I'm hoping she'll learn to trust us."

"But what if she wants to get married?"

His grandmother elbowed him. "Did you ask?"

"Kind of."

"Well, you'll be in a pickle if she says yes. But I have a suspicion there's a reason she didn't jump at your offer. Now take me on home. I'm tired through and through."

Henry stood and helped his grandmother to her feet. His head spun as they left for the farm. This situation was getting more and more complicated by the minute.

Margaret woke the next morning stiff and rumpled from sleeping in a chair in Mayfair's room. She'd fallen asleep holding her sister's hand but had released it at some point. The hand was still there, pale against the sheets, unmoving. Margaret went in the bathroom to splash water on her face, and when she came out, Henry and Emily were walking through the door. Emily hurried over and gave her a hug. Henry waved feebly from the doorway.

"I had Henry bring me out first thing. Did you sleep here last night?" She held Margaret at arm's length. "Of course you did. Where else would you be? Just let me tell Mayfair good morning, and then we'll go find you some breakfast."

"I'm not hungry."

Emily smoothed Margaret's tangled hair back from her face. The touch was almost too tender for Margaret to bear.

"I know you aren't, but you'd better eat. Henry can stay here with Mayfair."

Henry smiled and nodded in a way Margaret supposed was meant to be encouraging but mostly looked goofy. She almost smiled at his obvious discomfort. He must not like hospitals, but then, who did? She was about to agree to breakfast when a wave of sound washed down the hall and into the room. Moments later Mom swept into the room with two nurses in high dudgeon and Dad bringing up the rear. They all seemed to be talking at once.

Henry put his fingers to his lips and whistled. All their heads snapped his direction at once. He turned red.

"Sorry. I thought all that racket probably wasn't good for anybody, least of all Mayfair."

Lenore moaned and sagged across the foot of her daughter's bed. "Oh, my baby. Why can't you wake her up?"

The older nurse tapped her foot. "As I tried to explain —"

"Oh, don't start with all that medical mumbo jumbo again. I just want my baby awake and in my arms." She pulled out a lace-edged handkerchief and dabbed at her eyes. Her gaze fell on Margaret. "And you. How in the world did you let this happen?"

Margaret recoiled and felt Emily slide an arm around her. She wanted to defend herself but knew better than to speak. There was no reasoning with Lenore Hoffman when she got like this. Margaret noticed that her father had receded into the corner, where he gazed at his youngest child with something like sorrow on his face. Margaret felt a moment's vindication. He should feel bad.

"Why can't anyone give me answers?"

Margaret turned back to her mother, who apparently felt she'd fallen out of the spotlight for a moment. Emily stepped forward and took Mom's hand.

"You poor thing. This must be so hard on you. I hate to see you like this. It must be upsetting to be here watching your child suffer. Why don't you come with me, and we'll get a cup of coffee." Emily tugged Lenore to a standing position. "The doctor should be around soon, and perhaps he'll have news to share with Margaret. Then she can tell you."

Mom sniffled and clutched her handkerchief. "I truly can't bear to see her like this. You're right. I doubt I can swallow anything, but perhaps we could try a cup of coffee."

Margaret watched the two women move toward the door as though her mother were infirm. Emily turned just before they disappeared and winked at Margaret. As the two turned into the hallway her mom called back.

"Wallace, get out here. I need you."

Dad closed his eyes and stood still for a moment, like a rabbit trying to avoid its prey by not moving. But when Mom hollered again, he sighed and moved toward the door. As he passed Margaret, he reached out and patted her shoulder. Then he was gone, too.

Henry looked at Margaret with a slightly stunned expression. "Holy cow," he said.

"Yeah."

"Hey, I can go get you something to eat and bring it back."

"Honestly, I don't much want to eat. And

the nurses were nice enough to bring me a sandwich last night. Maybe they'll think to bring me a biscuit or some cereal this morning."

Henry stepped over and touched Mayfair's hand gently. "Has she moved at all?"

"No. Sometimes I see her eyes moving behind the lids — like she's dreaming. I'm hoping that's a good thing."

"It seems funny . . ." Henry trailed off and cocked his head to one side.

"What does?"

"Well, not funny, maybe strange. It seems she might have made other people better, but now she's sick. Seems she can heal everyone but herself."

"Or that she absorbed their sickness," Margaret said. She wanted to clamp a hand over her mouth. That was ridiculous.

"Yeah, something like that. I mean, why would God let other people get well but not Mayfair? He's supposed to love everyone. Why would He help mean old Clint Simmons' wife and not someone as sweet as Mayfair? I don't get it."

"Maybe it's not God. Maybe it's coincidence. Maybe God doesn't care, and it's all just chance." Margaret flopped back down in her chair and rested her head on the edge of the mattress.

"Like Dad dying," Henry said. "I wish Mayfair had been there for him."

Margaret looked up at Henry. "You think she could have healed him? What did he die of?"

"They think his heart gave out. He was born with some kind of defect. It kept him out of the war, and I guess his heart just couldn't keep going."

Margaret smiled even though she felt sad. "Well, Mayfair has certainly touched a lot of hearts." She reached across the bed and grasped Henry's wrist. "I'm sorry she wasn't there for your dad."

Henry slid his fingers around Margaret's and held her hand. "Me too. I guess it could all just be coincidence — Angie's mind getting better, my hand healing so fast, the little girl with the bee sting — but somehow I think it's more than that."

He squeezed Margaret's hand, and she felt her pulse race, her heart flutter. Why, oh why, was he being so sweet? She wanted to be mad at him and the rest of the world. He cleared his throat.

"I've been thinking, though."

Margaret looked at him expectantly, afraid if she spoke he might release her hand.

"Your parents." He nodded toward the door. "Well, I'm just really lucky to have the family I do. I've got great memories of my dad. I can't count how many times he told me he loved me or that he was proud of me."

Margaret felt tears prickling her eyes. She wasn't sure if she was crying over Henry's losing his father or her never really having much of one.

"Anyhow, I've just been thinking that your parents aren't like mine." He gripped her hand a little tighter and looked right at her. "And I wish it could be different for you."

She gazed back into those eyes the color of rich brown soil ready for planting, and it was like something electric passed between them. Something powerful, something that felt like . . .

Mayfair moaned softly, and her eyelids fluttered.

24

Henry hated to leave the hospital, but he needed to tend the animals. Grandma opted to stay in hopes that Mayfair would fully awaken. She seemed to be more responsive but still wasn't really aware. When Margaret gripped her sister's hand, Mayfair squeezed it back, and they all thought she turned her head toward Margaret's voice, but it could have been involuntary. The hospital staff acted as if they didn't want to get anyone's hopes up, but Henry knew Margaret's hopes were high.

Bertie met him at the cowshed, clearly eager for her milking. Henry rubbed her neck and led her into the stall where he tucked his head into her side and fell into the rhythm of milk striking metal. It was lonesome on the farm, knowing that everyone was at the hospital. No grandmother in the main house. No Margaret and Mayfair in the little gray house.

Just Bertie chewing her cud.

Henry thought about that moment before Mayfair's eyelids fluttered. He wasn't sure why he'd taken Margaret's hand, only that it had felt right. It wasn't like sparks flew or anything. And yet there had been an attraction. He guessed maybe he found Margaret's devotion to her sister and her sensible way of looking at the world appealing when his own world felt so upside down. He liked her willingness to work hard and take care of his grandmother. He admired the way she had stepped away from her awful family but not from Mayfair. And although he still wouldn't call her beautiful the way some of the girls at school were, with their perfect hair and short skirts, he guessed she was prettier than he'd realized. Even her freckles had grown on him. He couldn't quite remember what he'd admired about porcelain skin.

Bertie mooed and looked at him over her shoulder. Henry realized although he'd finished milking, he was still leaning into the cow's warm flank. He gave himself a shake and stood, patting Bertie and talking to her as he let her back out into the pasture. She ambled off a few feet and stopped to crop grass as though she liked his company as much as he did hers.

An image of life on the farm with Margaret flashed through Henry's mind. He'd carry the brimming bucket to the house. She would take it from him, strain it, and leave it for the cream to rise. They'd sit down to supper together and talk about the farm and their plans for adding livestock and maybe some field crops, now that it was early spring. She'd wash the dishes while he listened to farming updates on the radio. Maybe they'd talk over what they heard. And then it would be bedtime.

Henry flushed and hurried for the house. He was an idiot to even entertain such thoughts. If he married anyone, it would probably be Barbara. He slowed and tried to picture her the way he had Margaret. No good. All he saw was a flustered young woman trying to care for a baby while burning the biscuits. He didn't have high hopes for Barbara's domestic skills. He guessed for now he'd just pin his hopes on Mayfair getting better and pray that maybe God would take care of everything else, too.

Mayfair kept opening her eyes, though she seemed to be having a hard time following movement. She'd try to watch Margaret as she walked around the room, but her eyelids would hang, and she'd have to blink and try again. She still hadn't spoken, but she was getting more consistent when Margaret asked her to squeeze her hand.

Mom and Dad had gone home so Mom could lie down. She'd left strict instructions to call if there was any change, but Margaret took that to mean she should only call if there was an opportunity for Lenore to come back and be the center of attention. She thought Mayfair's improved responses would likely offer just such an opportunity, so she didn't call.

Perla had come to join Emily, and both women went to pick up supper at a nearby diner. The consensus was that Margaret needed to eat something other than hospital food. Margaret didn't much care but was glad for a moment alone with her sister. She pulled one of the uncomfortable plastic chairs over to the bed and twined her arm with Mayfair's. Her sister turned her head but seemed to struggle to focus. She closed her eyes and squeezed Margaret's hand. It felt like a hug.

"Were you listening to Henry and me?" Margaret asked. "When we were talking about you? It's the funniest thing, the way people seem to get better when you're around. And then you get worse. Could you tell Henry held my hand?" Margaret stroked

Mayfair's arm. "I don't know why he did it, but it was nice. I can't decide if I like him or not. I mean, I like him — even when he's an idiot — but sometimes I feel there could be more. Like we could . . . Well, that's probably silly. But when he held my hand like that, it seemed as though I could see a future with him in it. And maybe children — a girl and a boy, I think."

Margaret laid her head down on the cool sheet. It smelled perfectly clean. Mayfair sighed. It was a sweet, contented sound. A single tear rolled down Margaret's nose, much to her surprise. Where had that come from? She heard a sound at the door and sat up. Clint Simmons pushed a wheelchair into the room. Beulah sat in it, all smiles.

"Oh, my sweet, sweet friends. I'm so glad to see you. How is she?" Beulah reached toward Mayfair as though she could hurry Clint closer to the bed.

Margaret swiped at the dampness on her face and smiled. "She's better but not quite well yet. I'm hopeful she'll be her old self soon."

Clint wedged the chair in as close to the bed as it would go. Margaret placed Mayfair's hand in Beulah's and watched tears rise in the older woman's eyes.

"She squeezed my hand. Oh, and her eyes

are sneaking open." She waved at Mayfair. "Don't you put yourself out, sweetheart. I don't need to look into your eyes to feel your love. You rest."

Something like pain passed over Beulah's face. Margaret laid a hand on her knee. "Are you all right?"

Beulah brushed her concern away. "I'm better than I've been since I can't remember when." She glanced back at Clint and smiled. "There's more to being all right than feeling up to dancing a jig."

Margaret snuck a glance at Clint, who was looking at Mayfair with an expression she might call concern. When he realized he had Margaret's attention, he averted his gaze, quickly looking out the window instead. His hand slipped from the handle of the wheelchair to his wife's shoulder. She placed her fingers over his.

An inner light seemed to come on inside Beulah. "Yes, indeedy, I'm finer than frog hair. Now, what does the doctor say about this precious child?"

"He says it may take some time, and there could be some lasting effects, but now that she's awake, he's hopeful she'll have a full recovery."

Margaret didn't dare share the whole truth in front of Mayfair. The doctor said there could be some long-term impact on her sister's speech and motor skills, but she wanted Mayfair to think all would be well. She turned the conversation back toward Beulah.

"But what about you? How are you feeling?"

Beulah smiled even wider. "I'm feeling like the Lord has blessed me enough for two lifetimes."

Clint whipped out a handkerchief and blew his nose, a great honking sound that made Margaret cringe. Beulah looked up at him like he hung the moon.

Margaret wasn't sure how to respond. She'd been to the Simmonses' house, seen how they lived and how they acted. How could Beulah feel blessed?

Perla and Emily returned, and Margaret felt a strange tension fill the room. When Beulah saw Emily, she held her arms out, and the two women hugged like sisters reunited after years apart. Clint took a step back, though he kept one hand on the wheelchair. When Emily straightened from greeting Beulah, she looked him in the eye.

"It's good to see you, Clint. I'm so glad the two of you came to visit Mayfair."

He cleared his throat with a great racket and nodded. "Child like that — she makes you think about what's true and what ain't. Guess maybe it's time for some of us to move on."

Emily nodded. "I'm glad."

Margaret wondered if they were talking about Clint's first wife dying in childbirth. Had Clint just let a couple of decades' worth of anger slide away? She looked at him more closely as he gazed out the window again. Maybe there was a softening there around his thin lips. Maybe the light in his eye wasn't the fire of anger anymore. Maybe miracles did happen.

"Marrrr . . ."

Margaret whirled toward her sister, who was trying to speak. Her face contorted, and she scrunched her nose. "Luuuuuff." She took a breath and closed her eyes. "Luuuff alllll." She lifted one hand and waved it back and forth.

Perla took the child's hand. "Are you saying you love us all?"

Mayfair nodded, her head jerking, and opened her eyes, managing to focus on Perla for a moment. "Yesssss."

"We love you, too, sweetheart. So very, very much."

Margaret swallowed the tears gathering in the back of her throat and looked around the room. Well, they were a motley collection of people and certainly not kin, but somehow it felt like family. She wished Henry were there. Somehow the moment was incomplete without him.

As the day wound down only Emily remained to keep Margaret company at the hospital. She tried to talk Margaret into coming home with her.

"You need a good night's rest, and I know you won't get that here. I can stay with you in the gray house, or we can send Henry over there, and it can be just the two of us at my house. Either way, I know you'll rest better."

"I appreciate it, Emily, but I really do want to stay here with Mayfair. I wouldn't sleep a wink for worrying about her."

Emily stopped fussing and put an arm around Margaret's shoulders. "I understand. I'd likely do the same."

Henry appeared in the doorway, beat-up John Deere cap in his hand. He looked at Margaret, and then his eyes slid away. "You ready, Grandma?"

"I am. Mayfair's had a good evening, but it's time to let these girls get their rest."

Henry nodded and looked at Mayfair. "She sleeping?"

"I think so," Margaret said. "She's still

having a hard time focusing, and I think it wears her out."

"I'll be keeping you both in my prayers," Henry said. "I'll be downstairs, Grandma." He disappeared and Margaret suddenly wished him back.

Emily hugged Margaret good-bye, patted Mayfair's shoulder, and smoothed her silken hair across the pillow. "I expect we'll be back tomorrow."

Margaret sat down in the dim quiet room beside her sleeping sister. Something was different. She couldn't remember Henry ever talking about praying — for her or for anyone else.

25

Henry let his grandmother out at the front door and then drove the truck over to a stand of pines. The weather looked like it might turn, and he wanted to leave it under the shelter of the dense branches.

When he switched off the headlights and got out, he felt more than saw someone in the shadows. "Who's there?" He wished he had his rifle.

"Pipe down. It's just me." Charlie stepped into the moonlight.

"What are you doing here? Get lost on a whiskey run?"

Charlie smirked. "Ain't never got lost in my life. Anyhow, Pa seems to be letting the business slide. Might be a chance to step in and pick up the slack, make some real money. Think you might want to go partners?"

Henry considered that he could give the money to Barbara and her child or maybe help Margaret with Mayfair's hospital bills, but he quickly discarded the notion of partnering with Charlie. "Reckon I'll find something honest to keep me and anyone else who needs it."

Charlie slid closer. "You going to marry her, then?"

It was on the tip of Henry's tongue to say he would, even though he was pretty sure the baby wasn't his, but deep down he knew Barbara wasn't the girl he wanted to marry, and he thought she might not want it, either. Still, he wasn't going to tell Charlie all that. "I might."

Charlie scuffed his boot along the dirt floor. "How's your ma feel about that?"

"She wants me to do what's right."

"You could probably get off just giving her a wad of cash and sending her away. I expect she'd go."

"You think?" Henry scratched under his cap. What was Charlie getting at?

"You do a couple of runs with me, and we could pile up enough cash to convince her to take the money and skedaddle. I could handle the, ah, finances for you."

Henry thought about his vision of living on the farm with someone like Margaret. Or maybe not just like Margaret. Maybe it could be Margaret. He buried that idea, planning to dig it up later when he had more time to go over it. Right now he couldn't shake the feeling that Charlie was working an angle, and he wanted to know what it was.

"What did you have in mind?"

Charlie sidled closer. "Two big runs back-to-back. One to Jack's place tomorrow night, then we do a drop-off at that cemetery you did once before. It'll all be over before sunrise, and the payout oughta be enough to put you in the clear."

"What if Barbara won't go for it? That's a big risk to take on the off chance she'll grab the money and run."

"I been knowing her a long time. I think it's a sure thing, but just ask her if you want to."

Henry rolled his head from shoulder to shoulder, thinking. It was just one night, and even if Barbara wouldn't take the money and go, it would still come in handy.

"How much are we talking about?"

Charlie named a figure, and Henry whistled. How could he pass that up?

"All right, but this is the last time."

Charlie slapped him on the back. "We'll take the Barracuda. I'll meet you at the bridge down on Laurel Run at midnight tomorrow."

Henry had the uncomfortable feeling he'd struck a deal with the devil, but he shook it off and went on into the house.

Henry woke the next morning to find a fine dusting of snow over the greening grass. When his grandmother referred to it as "poor man's fertilizer" he thought to get the tractor out and plow the garden.

"That'll be fine. I'll get Perla to take me to the hospital. You just stay home and be a farmer today."

Henry smiled. He couldn't think of anything he'd like better than riding the tractor up and down the garden rows, the sun warm on his back, getting the soil ready for spring planting. He felt like winter might really be over, like his life might finally be coming together, and like all of his problems had a solution.

When Grandma came home that evening with the news that Mayfair had spoken a few words and seemed to be getting some of her dexterity back, he felt that God really was smiling on him. He remembered telling Margaret he'd pray for her and Mayfair, so he whispered a quick word of thanks and felt even better about himself.

Grandma turned in early that evening, which suited Henry just fine. He hoped she wouldn't even know he was gone overnight. He'd left the truck on the crest of the hill that ran down to Laurel Run. He figured he could put it in gear and coast a good way before starting it up. He was at the bridge ten minutes before midnight feeling pretty invincible.

Charlie rumbled up in the Barracuda. "Good. Give me a hand." He pointed to the bridge in the moonlight.

Turned out the moonshine was stashed underneath. Henry helped load, wondering what made this run so valuable and why they didn't load up at Clint's house. He started to ask the question but knew from experience this wasn't the sort of enterprise where folks appreciated questions. He clamped his mouth shut and finished loading.

They made it to Jack's backwoods bar without incident, unloaded, and then Henry figured they'd head back to Clint's or the bridge for the second load.

"Hold on." Charlie laid a hand on Henry's arm. "Second load's here."

Now Henry was really confused. Why would they deliver liquor and then take more away? Charlie pointed at some crates. There were only a few, and they didn't weigh nearly enough. Henry was getting a bad feeling, but he knew better than to cause a stir. Jack looked grim and Charlie surely wasn't offering any additional information. Henry noticed there was a shotgun in the backseat of the car that he hadn't seen before. His earlier feeling of well-being was long gone.

"You drive," Charlie said, tossing the keys. "I ain't been to the church before."

"Same stone?" Henry asked.

"Yup. Bert Williams or something like that."

Williamson, thought Henry, but he didn't correct Charlie.

They drove in silence, Charlie tapping his fingers on the armrest and Henry trying to puzzle out what he'd gotten himself into. He thought about Raymond Sawyer, the preacher at the Baptist church. What was the Scripture he pointed out? Oh, yeah. Esau scorning his birthright. He'd looked it up later and read the whole story, and now it came back to him. Esau had been so worried about filling his belly that he gave up his rights as eldest son. Henry wondered what his rights and duties were as his father's only son. To inherit and run the farm? To take care of his sister, mother, and grandmother? To be the spiritual leader of the family?

As he sped through the night with who knows what in the trunk of the car, he didn't feel like much of a leader. He felt he was trying to take the easy way out. Well, once they got through this, he was never going to do anything shady again. And he was going straight over to see Barbara first thing in the morning to reaffirm his willingness to take care of her and the child, no matter whose the child was. He felt a pang, realizing he might be giving up a great deal, but he also felt kind of noble, and the car seemed to fly even faster with the impetus of his resolve.

The moon had set by the time they reached the cemetery, and Henry felt weary. He was a fool, but he'd make the best of a bad situation. He figured the only way past this mess was through it. He took a few minutes to find the stone with Bert's name on it. Charlie seemed to be getting antsier by the minute. Henry whispered a prayer, asking for help and forgiveness all in one breath. This praying business was getting easier.

They were carrying the last crates of whatever they were delivering to the stone when a spotlight mounted on the corner of the church building flicked on. A voice spoke as though from heaven.

"Freeze, boys. Stay where you are."

For a moment, Henry thought God was finally calling him to task, but then he realized it was Sheriff Pendleton with a bullhorn. He wished it were God instead.

The little gray house looked like heaven to Margaret in the morning light. She was only stopping by to bathe and get some fresh clothes, but it still felt like home. Mayfair had also asked for some books, although Margaret wasn't sure she'd be able to read them. Maybe she'd read aloud to her sister. She smiled at the thought. It had been a long time since they'd done that.

Finished with her tasks, she headed out past Emily's. Perla's car was in the driveway, and Margaret decided to stop in and give the women an update. She'd talked to her parents the evening before, and they'd barely seemed interested. It would be nice to talk to someone who really cared.

She stepped into the sitting room and followed voices toward the kitchen. Emily and Perla sat at the table sipping coffee with a third woman, who was much younger. Maybe even younger than Margaret. She'd never seen her before, but she was immediately struck by how pretty the girl was, although there was a sharpness to her features, too, like she was bracing for something painful. This must be Barbara.

Margaret smiled. "Good morning. I thought I'd stop and let you know how Mayfair is."

Perla jumped to her feet and gave Margaret a quick hug, then fussed over getting her a cup of coffee. Margaret wondered if she was imposing. Emily sighed and pinched the bridge of her nose.

"Margaret, this is Barbara."

"Nice to meet you," she said, nodding to Barbara. "I hope you're enjoying your stay."

Barbara snorted in a most unladylike way, and Margaret felt silly. She began to feel less like family and more like a clumsy neighbor who doesn't know when to butt out.

Perla pressed a cup of coffee into her hand, and Margaret set it down on the counter. "You know, on second thought I'd better get on to the hospital. Mayfair really is much better, and I hate to be away too long. It was nice to meet you, Barbara."

The girl stood and Margaret thought she was going to shake her hand, but she smoothed a hand over her belly instead. Although Margaret knew she was pregnant, seeing the evidence was something of a shock.

The phone rang, and Emily muttered something that didn't sound nice under her breath. "Margaret, wait right there. Perla, would you get that?" Emily stood and guided Margaret into the sitting room while Perla picked up the receiver and spoke into it.

"Emily, it's Henry," Perla called from the kitchen.

Emily sighed and closed her eyes. "What now?"

"He's been arrested. We have to get down there right away."

Margaret walked up the stairs to the second floor of the hospital. She could have taken the elevator, but she wanted to keep moving. She wasn't sure she could stop even when she got to Mayfair's room. Although she'd known there was no hope for her and Henry, meeting Barbara and seeing her swelling belly had truly driven the fact home.

And now he'd been arrested. For what, Margaret didn't know, but did it even matter? She'd been entertaining romantic thoughts about a cad and a lawbreaker. She should be glad she'd found out what kind of man he was before she'd really lost her heart. She stopped and leaned against the wall near the door to the second floor. A nun popped through and seemed startled to find her there.

"My dear, are you all right?"

Margaret straightened up and smoothed a hand over her hair. It was raining outside, and she probably looked like a bedraggled mess.

"I'm fine." The words came out as a whisper. She cleared her throat and tried again. "Fine," she said brightly.

The nun looked her up and down and reached out to take her hand. "You are not fine. Can I pray for you?"

Margaret wanted to jerk her hand away and run from this kind woman. She was short and looked soft, though not overweight. Her eyes were spectacularly blue, and Margaret almost could see her reflection there. It made her heart hurt.

"Okay."

The woman gathered both of Margaret's hands in her own and tucked them under her chin. She closed her eyes, so Margaret did, too.

"Father in heaven, your daughter is suffering a pain that only you know and understand. Her heart is heavy, and she needs the comfort that your Spirit provides. Give her peace today and wisdom for the days ahead. In your son's holy name I pray, amen."

Margaret stayed with head bowed and eyes closed. She felt as though someone who loved her had wrapped their arms around her. She didn't want to leave the stairwell. She was afraid if she moved she'd burst the fragile bubble of peace that had formed around her. The nun didn't seem in any hurry, either.

At last Margaret lifted her head and looked into those cerulean eyes. "Thank you."

"Oh, my dear, it's a gift for me to talk to our Father on your behalf."

Margaret moved through the door and into the hallway. She eased toward Mayfair's room, afraid the tenuous peace might evaporate. But somehow it seemed to grow stronger, more tangible, the closer she got to her sister. When she entered the room, Mayfair was sitting up, smiling. And Margaret somehow found the grace to hope Henry wasn't in bad trouble and that he might even find happiness with Barbara.

On one hand, jail wasn't as bad as Henry imagined. It seemed everyone who worked there had known his father and regretted having to lock him up. They were as nice as they could be under the circumstances, bringing him food and making him as comfortable as the accommodations would allow. On the other hand, jail was infinitely worse than he imagined. He had never felt quite so alone in all his life. And when, for just a moment, it crossed his mind that he was glad his dad wasn't here to see him, it was the lowest point of his life. Or so he thought, until his mother and grandmother appeared on the other side of the bars.

"Henry, are you all right?" Mom asked.

All he could manage was a nod of his head. Then he stared at the floor between his feet.

"What were you thinking?"

He wasn't sure which one of them spoke the words. He looked up at the little window high in the wall behind him. "I guess I wasn't."

"Oh, Henry. Marijuana. This is serious."

"I didn't know," he mumbled.

"What's that you say?" That was definitely Grandma.

"I said I didn't know it was marijuana. I thought . . ." Well, it really wouldn't do to explain that he thought he was bootlegging moonshine.

"Never mind. The main thing is to move forward from this point. I'm not sure what

347

26

A door clanging open awakened Henry. He blinked, trying to get his bearings. Sheriff Pendleton stood there, legs wide and hands on his hips.

"Get on up. I'm running you home."

Henry blinked and sat up. "What?"

"Seems you were an unfortunate bystander in a criminal operation. Wrong place. Wrong time."

"Well, yeah, I didn't know there were drugs, but why are you letting me go? I mean how did you know?"

The sheriff scratched his head and sighed. "Son, I would have bet my last dollar Clint Simmons would do everything in his power to make sure a Phillips rotted in jail. But I'd have lost that bet. Seems old Clint knew what his boy was up to and knew he'd wrangled you in on the deal."

"Clint told you . . . what?"

"Well, I'm still thinking you might not

have been one hundred percent aboveboard with whatever was going on, but I tend to believe you didn't know anything about the drugs. And with the information Clint, uh, persuaded Charlie to share about the men who are running the operation, well, I see no reason to keep you locked up." The sheriff swung to the side and motioned for Henry to come out of the cell.

"Now I'm going to run you to your grandma's house, and I aim to lecture you pretty hard most of the way." He started toward the door, and Henry jogged to keep up. "But if I find you in my jail again, I'm going to throw away the key, no matter what."

"Yes, sir." Henry wondered where his truck was.

They got to the parking lot, and a man stood there leaning up against Henry's truck.

"Howdy, Ray, I didn't know you were planning to come around this morning," the sheriff said.

"Sheriff, when you work for the Lord, you don't know your own plans most days. I just go where He sends me. This morning He told me to bring Henry's truck on over." He looked past the sheriff. "Hey, Henry."

With a start, Henry realized it was the

preacher from the church where they'd been delivering the moonshine — or marijuana, he guessed.

"Hey."

"Ray, I was going to lecture this boy all the way home. If I turn him over to you, reckon you could handle that for me?"

"I've been known to preach a sermon or two in my day. I think I can take care of it."

Sheriff Pendleton tipped his hat and headed back toward the courthouse.

Ray opened the door to the truck. "You want to drive? I preach better when it's all I'm doing. You can run me back to the church on your way home."

Henry slid behind the wheel. "How'd you get my truck?"

"I was there when the sheriff apprehended you last night. He confiscated your keys, and I rode with the deputy who went to pick up evidence at the bridge. We found your truck, and I offered to drive it."

"How'd you know about the bridge?"

"Sheriff's been trying to get those boys growing weed for a while now. Guess you got tied in at just the wrong moment. He knew about the bridge, the drop-off at the cemetery, and young Charlie's involvement." He grinned as Henry started the truck and pulled out onto the road. "You,

351

on the other hand, were unexpected. There was supposed to be somebody else with Charlie last night."

Henry opened his mouth to ask who but decided he didn't want to know. "Now what?" he asked instead.

"Well, I suppose that's up to you."

"Aren't you supposed to lecture me or something?"

Ray chuckled. "I could do that. You want me to?"

"I guess not. Seems I've got a pretty good idea about the mistakes I've made."

"I take it you're talking about more than getting tangled up with Charlie Simmons?"

"Yeah, though I'm surprised his dad helped get me off the hook."

Ray put one booted foot up on the dashboard. "I've got the feeling ole Clint has seen the light. I been praying for that as long as I can remember." He let a beat of silence roll by. "How about you, Henry? You seen the light?"

"I'm a Christian, if that's what you mean." Ray didn't comment, and Henry felt compelled to explain. "I mean, I've been going to church all my life. I know about Noah's ark and David and Goliath, stuff like that. I even looked up the one about Esau after you read me that Scripture a while back."

Ray nodded his head. "Those are some good stories. As it happens, I did preach on ole Esau the Sunday after we met."

"Yeah? Was it any good?"

Ray chuckled. "Well, I didn't notice anybody dozing off, but you never know. God works in His own way, and it's almost never the way I expect." He took his foot down from the dashboard and sat up a bit straighter. "The thrust of the sermon was that Esau pretty much ruined things for himself because he was focused on his physical wants rather than his spiritual needs. Gave up his birthright — his future — to satisfy his belly."

Henry pondered that. "I read on ahead. Seems like it turned out okay for Esau. He got a big family and lots of land, and his brother Jacob was even kind of afraid of him when he finally came on home."

"True, true. I'm not saying Esau had a bad life. He just didn't have the life he was born to. Seems to me he had to go through a whole lot of aggravation and disappointment just so he could eat a bite when he was hungry. Might have been worth waiting till he could get a sandwich later on."

Silence stretched long in the cab of the truck. Finally Henry cleared his throat.

"You think everybody is born with a purpose?"

"Oh yeah."

"How do you know what it is?"

"What satisfies you, Henry? I'm not talking about being happy or pleased. I'm talking about deep down in your bones satisfied."

Henry thought about that. He'd been trying to feel as little as possible since his dad died, but maybe there had been a time or two . . . When he played his fiddle. When he was showing Margaret how to milk Bertie. That time he was fixing fence with Mayfair and could look back down the line to see what they had accomplished. When he plowed the garden the other morning and the rows ran straight and dark with the promise of future crops . . .

"Can't think of anything?" Ray interrupted his thoughts.

"I guess I can, but it doesn't seem like much of a purpose, not like those guys in the Bible."

"God only called one man to build an ark, Henry. Whatever His purpose is for you, it's different from anyone else's. You ponder on what makes you feel satisfied. That ought to at least point you in the right direction."

Henry let silence fill the truck again. This

time, neither man broke it.

A week later, well into April, Mayfair was ready to go home. She was able to speak pretty well, although sometimes she seemed to lose words or get lost in the middle of a sentence. She also walked with what Margaret had come to think of as a stutter. She'd be moving along pretty evenly when her left foot would hang as though an invisible hand were holding it down. After a moment's hesitation, she would typically resume forward motion. Margaret hoped everything would work itself out once they got home and life began to feel normal again.

A week or so earlier, when Lenore and Wallace stopped by for what Margaret had come to think of as her mother's drama fix, Dad had quietly suggested Mayfair come back to her parents' house. Lenore had been down the hall working the nurses' station for sympathy, which the nurses were learning not to give, when he made the offer.

Margaret took her father's hand. She couldn't remember the last time she'd touched him. "Dad, you know it's not a good place for her," she'd said. "But it's good of you to ask." She wasn't sure where that last thought had come from, but it seemed to please him. He'd squeezed her hand, and she thought his eyes glistened, but it could have been her imagination.

"Home again, home again, jiggety jig," Margaret sang as she pulled the Volkswagen up to the door of the gray house. Mayfair giggled. "Oh, it's good to have you home again."

"It's good to be . . . home."

There. The hesitation. Although it might have been emotion. Margaret tried to act unconcerned. The doctor told her she shouldn't fuss over her sister unnecessarily, just support her and assume she would continue to heal. She also had strict instructions to keep Mayfair's blood sugar under control. Another episode could be life-threatening.

It was evening, and although the days were getting longer, it was already dim inside. Margaret fumbled for the light switch, and when she flicked it on, voices shouted, "Welcome home."

Emily, Perla, Henry, and Frank and Angie Post crowded near the little table, which was loaded down with enough food to feed them for a week. There were Mayfair's favorite fried pork chops, cheesy scalloped potatoes, green beans, angel biscuits, and a coconut layer cake.

"We wanted to make sure you came home to a good meal," Perla said. "I hope you're hungry."

"What? No . . ." Mayfair shook her hand as she looked for the right word. "Jell-O?"

They all laughed, and Emily folded Mayfair in a big hug. "I can't begin to tell you how much we've missed you. My house is just empty without you girls in it."

Margaret shot a glance at Henry. It wasn't empty. He was there. She wondered where Barbara was. As though on cue, the pregnant girl materialized in the doorway, looking uncomfortable.

"Hey," she said.

"Now that you've met, we insisted Barbara come with us, although it took some doing. No sense in her sitting at the house alone when we have something this wonderful to celebrate," Perla said. "I hope that's all right?"

Mayfair smiled a brilliant though slightly crooked smile and took a step toward Barbara, but her left foot stuck. Margaret took the chance to move into the gap. She took Barbara's hand and pulled her toward the table.

"We're so glad you came. These folks are known for taking in people who need a family. I'm glad they included you. We can't

357

have too many people celebrating Mayfair's return home."

Barbara's chin quivered, but she seemed to gather herself. "Thank you," she whispered.

"Let's bless this food and eat," Emily said. "Before it gets cold."

Henry thought Margaret was magnificent the way she pulled Barbara in and made her feel part of the group. He'd been trying to warm up to Barbara in case she decided to marry him. He wished she'd decide one way or the other, but any affection he'd managed to dredge up was eclipsed by what he felt for Margaret just then. He was still trying to figure out his purpose, but whatever it was, he had a strong feeling Margaret was part of it. He suddenly understood how Esau must have felt when the reality of giving up his birthright came home. What had he thrown away?

Henry tried to eat, but the food stuck in his throat. He was so glad to see Mayfair at home, laughing and talking and smiling, but the reality of his mistakes was becoming all too real to him. What if he'd gone back to school? He could've written Margaret long letters and then spent time with her when he came home on break. He would have had the satisfaction of knowing she was with his grandmother while he was away. Once he had his degree, they would have gotten married and run the farm together — with a room for Mayfair. Something broke open in Henry, and it was all he could do not to cry right there in that room full of laughter.

His father had felt this for his mother. This is what had been lost when his dad died. The memory of love had to be what his mom carried in her heart even now, a memory that clearly sustained her. Henry had vowed never to love anyone the way he loved his father. What he had failed to do was vow never to love anyone the way his father loved his mother. He thought he might die, but instead, did his best to choke down a slice of coconut cake.

27

Margaret tried not to fuss over Mayfair too much. Their routine had more or less returned to what it had been before the trip to the hospital. When Mayfair wasn't in school, they spent their time with Emily, and Mayfair was taking more of an interest in the garden. She and Henry pored over seed catalogs, planning rows of corn, tomatoes, beans, lettuce, carrots, squash, and she didn't know what all. Mayfair had her heart set on growing watermelon, and although Henry said he thought they might be too far north, Margaret could see Mayfair would get her way.

Their parents seemed content with a weekly phone call, and already Margaret could sense that soon, calling once a month would be more than enough.

It was a rare Sunday at home when Mayfair began talking about Beulah, whom they'd visited the day before. "She's not going to live much longer, I think."

Margaret looked up from where she'd been darning one of Henry's socks. He didn't know she had his socks, but when she saw the raggedy pair in the laundry room at Emily's, she decided to repair them.

"What are you talking about? I thought you —" She'd never really talked to Mayfair about healing people.

"You thought I healed her?"

"Well, people do sometimes seem to get better when you're around." Margaret flushed and bent back over the sock with a light bulb stuck inside to fill it out. She liked the tick, tick of the needle against the glass.

"It isn't me. It's just that sometimes I think about Jesus, and it seems to rub off on people."

Margaret tilted her head so she could see her sister. She wanted to ask what in the world Mayfair was talking about but bit her lip and waited instead.

"It's like Jesus' name inside my head makes things, people . . . smoother. Makes them fit."

"Then why do you think Beulah is going to die?"

"Her body isn't what needed smoothing out. It was inside — the real her. And now she's smooth." Mayfair smiled as though

361

she had explained it all and it was the most wonderful thing ever. Then the smile faded. "But Clint isn't all the way smooth yet. He'll be sad when she dies."

Something struck Margaret. "Can you tell whether or not anyone is . . . rough, I guess? I mean, like me? Or Mom and Dad?"

"Sometimes it's harder when I really love someone."

"So you couldn't help me if I were sick? Or . . . rough?"

Mayfair shrugged. "I don't know. But Jesus could, and that's the main thing."

"But what about Mom and Dad? Seems like you could smooth them out a bit."

"You have to want to be better." Mayfair yawned. "Can we have waffles for breakfast in the morning?"

"Sure," Margaret answered.

Her darning lay forgotten in her lap. Did she have rough edges that needed smoothing out? She'd always been healthy, except that time she thought she had appendicitis, but could she be like Beulah and need healing somewhere inside? And if she needed it, did she want it? She went into the kitchen to gather what she would need for breakfast in the morning, then fell into bed troubled over her own rough edges.

■ ■ ■ ■

Barbara's belly seemed to grow rounder by the minute. Henry wanted to press her for an answer to his proposal but was afraid she might see that as enthusiasm on his part, and he'd lost even the little enthusiasm he'd once mustered. After plowing his mother's garden for the second time, he watched Barbara waddle onto the porch to sit in the sun, her hand pressed into the small of her back. Since the night she was included in Mayfair's homecoming, she'd been quieter, more helpful around the house. He thought his mom was beginning to think of her as another daughter. Sadie called once a month and wrote a letter each week, but having someone around to take care of seemed to make Mom happy.

"Henry, call Barbara in for supper," his mother hollered from the kitchen. The weather was so mild, she'd left the door open.

Barbara heard and stood with a grunt, then shot him an embarrassed look.

"Not too graceful these days," she said.

"When's that baby coming, you reckon?"

She looked at the floor. "Guess it might be earlier than I expected. You never know about these things."

Henry thought he did know and decided to offer a jab. "By my count you should have a ways to go yet."

Her color deepened, and she looked like she might turn and run. He immediately felt bad, but if this baby really wasn't his, he might like to hang his hat somewhere else. He thought about how Mayfair healed his hand and wished she could heal something like this. He took a step toward Barbara, hand extended.

"Don't you lay a finger on her, Henry Phillips, or I'll cut it off."

Henry whirled toward the voice and saw Charlie coming around the corner of the house. "She's my woman. You back on off."

Charlie steamed up onto the porch and planted himself in front of a shocked-looking Barbara. He spread his legs and stood with hands on hips. "I'm claiming what's mine."

"What are you talking about?" Henry asked. Mom appeared in the doorway but didn't interfere.

Charlie half turned toward Barbara and looked at her belly, then into her eyes. Hope bloomed there as Charlie took her hand.

"Baby's mine. We thought, well, the plan was —"

Barbara cut in. "I was already pregnant that night, Henry." She glanced at Charlie. "With his baby, but he wasn't in a position to do right by me, so we figured on getting someone . . . upstanding to step in." She lowered her eyes. "I did my best to get you into bed with me that night so you'd think the baby was yours."

A wave of relief washed over Henry, and he felt his knees go weak. He sat down hard in the porch swing.

Charlie took over again. "We figured you'd marry her, or at least give her some money. Then she could run off with me." He scuffed his boot. "Except I got arrested trying to raise the money to run off." He brightened again. "But since Pa sorta encouraged me to turn in the guys running the dope, all I have to do is testify against them and do some community service."

"You kids come in here and eat," Mom said through the screen door. "It's getting chilly."

Charlie jumped. Henry guessed he hadn't seen her there. "Eat? You want us to eat with you?"

"If you don't, I'm going to have a whole bunch of food going to waste. Get on in here."

Charlie looked at Barbara, and she

shrugged. "They're nice. That's why I haven't married Henry. I felt bad 'cause he was so nice to me. I hated to do it to him." She glanced toward the door. "To them."

Henry felt like whooping for joy. Being nice had finally paid off. "Come on in here," he said, grinning. "I guess we all need to do a little repenting today, and it's easier done on a full belly."

Two days later Henry realized that his knowing Barbara's child belonged to Charlie and the rest of the world knowing it — namely Margaret — were two different things. How did you go about telling the girl you loved you weren't going to be a daddy? Especially when you'd been in a position to believe you might be? He still wasn't sure he'd actually, well, you know, with Barbara, and he didn't have the guts to ask her. Somehow it didn't seem like polite conversation.

Henry decided to go see Frank. The old man had proven to be a good source of advice in the past, and what would it hurt now? He needed someone else's opinion. Someone not his mother or grandmother.

Charlie and Barbara were planning to get married down at the courthouse and then they'd head for Detroit. Charlie seemed to think he could get a job in a car plant, and Barbara thought she'd make a fine waitress until the baby came. Besides, Charlie didn't want to be around after he gave evidence against the guys running drugs. Henry marveled that they really and truly seemed to love each other. Who would have guessed?

The upshot was, his mother acted like she was losing her last child. And she acted a little bit mad that Henry wasn't giving her a grandchild after all. He shook his head. Life was confusing.

When he arrived at the Talbots' — or Posts' — Frank and Angie were out in the side yard where a swing hung from a tree. Angie sat, holding the ropes tightly, while Frank pushed her forward ever so gently. She smiled at Henry as he approached.

"When's the last time you saw an old lady in a swing?" she asked.

"I guess maybe never," Henry said.

"Get an eyeful while you can. Every time we come out here, I figure it'll be the last time, but somehow Frank talks me into it again."

Frank laughed. "Keeps her young." He stilled the swing. "But you probably didn't come out here to watch us play."

Henry shrugged and squinted up at the sun that was warming the earth and coaxing green out everywhere. "Guess it's as good a reason as any, but I was looking for a piece of advice."

"Well, now, that's something we have a surplus of. Come on up here on the porch with us, and we'll give you all you can carry," Frank said with a wink.

They settled onto the porch where the sun slanted under the roof. Henry breathed in the smell of damp moss and fresh dirt that always seemed to hail spring. He guessed Frank and Angie had traveled a lot of miles to get to this point, and he hoped he might be in the same position one day.

"I don't know if you've heard, but Barbara is marrying Charlie Simmons. Guess that's his baby she's carrying."

Angie pursed her lips, and Frank nodded. "We might have heard something along those lines."

Henry was trusting the town gossips to have done their job. "So I'm free to, well, look elsewhere for a wife."

"You have anyone in mind?" Frank asked.

"Could be. Could be. It's just she's probably not thinking too highly of me right now, what with this business of how I might've fathered the child." Angie averted her eyes, and he flushed. "Anyhow, I'm trying to figure out how to change her opinion of me."

"What's her opinion of you?" Frank asked.

Henry stumbled over his answer. "Well, I guess she thinks I — that is, I don't know exactly, but I guess it's probably not good."

"You guess. Son, never guess where a woman is involved." Frank made a face when Angie poked him in the ribs. "If you want to know what a woman's thinking, you'll have to ask her at least three times."

Angie huffed. "Don't listen to his nonsense. He delights in it." She glanced at her husband. "But he is right that the best way to know what a woman thinks or wants is to ask her. We don't always know right off, but asking usually sets us to thinking."

Frank cut in. "And by the third time you ask her, she'll have settled on something."

Henry smiled but didn't think this was going to be much help.

"Of course, there's always the grand gesture," Frank said.

"The what?" Henry asked.

"The grand gesture. When Casewell was courting Perla, he picked her a big bouquet of flowers and made homemade candy. It might not sound like much now, but for Casewell, it was an undertaking."

"And I heard he messed it up," Angie said.

Frank took his wife's hand. "We men get things wrong sometimes, so you ladies can feel superior."

"*Pshaw.* Casewell was a lost sheep, and Perla rescued him. I don't care how it seemed to anyone else, that's how it was."

Henry wasn't sure this was helping his problem, but he liked hearing about his parents. "After Dad made the grand gesture, did Mom marry him?"

"Ha. She ran away right after that," Angie said.

Frank raised a finger in the air. "Which brings me to the real grand gesture. Casewell drove across the state of West Virginia to find your mother and bring her home."

"He did?"

"Yup. Perla was riding the Greyhound bus to Ohio, and he managed to catch up with her and Sadie — who must've been five or so back then — and hauled 'em back. Didn't give her another chance, either. They got hitched right after that."

"Oh, that was the loveliest wedding." Angie sighed. "The way people turned out for it. I guess it was almost as nice as ours."

Frank pulled Angie closer. "But not quite." They exchanged a look that made Henry feel like a third wheel.

"So you're saying I should ask Margaret how she feels, and if there's any hope at all, come at her with some grand gesture?"

Frank's eyes twinkled. "Margaret, is it?"

Henry felt stupid. "Oh, well, I —"

"No, we won't say anything. Just glad to see you've got some sense after all. You made us wonder a time or two. Guess you're like your pa that way."

Henry stood. "Thanks for the advice. And the stories about Mom and Dad. If they turned out all right after a start like that . . . well, maybe there's hope for me."

"Oh, Henry," Angie said, leaning into her husband's side. "There's always hope."

28

Mayfair was with Henry, planting the garden, when Barbara knocked on Margaret's door. When she saw who it was, Margaret wished she could hide, but she was pretty sure Barbara had seen her through the window. Being nice was one thing, but forming a friendship with someone carrying Henry's child wasn't at the top of her list of things to do.

"Hey there, Barbara." Margaret opened the door and positioned herself in the opening with a bright smile pasted on her face. "What can I do for you?"

Barbara glanced over her shoulder at a car Margaret didn't recognize. "There's something you ought to know, if you haven't heard already."

"Oh?"

"Yeah. Can I come in a minute?"

Margaret forced a smile and motioned Barbara inside. She'd hear her out, but she wasn't going to offer her anything.

Barbara waddled in and looked uncertain. Margaret pulled a chair out from the table and invited her to sit.

"Oh, thank you." She patted her belly. "This is getting to be quite a load."

Margaret felt her smile slide. "I imagine it is."

"This," she patted her belly again, "is actually what I want to tell you about."

Margaret couldn't imagine what the baby had to do with her.

"It's not Henry's."

"What? What's not Henry's?"

"This baby." Barbara glanced toward the door. "It's Charlie's. He's out there waiting on me. We're going to get married down to the courthouse, and then we're headed north." She creased the oversized blouse she was wearing, folding the fabric between her fingers. "Only I seen how Henry's been looking at you, and I wanted you to know he and I . . ." She blushed. "Well, what happened between us was all my doing. I tricked him, but now folks know the truth, and Charlie and me are gonna make a go of it."

"But why?"

"Charlie thought Henry might give me some money or maybe even keep the baby once it was born." She hung her head. " 'Cept I don't want that. This baby is mine."

There was a fierceness in Barbara's voice that Margaret found herself admiring. "What changed?"

"Charlie did." She smiled and looked up. "Maybe God ain't turned His back on me, after all. Anyhow, we're getting hitched, and just in case you had any feelings for Henry, I wanted you to know the truth."

"I appreciate that, although I don't think there'll ever be anything other than friendship between Henry and me."

Barbara heaved herself up out of the chair. "Oh, I don't know. I'd say that boy's sweet on you. Guess all you have to decide is do you want him."

Margaret watched Barbara walk toward the car. Charlie leapt from the driver's side to open the passenger door and help her ease her bulk inside. He laid his hand on her belly and kissed her slow and soft. She watched them drive away and was surprised when it occurred to her to say a prayer for their future. And for the baby. Even a month ago she wouldn't have given the couple much of a chance, but after today — well, stranger things had happened. At least they seemed to like each other. That was more than her own parents had going for them.

She slid into the chair Barbara vacated. Could there be a future for her and Henry? Even if he hadn't fathered the child, he'd put himself in a situation where he thought it a possibility. Did she want a man like that? Then again, she might've made a mistake or two herself along the way. Of course, just because Barbara said Henry liked her didn't mean he did.

She reached in a pocket and pulled a hair band out, securing her hair in a ponytail. What she needed to do was wash windows. She'd put it off when it was colder, but the weather was fine now, and some spring cleaning was in order. Her mind might not be clear, but her windows soon would be.

Perla brought word when she heard at the grocery store that Beulah died. Margaret was surprised at the stab of pain she felt at the news. She'd grown fond of Beulah and their visits out to the Simmonses' place. Even Clint had seemed, if not friendly, at least tolerant of them. She wondered if he'd be mad that Mayfair hadn't healed his wife.

"They don't have a church, so we're going to make sure they get plenty of food," Perla said. "The funeral's in the morning. We'll carry food to the house for everyone to eat afterwards."

Emily added, "And we'll make sure there are plenty of people to eat it. Clint might've had a limiting effect on Beulah's social life, but I know people loved her. We'll get up a good turnout."

And they did. Most of the town of Wise turned out for Beulah's funeral. Clint sat stiff in the front pew with Harold beside him. Charlie was already in Detroit, and with Barbara having some issues, they didn't dare travel. Margaret felt a little bit bad for him. It must be hard to miss your own mother's funeral, especially if you actually liked her.

Henry couldn't believe he was going to this much trouble for the Simmons family. He did feel bad for them. He knew what it was like to lose a parent if not a wife, but still, they were moonshiners and had caused him more than a little grief. Of course, he'd asked for a fair amount of it.

He carried the last cardboard box loaded with food out to the car and set it in the trunk. It wouldn't slide around. There were too many other boxes filled with dishes in there. Whatever his mother was cooking, it seemed never-ending.

The minute the preacher said "Amen" at

the funeral, Mom rushed him out of the funeral home and back to the house to load up the car. Now they were flying over dirt roads to the Simmonses' place. Henry thought of all the other times he'd made this trip. He never imagined his mother would make it with him.

Grandma was already there. Margaret had driven her and Mayfair over while Clint was still shaking hands and trying to get away from the crush of people who turned out. Henry guessed Beulah was more popular than her husband.

As soon as he put the car in Park, the women began unloading the food. He could swear they took out more than he loaded, but he guessed it was just his imagination. He caught Margaret's eye, and she smiled at him. It was kind of a shy smile, as though she was a little bit embarrassed. He guessed she still felt funny about Barbara. He wished he could tell her how things were, but maybe she'd heard by now. Of course, even if she had, he still didn't come off as the hero of that story. He grabbed the last box and toted it inside. Maybe time was what he needed. Maybe he should go back to college and write her those long letters he'd been imagining. She'd probably like that.

He watched Margaret move around the

Simmonses' kitchen with his mother and grandmother. They were like dancers performing an intricate choreography that would ultimately feed most of Wise. Mayfair sat at the table and watched, clearly delighted with all the goings-on. He wondered why she looked so happy at a funeral, especially since she'd gotten so close to Beulah.

When Clint and Harold came in the front door, the old man looked bewildered by the house full of food and women. Henry suspected it was the cleanest the place had been in at least a decade. He felt a moment of panic when it occurred to him that someone might stumble on the still out in the woods. He sidled over to Clint.

"Do I need to make sure folks steer clear of the, ah, works out back?"

Clint ran his fingers through his slicked-back hair. "Naw. Took it down about a month ago. I closed up shop when Charlie left. Been meaning to give it up for a long time, and it —" He coughed and blew his nose in a handkerchief. "It seemed to make Beulah awful happy."

"Oh. Well, that's good." Henry couldn't have been more surprised if Clint had said he was taking up disco dancing. "Guess I'll get a bite to eat, then."

"But who are all these people?" Clint asked. "And where'd all that food come from?"

"Mom and Grandma decided Beulah needed a proper sendoff. I guess when they decide something like that, it's going to happen."

Clint grunted. "Guess I can stand it for a little while."

He pulled a flask out of his coat pocket, sloshed whatever was in it into a mug, and topped it off with coffee. His look let Henry know in no uncertain terms that he should keep his mouth shut. Henry eased away as others stepped in to offer their condolences. He wondered how long Clint could stand all the socializing. He'd probably pull out a shotgun and run them all off before the day was out.

He snagged a fried peach pie and stepped out back for a breath of fresh air. The spring sunshine warmed the dirt-packed yard, where Clint's hunting dogs had worn the grass away. A woman sat in an old chair with missing slats. A hound had his head in her lap, looking blissful as she caressed his ears. Henry felt his heart leap when he realized it was Margaret.

"Hey, there," he said, swallowing his last bite of pie.

Margaret turned, and he saw that her freckled cheeks were tracked with tears.

"Oh, hey, what's wrong?" he asked.

She swiped at her face and bowed her head over the dog. "I guess I miss Beulah more than I thought I would." She sniffled. "She was always so glad to see us, and it made her happy when I helped put things to rights out here. Seems lonesome without her."

Henry glanced back at the house overflowing with people. He guessed he knew what it felt like to be lonesome in the middle of a crowd. He squatted down next to her chair and scratched the hound's shoulder. The dog began to pat the ground with a hind foot.

"I'm still awful lonesome for Dad. But I guess, maybe, it's good that he went like he did — in his sleep in his bed in his own house. I've been talking to that preacher, Ray, and maybe when you're a person of faith, dying isn't such a bad thing. It's just rough on whoever's left behind. Beulah sure seemed to love the Lord."

"Are you a person of faith?" Margaret asked. Her hand still rested on the dog's head, and Henry saw that he could move his own hand a little and touch her.

"I'm trying to be one. Guess I have a ways to go."

"Me too. When I thought Mayfair might die, I talked to God a lot and sometimes . . ." She raised her eyes to treetops unfurling their new spring leaves. "Sometimes I thought He was listening and maybe, just maybe keeping Mayfair alive not for her sake, but for mine. I guess I owe Him for that."

"Mayfair's pretty special. Guess we all owe Him one there."

Henry swallowed and let his fingers slide over Margaret's. He felt her stiffen and then relax. He snuck a peek at her face and thought he saw a smile. He tried to think of the words that would let her know how he felt, but before he could open his mouth, his mother hollered from the back door.

"Margaret, I think something's not quite right with Mayfair. You'd better come."

Margaret whirled from the chair and ran toward the house.

When Margaret pushed her way into the living room, she saw Mayfair sitting in the middle of the floor with a funny look on her face. Clint was crouched in front of her with a mug in his hand. He tipped it and whatever was inside ran down Mayfair's chin. He spoke so softly Margaret couldn't hear, but she instantly wondered if he'd been drinking, and it struck her that alcohol was about the worst thing anyone could give Mayfair.

"No," she cried out, fighting her way forward.

Clint gave Mayfair another sip, and it looked like she swallowed most of it.

"What are you giving her?" Margaret towered over Clint, hands on her hips. "Someone bring me some punch or orange juice. Now."

Mayfair blinked slowly and tilted her head up to look at her sister. "More," she said.

Clint looked Margaret in the eye as he gave her sister another swallow. Margaret wanted to knock the cup from his hand but hated to make more of a scene than they already were.

"You'd better not be giving her moonshine," she hissed as Perla pressed a cup of punch into her hand.

Clint rose to his full height and looked down at Margaret. "It's grape juice," he said. "Made it myself." Then he walked out of the room.

Everyone stared at Margaret as she helped Mayfair to the sofa where she'd visited with Beulah so many times. She tried to ignore the looks. Everyone knew how sick her sister had been. Of course she was going to be cautious. Gradually, the hum of conversation resumed, and Margaret gave Mayfair her full attention.

"How are you feeling?"

"I'm okay. Clint seemed to know what was happening before I did." She smiled. "He's so nice. I'm glad he and Beulah got better before she died."

"What are you talking about? Beulah didn't get better."

Mayfair smiled. "I'm sleepy. I don't think Clint would mind if I took a nap in Beulah's room."

"Oh, I don't know if —"

"Come get me when you're ready to go." Mayfair walked gingerly into the bedroom and settled into a rocking chair. She drew an afghan over her knees and closed her eyes.

"I think she'll be fine, sweetheart." Margaret hadn't seen Emily approach. "Clint was there so quick, I don't think it was much of an episode at all. I don't know how he knew, but thank goodness he did."

Margaret nodded and looked around, feeling lost. She wanted to thank Clint, maybe even apologize. But she didn't see him anywhere.

29

Mayfair sat curled on the sofa reading *Alliance Life* magazine. She'd asked Margaret to subscribe to it for her, and although Margaret didn't know why her little sister would want to read a missionary magazine, she was happy to put in the order. Watching Mayfair get lost between the pages, she was beginning to wonder if her sister didn't have dreams of her own.

Margaret, on the other hand, still had the same dream — to live out her days on this farm. Originally, she'd thought any farm would do, but now she was in love with the Phillipses' family land, and maybe the Phillips family, as well. She glanced out the window at the greening countryside as she rested her fingers. She was trying to crochet some place mats for the table, and it was more challenging than she anticipated.

Her thoughts turned to Henry, who seemed different lately. When he'd held her hand at Beulah's funeral, she'd felt the most wonderful tingling deep in her belly. It was a little scary, but she wouldn't mind feeling it again. Was it wrong to imagine marrying him so she could stay on the farm? She liked him in spite of all the mistakes he'd made in recent months. She might even feel something more than liking.

She sighed and picked her crochet hook up again. Why had she chosen a pale yellow? It would surely show stains. But it was too late to turn back now. She was almost finished with the first place mat. One more, and she and Mayfair could use them, even if they weren't perfect.

She glanced out the window again. It was open a crack, and the spring air carried the aroma of lilacs inside. Margaret closed her eyes and breathed it in. Getting married in the spring would be nice. There were so many flowers, and the world looked soft and new. She grimaced and gave herself a mental reprimand. Idle daydreams were a waste of time.

As she opened her eyes, she saw movement. She could have sworn a man had just walked by and ducked behind the shed where she parked the car. A chill ran up her spine. It was probably Henry. He'd come knock on the door in a minute, and she'd ask him in and give him a piece of cake.

But Henry didn't come, and Margaret saw movement again. She could swear someone was inside the shed. There were cracks in the boards and, there, a shadow. She glanced at Mayfair, who seemed oblivious. She laid down her work and stretched.

"I'm going to get a breath of air," she said.

Mayfair nodded without looking up from the article she was reading. Margaret stepped outside and walked around the house toward the shed. She heard the clank of metal and froze, her heart in her throat. Someone was out there. *Let it be Henry,* she prayed, stiffening her spine and walking as though she were confident of who she would find.

"Hey, there."

Margaret meant to scream, but all she could manage was a squeak. Henry stepped around the corner of the house behind her. "Thought I saw you. Whatcha doing?"

She pointed a shaky finger toward the shed. "I heard something, saw something. I thought it might be you."

Henry wrinkled his brow and stepped between Margaret and the outbuilding. "Stay here."

Although she was hugely relieved, Margaret's heart still raced. She glanced back at the house. She could see Mayfair's dark head bent over her magazine. It was probably an animal. A stray dog or a raccoon. Henry reached the side of the building and cautiously peered around the open end where she drove in and out. His posture immediately relaxed, and he spoke, stepping into the space.

Margaret released the pent-up breath in her lungs. It took a moment for her breathing to even out, then she started forward. She could hear Henry and what sounded like another man. She rounded the corner and froze.

Henry almost laughed out loud when he saw who was in Margaret's car shed and what he was doing. "Well, howdy. Looks like you've tackled a job there."

Clint wiped his hands on a greasy rag. "Heard her drive away from the house the other day. Valves were making way too much noise. Reckon she don't know about adjusting them."

Margaret stared when she saw Clint with the engine compartment open on her car.

"When's the last time you adjusted your valves?" Henry asked.

"What?" Margaret looked as though he were speaking a foreign language.

"Your valves." He pointed toward the engine. "You should adjust them at least once a year, probably more than that."

She shook her head and looked at Clint. "Why didn't you come to the house?"

He grunted and leaned back down to tweak the final valve. "Didn't know if you'd take kindly to me helping, so I thought I'd ease on in here and do this little job. They were pretty bad, too. Needed doing."

"But why?"

Clint looked at Margaret and then back at the car. "Your sister's done more for me and mine than I could have deserved in three lifetimes. I wanted to do something to earn it." He threw the rag down and stuck a wrench in his back pocket. "Not that I ever could."

"I don't understand. I thought you wanted her to heal Beulah."

Clint slammed the lid, then turned and leaned against the car. "And so she did. Only she did even more than that. She managed to fix a lifetime of me being mad about Esther dying and taking it out on everyone around me."

His first wife, Margaret remembered. "How did she do that?"

"Don't know. When I was driving around that night and she just showed up to come go with me, I guess that was the first thing. Then the way she made Beulah light up . . . it was like I seen her for the first time. And maybe I robbed her of the good she deserved. I even made my boys scornful of her." He looked out into the pasture where a doe and a fawn grazed in the edge of the field. "Even that deer out there had it better than poor Beulah. I was a sorry son of a . . . well, I knew I needed to do something different."

"Because of Mayfair?"

Clint pounded his chest with his fist. "She fixed us here. Don't know how it happened. Don't know if she even meant to do it, but watching her pour love out over the sorriest family in Wise made me want something different."

Margaret felt tears prick her eyes. Could Mayfair have made such a difference? Just by being nice?

Clint stood and pointed at Henry. "Son, I seen the poison you been carrying around since your pa died. It's the same mess I shouldered for way too long. I took advantage of what I saw in you there for a while." He grinned. "You could have a real future in moonshining if you don't aim to walk the narrow path." The smile faded. "But I reckon I been seeing a change in you

389

here lately." He eyed Margaret. "Might have something to do with the company you keep."

Henry, who had been watching Clint and Margaret like it was a sporting event, dropped his mouth open. "There's nothing wrong with me."

Clint's laugh sounded like a bark. "Son, what you mean to say is there's nothing wrong with you that a good woman can't fix." He grinned. "If you ain't too stubborn to take advantage of it, like me." He slapped his hands together. "Car should run better now. I'll come again in six months or so, if you'll let me."

Margaret searched for words. "That would be fine," she finally said.

Clint nodded once and walked toward the woods. There was a logging road down that way, and she saw sunlight glint on metal. He must have parked there. For a moment she wondered if he'd done something to hurt the car, then felt ashamed for even letting such a thought run through her mind. Something told her Clint was a changed man.

Henry watched Clint disappear into the trees, heard a car door slam and an engine start. He looked at Margaret, who was also looking toward the trees. He'd never really noticed her in profile before. Her freckled nose turned up a smidge on the end, and when she held her chin up like that — well, she was beautiful.

"Margaret, I —"

She turned toward him with an expectant look. "Yes?"

"I need to tell you something."

She smiled. "I hope you're not going to tell me to avoid Clint Simmons, because I think he and I are going to be friends." She tossed her head. "Of a sort."

"No, no. I just wanted to tell you . . ." He felt as if he'd swallowed a big wad of biscuit dough and couldn't get any words past it. He coughed, and Margaret stepped forward to pound him on the back.

"You okay?"

"Yeah. What I'm trying to say is . . . I'm going back to school." He choked again. Where in the world had that come from?

"Oh. Well, that's great. I think you should." She looked a little uncertain. "That is, if you want to."

Henry let out a gusty breath. "You know, I think I do. Somehow I want to finish something." He rubbed the toe of one boot down the back of his pant leg. "Do you . . . would you mind if I wrote to you from school? Maybe come see you when I'm home?"

Her face bloomed in a smile that made Henry's feeling of being an awkward fool fade.

"I'd like that."

Henry reached out for Margaret's hand, and she slipped her fingers into his. He was surprised by how delicate her fingers were and how it made him feel strong. Like maybe there was more in life to look forward to than he'd allowed himself to think.

30

"Summer classes start May 18. If I work hard, I think I can make up what I missed in the spring semester." Henry and Margaret sat on a rock outcropping overlooking the valley spread out below. "Of course, I'll have to meet with Dr. Stanley and see if there's any chance of making up his class. He failed me last semester."

Margaret didn't say anything. She just reached over and squeezed Henry's arm where it was propped against his knee He was glad. He was tired of people giving him advice and telling him what he should do. Margaret somehow made him feel better just by being there. He glanced at her pretty profile. Maybe she'd picked that peacefulness up from Mayfair.

"What are you planning for the summer while I'm off in Morgantown slaving over my books?"

Margaret lifted her chin so that the spring

breeze pushed her hair back from her face. "I'm going to learn all I can about running the farm from your grandmother. We're getting a pig next week to fatten up for fall. There's the chickens, Bertie, the garden — I have a feeling it'll be more than enough to keep us busy."

Henry found Margaret's hand and twined his fingers with hers. He felt bold doing it. "But what will you do for fun?"

She gave him a teasing look. "That is fun, but I suppose I might write letters to a certain young man slaving over his books, too."

Henry's heart felt lighter than it had since before Dad died. He wondered that he'd ever thought Margaret was plain or prudish. He had the urge to brush a strand of hair out of her face and kiss her, but he turned back to the view instead.

"I'm hoping I'll have at least a little bit of time for music. Maybe I can get back in with Mort and those guys at the Screen Door."

Henry flashed back to the last conversation he'd had with his father. He'd argued that he had time to play music and study. He wished, more than anything, he'd stayed home that New Year's Eve and played with his dad. You never knew when it might be your last chance at something.

Margaret leaned over and bumped his shoulder with hers. "What deep thoughts are you thinking now?"

He looked at her, so very close, and without really even considering what he was doing, he leaned in to cover her lips with his. She gasped ever so slightly, making him want to deepen the kiss, but he pulled back instead. She had full soft lips that felt even better than he'd imagined. They were slightly parted now, maybe in shock.

"Is it okay that I did that?"

She blushed and leaned her head against his shoulder. "More than all right," she whispered.

Henry surveyed the world around them — the mountains flowing down to pastureland with a creek winding along. Cows were grazing, and he saw a deer in the shadows near the water. He could hear birds singing, and the air smelled sweet and clean. He inhaled deeply, feeling as if he was completely filling his lungs for the first time in years. He wrapped an arm around Margaret's waist and pulled her close to his side. Man, this last year of school was going to feel like forever.

The bend where Henry's truck disappeared

didn't change. There wasn't even a breeze to stir the leaves. Margaret stared, thinking there should be some sign, some indication that a man who kissed her had just gone by and would hopefully come back that way before long. She wanted something — some proof that she hadn't dreamed the whole thing.

She'd once thought Henry selfish and ill-mannered, but as the winter ended and spring bloomed, so had he. She closed her eyes and allowed herself to imagine that he really would come back for her. That he really would write and call and miss her while he was away at school. She felt a mixture of exhilaration and fear bubble through her. Her mother taught her long ago that if something seemed too good to be true, then it surely was. Mom also taught her that most everything was too good for her.

"Mom loves us. She just doesn't know how to show it because she's never felt like anyone really loves her."

Margaret jumped when Mayfair spoke. She turned to look at her healthy pink-cheeked sister. She hadn't had an episode in weeks, and being on the farm really seemed to agree with her.

"Mayfair, you're the lovingest person I

know, and you love Mom, though sometimes I wonder why. How come that doesn't do the trick?"

Her sister watched a robin land in the grass and snatch up a worm. "Sometimes it's hard to recognize love when you've never seen it before." She turned her attention to the bend in the road and pointed. An animal slipped out of the trees and crouched low in the road.

"Is it a dog?" Margaret squinted. The animal stood and shook itself, lifting its nose into the air in their direction.

"Yes, and I think it needs a home."

Mayfair whistled low and melodic. The dog pricked its ears and seemed to consider what to do next. After a moment's hesitation, it eased along the dirt road, hugging the tree line, in their direction. It stopped about a hundred feet out and considered the two girls.

"He's not sure of us," Mayfair said. She crouched down and began humming and poking in the grass like she was hunting for a four-leafed clover. "Get down, Margaret."

Margaret crouched down, too, feeling silly. Weren't you supposed to call the dog to you with your hand out? She watched out of the corner of her eye as the dog crept closer. Her knees were beginning to ache, and she eased on down to a cross-legged position.

"Don't look right at him," Mayfair said and resumed her humming. It sounded like a hymn, but Margaret couldn't place it. Oh, wait. Maybe it was "Come Thou Fount of Every Blessing." She forgot the dog, trying to remember the words. Something about streams of mercy and redeeming love. And there was another line . . . Yes. *Prone to wander, Lord, I feel it. Prone to leave the God I love; Here's my heart, O take and seal it . . .*

Something warm and soft touched her hand, and with every fiber of her being, she resisted jerking away. The dog sniffed her hand again and then Mayfair's. He sat and gazed at them, as though waiting to see what they would do next. Margaret looked into his big brown eyes and felt the strangest connection.

"Guess we'd better feed him, then."

Henry promised himself he wouldn't play at the Screen Door until he was confident that his classes were in order and his grades were where they needed to be. But since the summer classes didn't seem quite so challenging, he figured it was time for some fiddling. He'd still have to figure out what to do about Soil Genesis and Classification, but for now he felt like music. Mort had been glad to see him and said he'd be welcome to come sit in on a set any time. As Henry pushed open the door, fiddle case in hand, he hoped Mort had really meant it.

It was early, and the guys were tuning up. Mort waved Henry over and grinned. "Your timing's great. Our fiddle and banjo players are cousins, and their great-uncle up and died yesterday."

Henry started to say something about being sorry, but Mort cut him off. "No, no. He was a hundred two and glad to go, but the boys are at the viewing. We thought we might have to cancel this evening, then I remembered Gordy said he'd play banjo for us sometime, and now you come strolling in with a fiddle in hand. Guess the good Lord's looking out for us, after all." He waved toward a stool. "Pull on up there, and we'll warm up a little. Gordy should be along any minute."

Henry sat and pulled out his fiddle, running the bow across the strings to make sure he was in tune. He was so focused on making adjustments, he didn't notice when the man with the banjo arrived, but he surely noticed when the first few notes twanged out beside him. He looked up and into the face of Professor Stanley.

"Henry. I'm pleased to hear you opted to return and finish your degree. I thought I would have had a visit from you by now."

Henry swallowed hard and wished he could wipe his suddenly sweaty palms on his pants leg. "I've been meaning to stop by. I wasn't sure you'd be glad to see me after . . . well, after last semester."

"Henry, I'm always glad to see a student make a wise decision. Especially when it comes on the heels of a poor one. Now is not the time to negotiate, but if you come see me next Monday, we might be able to come to an understanding regarding credit for my class."

Henry feigned deep interest in his bow. "Yes, sir. I'll be glad for any opportunity —"

"Not now, Henry." Professor Stanley's — Gordy's — eyes twinkled, something Henry didn't think was possible. "Now is the time for some music."

And with that, Stan the Man launched into dueling banjos, nodding at Henry to pick up the response on his fiddle. After a moment's hesitation, he did, and before he knew what was happening, Henry and his professor were playing a mile a minute while the rest of the band whooped and hollered. Henry felt his heart take flight with the music. Yes, indeed, the world wasn't always what it seemed. He wished Margaret could see him now.

Margaret washed her face and started over with the eyeliner. She'd never worn much makeup and didn't seem to have the knack for applying it. She was almost tempted to call her mother and ask what the trick was. Lenore's makeup was always perfect. She leaned toward the mirror. A raccoon. She looked like a spotted raccoon.

Piebald thumped his tail at her. Once the dog accepted Margaret and Mayfair, they fed him and fussed over him. A search for an owner came up empty, so the girls adopted him and named him Piebald — or just Pie — because he had more freckles than Margaret did. Margaret expected him to bond with her sister like most animals did, but he seemed really and truly attached to Margaret. And he had surely found an easy home in her heart.

"Pie, I'm a little nervous about seeing Henry. What if he's changed his mind about me?" The dog cocked his head as if trying to understand. "What if he met someone prettier or smarter or just, I don't know, better?" Pie sighed and rested his head on his front paws.

"At least you love me. Don't you?"

Pie thumped his tail again and rolled his eyes in Margaret's direction. She took that as a yes.

"Henry just pulled into the driveway." Mayfair stuck her head through the open bathroom door, then stopped and looked concerned. "Are you going to wash your face?"

Margaret flushed and began wiping away the attempt at makeup. "I'll be right there."

Face clean and freckles likely glowing, Margaret walked into the kitchen just as Henry burst through the door. His eyes lit up when he saw her, and he leapt forward to wrap his arms around her and spin her in the air. She was sure her foot would whack into the stove or the table, but he completed his circuit, set her back on her feet, and planted a kiss on her forehead. It was unexpectedly tender and sweet, and Margaret thought she might cry.

"It's so good to see you," he said, his face pressed into her hair. "You smell good."

"Baby shampoo," she blurted, then clamped her lips shut. Of all the things to say. "It's good to see you, too."

"Mom and Grandma say you two should come to the house for supper tonight. There's fried chicken, potato salad, and graham cracker pie. I'm going to make up for having to eat in the cafeteria or suffer my own cooking."

"That sounds good." Margaret started to ease out of Henry's arms, but he tightened his grip and caught her eye.

"I've missed you." The brown of his eyes seemed to get richer. "More than I thought I would."

Margaret tried to relax but wasn't sure how to react. She'd never had a boy — a man — talk to her like this. "Me too," she whispered, surprised at how husky her voice sounded.

Henry dipped his head and brushed his lips across hers, but before she could even begin to catalog the wonderful feelings coursing through her, a deep growl sounded near her feet. Then a warm doggy body began to wedge between them. Margaret released Henry and stumbled back a step. Pie sat practically on her feet and eyed Henry like he was a fox in the henhouse. Henry stepped back and blinked.

"This must be the dog you wrote about."

"Piebald — yes. He showed up the day you left for school. I guess he's kind of attached to me."

Henry stepped forward, and Pie curled his lip. "Will he bite?"

"He never has," Margaret said. "I'm not sure what's gotten into him."

Mayfair popped into the kitchen and scratched Pie behind his ears. "He just wants to make sure Henry's intentions are good."

Henry bristled. "The dog's worried about my intentions?"

Mayfair shrugged. "He loves Margaret. That's what you do when you love someone."

"Whatever." Henry's romantic mood seemed to evaporate. "Do you two want to walk over to the house with me?"

"Sure," Margaret hurried to answer. She rubbed Pie's head, trying to soothe and reassure him. She wanted to tell the dog Henry's intentions were honorable, but it seemed a silly thing to do, so she just told him to stay and followed Henry out the door. And anyway, she didn't actually know what Henry's intentions were.

The week at home between summer and fall semesters wasn't nearly long enough for Henry. He'd meant to plow under the beans now that Margaret and Grandma had finished picking and canning them. It would have meant room to get in some fall crops, but the time flew, and he didn't get to it.

He also hadn't spent as much time with Margaret as he wanted. Well, not alone, anyway.

Henry was surprised at how much he enjoyed being around her. Mayfair had always had a calming effect on him, but Margaret used to get his dander up. He grinned to himself as he crossed campus for his early class. She still did. It's just that he liked it now. He'd even won that goofy dog over. Well, mostly. Pie still tried to get between him and Margaret every chance he had, but Mayfair helped out, taking the dog for long rambles around the farm.

Only nine months until graduation. Only June until he saw Margaret again. Professor Stanley let him make up his paper, and it turned out the old coot really had known his dad. Apparently they'd played together a time or two at bluegrass festivals, and Stan the Man had a lot of respect for Casewell Phillips. Henry wondered what else he didn't know about his father. He guessed he'd never really get over missing Dad, but he could think about him now without wanting to cry or kick something.

Life was filled with stuff you didn't expect — your dad dying, falling for a girl you thought you didn't like, playing music with your crusty old professor. Henry grinned.

31

Christmas wasn't quite what Margaret expected. While she wasn't entirely sure what she had in mind, it certainly wasn't a carved butter mold and never being alone with Henry. She tried to tell herself that the butter mold was thoughtful and practical. She enjoyed making butter and was even selling some. It would be nice to shape pretty, one-pound rounds with a flower pressed into the tops. It just wasn't . . . romantic.

And while Henry had been plenty happy to see her, he didn't seem to mind that they were never alone. He held her hand and told her all about his classes and how he'd been able to keep his grades up while playing at the Screen Door with some bluegrass band he was all excited about. But they hadn't had more than ten minutes to themselves, and although Henry kissed her like he meant it, it wasn't like he was trying to arrange time for more kissing. Wasn't that what boys did?

Confused. Margaret felt confused. Henry acted like she was his girlfriend, but he also acted like his focus was on his life back at college. He'd milked Bertie a few times and admired the hog, but he didn't seem excited about Margaret's plans for the farm. He'd listen like he was just waiting for his chance to talk, and then he'd launch into stories about the guys in the band or his roommate, who had three blond-haired, blue-eyed sisters who sang like angels.

Margaret wanted to ask Henry what he was feeling — what his plans were after graduation — but she was afraid she might annoy him. She was starting to get used to the idea that someone like Henry might be attracted to her, and she didn't want to spoil it.

"I was thinking about heading back a few days early." Henry walked beside Margaret, carrying the bucket from the evening milking. Margaret had been filling him in on how Bertie was doing now that she was pregnant again. The calf born the previous spring had been sold for enough to help pay the taxes on the farm. Margaret kind of wished they could have kept the little heifer — a gentle, sweet animal that followed

Mayfair around like Pie followed Margaret. She figured Henry hadn't heard much of anything she'd just told him.

"Really? How early?"

"Oh, I was thinking no later than the thirtieth."

"But I thought classes didn't start until January sixth?"

"They don't. I just feel like I need to get back there."

Margaret saw Emily watching them through the bay window in the dining room. Never a moment alone.

"But we've hardly had any time together. I thought we'd — I don't know — do something."

It sounded so very lame. What did she expect? A fancy dinner out? Long walks in the snow with the stars sparkling above and Henry's kisses to keep her from feeling the cold? Yeah, maybe she was expecting something like that. Margaret felt a spark of annoyance.

"Like what?"

Margaret was glad Henry held the milk bucket because she might dump it all over him given the chance. "Never mind. You do what you think is best." She picked up her pace, ignoring the confused look on Henry's face.

■ ■ ■ ■

As the end of the year loomed, Henry didn't think he could stand to be home for the anniversary of his father's death. He'd been trying to make excuses for leaving early, but everyone seemed to be annoyed with him about it. He wanted to tell Margaret how hard this was — the thought of being in the house with his mom just like the night Dad died. The thought of waking up on New Year's Day 1977 knowing he'd been without his father for a whole year and making a mess of things more often than not. Maybe he wasn't quite ready to admit that to anyone yet. Not even to Margaret.

He was going back to school, and that was that. Funny, a year ago they'd all been so eager for him to go, and now they acted like he should stay. Fickle. That's what they were.

Henry told everyone he was leaving on the thirtieth, but he had the feeling they didn't believe him. He slipped out of the house early that morning, his breath making clouds in the air. Tossing everything in the truck, he climbed in and started it up, grimacing at the noise. He thought he saw Mom's face in the window as he coasted down the driveway, but he told himself she'd understand his leaving like this. She probably wanted to be alone as much as he did. Maybe not alone, but maybe with people who could offer her some comfort. He wished he could, but Dad's death had left too big a hole in the world and in his heart. He pulled into the gas station in Wise to fill up before heading on to Morgantown.

"Thought you'd be sticking around for your ma's cabbage come New Year's."

Henry looked over his shoulder and saw Clint Simmons lounging against the wall of the small service station, a cigarette clenched between his lips.

"I need to get on back to school. One more semester, and I'll be done. Might even make some money on New Year's Eve playing down at the Screen Door." Henry didn't know why he was explaining himself to Clint.

The older man stepped closer, and Henry could see his normally wild beard was neatly trimmed, and his eyes looked clear. Cigarette smoke made Henry want to sneeze. "Your pa ever tell you how he got that scar on his jaw?"

Henry startled. That was the last thing he expected Clint to bring up. He ran a finger around the scar on his own chin. "No." He didn't mention that Frank told him.

"I give it to him. He stole moonshine and fouled up the still so bad we had to start over. Passed out drunk a stone's throw away, and I aimed to do him in. If it hadn't been for Frank Post interfering, you wouldn't have been even a twinkle in Casewell Phillips's eye. I always hated anyone with the name Phillips after that." Something sinister shone in Clint's face, then faded like a dying ember. "Guess I might've got over it, though. Seems hate works like poison from the inside out." He cleared his throat. "I never said so, but I'm real sorry about you losing your pa. Guess he made up for any youthful foolishness once he was growed. Guess you might take after him like that, if you learn to keep shy of folks like me."

Clint thumped Henry on the back once, flicked his cigarette butt on the ground, and then turned and went inside the station. The bell on the door clanged in his wake.

Henry swallowed hot tears and squared his shoulders. He rarely thought about Dad making mistakes — doing something as foolhardy as stealing from the Simmonses and getting fall-down drunk. He told himself that if he was making a mistake going back early, at least it wasn't one that could get him killed. He told himself he could save the money he earned playing music so he'd have more than his dreams to offer Margaret. He told himself maybe he could be like his father. He kept trying to convince himself all the way back to campus. When he arrived, he was as tired as he'd ever been.

Finding a good example of two people in love was proving a challenge for Margaret. It seemed that everyone she knew with a good marriage was now alone. Emily lost John years ago, Perla still grieved for Casewell. Even Clint Simmons had lost Beulah, although they certainly hadn't seemed happy together until the very end.

Maybe she could write to Barbara, who seemed much happier with Charlie than any of them ever imagined. They'd gotten a note saying the couple were doing well. Charlie had found a good job in a factory that let Barbara stay home and take care of little Lisa, who was proving to be an easygoing baby. Margaret wondered what it said about her that those two seemed to have their relationship figured out better than she and Henry did.

"Margaret, would you run this pot of soup over to Frank and Angie? He's had a cold

413

for a week now, and chicken soup might help." Emily stood in the kitchen holding a kettle with the corners of her apron. "I know you planned to deep clean the back bedroom, but that can wait."

"Sure. I don't mind."

Actually, Margaret was glad to get out and about. The winter had been cold and harsh, keeping them indoors more often than not, and she was feeling restless. Mayfair was at school at the moment, and when she was home, she spent most of her time writing letters to orphans in China or someplace. She'd been doing that more and more lately. Margaret was glad her sister had found something to be passionate about, although she kind of missed having her around all the time.

Ice crunched under her tires as Margaret pulled into the side yard of Frank and Angie's house. She wrapped her scarf more tightly under her chin and ducked her head to dart through the gusty wind into the warm house. Frank and Angie sat near the gas heater looking pleased to see her. Frank's nose was red, and he kept sniffling. Angie watched him, a look of concern painted across her face. Margaret realized she had just walked into an example of love in full bloom.

"Emily sent you some chicken soup."

"That's thoughtful of her," Angie said. She got up and tucked an afghan over Frank's legs in a little tighter.

"Stop fussing, woman." Frank made a shooing motion, but his eyes said he liked the fussing.

Angie kissed him on the cheek and resettled herself, waving Margaret to a chair as she did so. "It's too cold to be out on such a day as this, so you might as well sit and visit a spell. Get your mettle up before you go out again."

Margaret smiled her thanks. "Angie, can I ask you a personal question?"

"*Humph.* You can, but I may not answer it."

"Why did it take you so long to get married?" She was surprised at her own boldness.

Angie looked at Frank and then the floor. "Sometimes there are more important things than being married."

"More important people, you mean," Frank said.

Angie fluttered a hand at him. "Marrying the right person at the right time can be one of God's best gifts. But if the time's not right, it can ruin your life."

"But if you love someone . . . Didn't you

love Frank for a long time?"

"Oh, honey, I loved him and I hated him, and when he went away, I missed him so bad I wasn't sure I'd live." Frank grinned, and Angie glared at him. "Don't go getting the big head over there."

"So why did you wait so long?"

Angie straightened her shoulders and smoothed her skirt over her bony knees. "I loved my sister and the good Lord more." She shot Frank another look. "Take that, you old coot." Frank grinned and blew his nose in a red bandana. "Honey, God wants you to be happy, but His idea of what should please you and your own idea aren't always the same. And while the love between a man and a woman is pleasing, it surely isn't the be all, end all. I guess God wanted to make sure we had our priorities straight before He let us get together."

Frank honked his nose again. "And it was surely worth the wait," he said with a wink. Angie rolled her eyes.

Margaret visited a little longer and then drove back home through the biting cold pondering what Angie said. She'd been thinking that if only Henry would love her, she would know she was worth loving. But she was already loved by quite a few people — Mayfair, Emily, Perla — even Frank and

Angie. And maybe, just maybe, God loved her, too. She tried to think if she had any proof that He did.

Well, Mayfair seemed to be getting better. She hadn't had any episodes in a long time. She didn't think her parents much cared about her, but she did have a family in Emily, Perla, and Henry that made her feel welcome and cared for. And her dream of spending her days living simply on a farm seemed more possible than ever. She was practically running Emily's farm, and so what if Henry never came home? She could keep going as she was and maybe buy the gray house and a few acres one day.

Margaret began to feel good about her life. Angie had gone nine decades without a husband and seemed utterly content. What if a woman's worth wasn't defined by a man? That's what the feminists claimed, but Margaret wondered if those women were taking the idea far enough. A man didn't define your worth. God did. And supposedly, God thought highly of her.

The previous Sunday Margaret and Mayfair had sat in their now usual spot in the Phillipses' pew at Laurel Mountain Church. The preacher said something that stuck with her. *We love because He first loved us.* Maybe she couldn't really love

Henry or anyone else until she better understood how much God loved her.

Pulling into the driveway, Margaret sat for a moment listening to the ping of the cooling engine as the wind rocked the car. It would be nice if God would give her a sign, like a sudden stilling of the wind, or a rainbow, or a dove, or something. She saw Mayfair, home from school, move past a window in the gray house that had become so very much home for the two of them. The kitchen door opened, and Pie ran out to greet her as though she'd been gone a year. Then again, maybe the signs were all around her.

32

He probably should have let Mom make a bigger deal out of his graduation. Henry took his spot with the band mere hours after receiving his diploma. Mom, Grandma, Margaret, and Mayfair had all driven up to watch him that morning. They must have gotten up really early to make it in time. When he told them he wasn't coming home right away, it was clear they were disappointed. Or maybe mad, if the look on his mother's face was any indication. Grandma patted him and told him not to stay away too long. Mayfair sighed. And Margaret looked at him as if he'd kicked that spotted dog of hers.

But seriously. How could he bail on the guys in the band? They'd come to count on him, and he was making decent money. He told them all he'd call every day — well, at least every other — and he'd be home in a week or so. He didn't add that he wasn't sure he'd stay even then. If Mort offered him a permanent position, he'd be a fool to pass up a chance like that. The women in his life hadn't liked him running moonshine, but playing music — that was so respectable his own father had done it. Well, not for money, but still.

Of course, it would be hard to date Margaret. And he did want to date her. He was surprised by how much he'd missed having her around the last few months. Henry groaned and started tuning his fiddle. Why wasn't anything ever easy?

Henry poured his frustration and confusion into the music, and by the first break he felt wrung out. And not nearly as much better as he wanted to. He settled his fiddle into its case and stretched his arms. That's when he saw her. Margaret. Sitting at a table off to the side with a soda in front of her. She was watching him intently, and it gave him a start. Like he'd somehow conjured her up with his wishing. He ambled over to the table and slid into a chair, trying to act like he wasn't shocked.

"Well, hey, pretty lady."

Margaret gave him a sharp look. "You're not making fun of me, are you?"

Henry shifted. "No. Why would you think that?"

"It's not often I'm accused of being pretty."

Henry laughed, then saw she was serious. "Are you kidding? Of course you're pretty." He reached out to touch her cheek. "I can't get enough of your freckles, and you've got the cutest nose." His eyes drifted downward. "Plus, you — uh — well, trust me, you're pretty."

Margaret sighed. "Then why don't you want to come home?"

Henry wrinkled his brow. "What's one got to do with the other?"

"If I'm pretty enough, and you want to keep seeing me — which I kind of thought you did — then I'd expect you'd want to be where I am." Her cheeks burned scarlet, and she stared at her hands gripping the sweating soda glass.

"Hey." Henry reached out and tilted her face toward him. "I do want to be where you are, but this is where I can make money with my fiddle. And if I'm going to, you know, plan for the future, I need to make some money. We can still see each other." He tried a crooked grin. "Just maybe not as often as we'd like."

Unshed tears gleamed in Margaret's eyes. "I thought you wanted to come back and run the farm. I thought you got a degree in agriculture so you could do that."

"That's what I thought, too, but now that I have a spot in the band, well, it's really cool to be able to earn a living doing something I love this much."

"Is it a living? Really and truly?"

Henry slid back in his chair. "Well, maybe not yet, but if things keep going my way, it could be." He sat up straighter. "And you could move here. You could get a job, easy. Maybe even waitressing here."

Margaret looked at him sideways. "And where would I live? And what about Mayfair?"

It was on the tip of Henry's tongue to suggest she live with him. He'd known lots of guys who shacked up with their girls through college. But he caught himself. Margaret wasn't like that.

"Yeah, I guess I hadn't thought that one through." He heard the guys messing around on the stage again. "Hey, I've got to get back to it. Will you still be here when we finish?"

"No. I'm catching the late bus home. Your mom didn't want to leave me behind, but Emily said she thought it would be all right."

Henry felt desperation rise in him, but he wasn't sure why. He wanted to grab Margaret and insist she stay. He wanted to offer to drive her all those hours home after his set was done. He wanted . . . well, what he wanted was clearly more than he would get. He leaned over and gave her a lingering kiss. She started to pull away in the crowded room and then seemed to decide it didn't matter who was watching. When Henry released her, Margaret kept her eyes closed for another beat. Then she opened them and looked straight at him.

"I hope I'll see you soon, Henry Phillips."

"Yeah, me too."

And with that she was gone, just a half empty glass of soda to mark where she'd been. He wished he'd said something else, but he couldn't think what it might have been.

"What's the matter, Margaret?" Mayfair slipped up beside her sister and took the basket of eggs from her hand. The chickens were still laying well, even as the summer days grew warm. Mayfair wiped the eggs down one by one with a damp cloth and slipped them into an empty carton.

"Why do you think anything is wrong?"

"You have that faraway look in your eyes, like you can see something that doesn't fit."

Margaret sometimes found Mayfair's insights unsettling, but at the moment, she was glad her sister was so sensitive. "I thought maybe Henry liked me — I mean, really liked me. He's been writing and calling, but he doesn't seem to care whether or not he ever comes back to the farm. I'm beginning to think he likes that fiddle more than this place . . . or me."

Mayfair closed a full carton and reached for an empty one. "I don't think he does."

"Well, he sure acts like it."

"Don't you sometimes act one way when you feel another?"

Margaret, busy wiping down the counter where she'd finished with the day's milking, stilled her hands. Honestly, that's how her life felt most of the time, that one thing was happening inside while she tried to show something else to the world. "I suppose," she said slowly, turning to consider her sister. "So how do I know how Henry really feels?"

"Ask him." Mayfair took the empty basket and tucked it away in the closet near the front door. "I'm going to write some letters."

That girl and her letters to orphans. Margaret found herself staring vacantly into space again. Ask him. Well now, maybe she should.

■ ■ ■ ■

As soon as Margaret dropped the letter to Henry through the slot at the post office, she wished she could reach in and take it back. She was an idiot. What woman wrote to a man and asked him to declare his intentions? That's not quite how she'd phrased it, but it was basically what she was asking him to do. She leaned her forehead against the cool metal of the box set into the wall and wondered if Jeanine would give her the letter back. The postmistress took her job very seriously, though, and anyway, Margaret was too embarrassed to ask.

"You need some stamps or anything?"

Margaret jumped and saw Jeanine watching her from behind a pair of half glasses. "No, ma'am. Thank you."

Jeanine blinked once and resumed sorting the letters in her hand. "All right, then." She shot Margaret another look over the top of her glasses, and Margaret took it to mean she'd lingered long enough. She gave a halfhearted wave and walked out to her car. She had a few things to pick up for Emily before she headed home.

"Let the waiting begin," she said to no one. Or maybe to God. Somehow she felt

more and more like He might actually be
listening.

33

Margaret just knew it. He'd fallen in love with one of those blond songbird sisters of his friend from school and was coming home to tell her in person. Henry had finally written back, but he didn't answer her directly. He only let her know when he'd be home and wrote that he'd like to talk to her about something important. He had a degree plus a possible career in music and what did she have? A high school diploma and a willingness to work the farm. Oh, and lots and lots of freckles. Surely he wanted more than that. She'd make a fine housekeeper, but anything more? Nonsense.

Henry was due to arrive at his mother's house that afternoon, and then they'd come to dinner at Emily's. Margaret and Emily cooked all day as Margaret's mood sank lower and lower. She surveyed the table. There was a glazed ham from the hog they raised last year, the first of the summer squash, biscuits, and mashed potatoes made with cream from Bertie, whose second calf was finally old enough for them to resume milking. There were also strawberry preserves she'd put up the week before and a pound cake for dessert. It should have pleased her to look over that table, but she was pretty sure she couldn't eat a bite.

Since coming home from Henry's graduation Margaret had lost her appetite. She'd always enjoyed food, but the pleasure seemed to have gone out of it. That probably meant she really was in love with Henry. She didn't know for sure, but if her current level of misery was any indicator, then she was definitely gone on him. She almost wished he'd married Barbara and never given her any hope. Almost.

"Here they come," Mayfair called from where she was kneeling on the sofa to watch out the window. She practically danced into the kitchen, smiling and clapping her hands. "Henry's home," she sang.

Emily smiled and wiped her hands on her apron. "I declare, that child looks and sounds the way I feel."

Margaret did her best to smile. Her sister was on the cusp of annoying her. Mayfair tended to have a positive outlook, but today she was downright bubbly. They all hurried out of the house to greet Henry as soon as he stepped out of his truck. He grinned and waved, then walked around to open his mother's door. Margaret thought that was gentlemanly of him. She almost wished he'd act like a jerk instead.

Henry hugged his grandmother first, swinging her feet until she insisted he put her down. Then he practically tossed Mayfair into the air as her crystal laughter fell over them all. Finally he turned to Margaret and took both of her hands in his.

"I sure have missed you," he said.

Margaret felt a flutter and tried to push it down. He was just being nice. They were friends, and he was going to let her down easy. There was no need to pin her future on a boy — she looked at him more closely, okay, a man — who was only going to break her heart.

Henry winked, and Margaret's resolve proved to be made of timid stuff. She almost cried when he turned away and escorted the chattering group of women into the house. She brought up the rear, determined not to spoil the party for everyone.

The meal was filled with laughter and Henry's stories. Margaret felt everyone was looking at her but guessed it was just this feeling that Henry was going to break her heart that made her feel like the center of attention. Goodness knows, she'd never been the center of anything. Finally, the meal drew to a close, and Emily offered to make coffee while they went into the living room to enjoy their cake.

"Margaret, come show me the garden," Henry said.

Margaret looked toward her sister. "Mayfair's the gardener around here. I just do what she tells me. Maybe she should show you."

Mayfair rolled her eyes. "I promised I'd dry the dishes."

"And I'd rather you show me," Henry said, reaching for her hand.

Margaret let him lead her outside. The late June evening felt cool against her skin, and the dusk softened the world around them. Roses bloomed on a trellis at the end of the porch, and she caught a trace of their perfume.

"Garden sure looks good." Henry walked to the end of a row of tomato plants, releasing her hand. "You and Mayfair make a good team."

"I like being in the garden. It's . . ." Margaret searched for the right word. "Manageable."

Henry half smiled. "I don't think I've heard anyone describe a garden that way before."

"I guess I know what to expect from the garden. If I plant and water and weed, eventually I'll get a harvest. It's not like people. You never know with people." She ducked her head and stuffed her hands into the pockets of the skirt she'd put on for Henry's homecoming. Her mother bought it for her back when she thought buying clothes a size too small would make Margaret lose weight. Now it was almost loose-fitting.

"You look different," Henry said, cocking his head to one side.

Margaret looked at him and squinted. "What do you mean by that?"

"Well, prettier for one thing. Maybe sadder for another. Mayfair's okay, isn't she?"

"Yes, I think she's the healthiest she's been in a long time. We've been really careful about what she eats and getting her insulin."

Henry nodded, appearing to be only half listening. "Good, I'm glad. So what about you? Seems like you didn't eat much this evening."

Margaret shrugged and knelt down to nip suckers off the tomato plants. She was surprised he'd noticed. "I'm okay. I've learned a lot about keeping up a farm from your grandmother. I'm not sure what good it'll do me, but I like learning it."

Henry moved toward a hill of crookneck squash with its mix of blooms and ripening vegetables. The buttery blossoms were closing now against the dark. "Yeah, I thought for a while I might want to do something else — something more — than farm this place. But over the last month I've realized living here, working the land my father and grandfather worked, is exactly what I want." He shrugged. "Some of the guys think I should do something else. Maybe use my degree to go into research or teach, keep playing music, but . . ." He looked around at the closing of the day, the fireflies rising from the grasses, and the last trails of light slipping behind the horizon. Then he looked right at Margaret. "But this is what I really want."

Margaret swallowed past a lump in her throat. It was what she wanted, too, but she hardly dared hope Henry saw her as part of his dream.

"What about you, Margaret? What do you want?"

She cleared her throat. "What I have now is pretty great. But I don't guess I can live in your grandmother's cottage for the rest of my life. Who knows what'll happen down the road? I might have to work in a plant or something. I don't guess I'm qualified for much else. I could go to school, but I don't know . . ." She looked away, unable to meet his eyes.

Henry moved to the far side of the squash plant, and Margaret took a step that direction to pull a few weeds hiding under the broad leaves. Henry knelt down opposite and reached over to tilt Margaret's chin up. He looked into her eyes, and she felt tears begin to pool. She would not let them fall.

"What's that?" Henry asked, releasing her.

Margaret was confused. "What?"

"That," he said, pointing down.

Margaret looked and saw where some dollar weed had begun to encroach on the hill. He was pointing out a weed she'd missed? Seriously? She reached for the weed, and her eye caught on a squash blossom. It looked different. There was something inside — not an insect — something shiny.

With shaking fingers, Margaret reached into the flower and touched the cool metal of . . . a ring. It was a simple gold band with a small diamond. She looked at Henry.

He smiled. "Margaret Anne Hoffman, would you marry me and live on this farm for the rest of your life?"

433

■ ■ ■ ■

Henry lay in the bed he'd been sleeping in since he got too big for the crib he hoped was up in the attic somewhere. No way would he sleep tonight. When he drove home from Morgantown with that ring in his pocket — paid for with what he'd earned playing at the Screen Door — he'd felt one hundred percent sure that Margaret would say yes. But once he was there in the garden where he'd tucked that band of gold, he'd had his doubts.

Margaret had been different. She had achieved an almost fragile prettiness since he'd seen her a month before. She seemed smaller, less sturdy than he remembered. No less strong or capable, but somehow more feminine. The feelings she stirred standing there in the garden in that soft blue skirt and white blouse had surprised him. The first time he thought of Margaret as a potential wife, he'd seen it as a practical arrangement. But now . . . well, he supposed this was how a man was supposed to feel about the woman he was going to marry.

He hadn't known he wanted to marry her until he'd tried on the life of a musician for size. He'd been so certain it would be the right fit. He thought if he could play music while she waited for him, life would be just about perfect. But then she left on a bus for the farm, and somehow as good as the music felt, it wasn't enough.

And it wasn't just Margaret's presence that was lacking. He missed milking Bertie on dewy mornings. He missed stupid things like hayfields dotted with daisies. He missed watching the chickens peck the yard clean. He missed his mother and grandmother and Mayfair, and yes, Margaret most of all. He called and even wrote a letter or two, but he'd still catch himself playing those mournful tunes at the end of a set, wishing he could watch the sunset throw its reflection over the pond as if it had all the light in the world to waste.

And then Margaret's letter came like permission to come home and claim the life he wanted more than anything. It was when he made that decision that he felt not only the pleasure it would have given Dad, but the pleasure it did give God. He punched his pillow and rolled over. He was going to marry Margaret and make this farm their own. He couldn't wait.

They were getting married — in August. Margaret held her hand up, tilted her head to watch light catch in the diamond. Henry said he wished it were bigger, but playing music didn't pay quite as well as he hoped. He laughed and said he used the moonshine money to pay off his tuition, and she'd just have to wait for him to earn some honest money. She didn't care one way or the other. She was getting married, and they would live here in the little gray house together. And Mayfair could stay as long as she wanted.

Margaret would call this a dream come true, if she'd ever had the courage to dream anything as good as this. She went to get ready for bed, although she doubted she'd be able to sleep a wink.

The next morning, Margaret felt shy when Henry came by the farmhouse as they were finishing breakfast. He said he'd already eaten, but he managed to force down a stack of Margaret's buttermilk pancakes with maple syrup just the same. He was halfway out the door when he ducked back in.

"Oh, yeah. Mom wants to do an engagement party for us," he said to Margaret. "Sadie's coming home for the Fourth of July, and she figured it would be the perfect time. I'm not sure she'll be able to come again for the wedding, so Mom wanted to have a party now." He rolled his eyes. "I guess this is the kind of thing you girls like to do."

Margaret smiled. She liked being included in "you girls." She'd always felt kind of alone before this. "Sounds great. I'll give Perla a call."

Henry nodded and headed out to start the day's chores, Mayfair on his heels. Margaret smiled. What were the odds that she would find a good man who loved her and her sister? She still wasn't a hundred percent sure what Henry saw in her, but she hoped whatever it was would last forever.

Henry didn't know about this engagement party business. Wasn't a wedding enough? Still, it was worth it to come out on the other side with the woman he loved. He laughed aloud as he finished hoeing the row of popcorn Mayfair insisted on planting. Who would've thought? Before Dad died he'd barely noticed Margaret, but somehow that morning — the worst morning of his life — she'd come to his attention. And he'd been noticing her more and more ever since. He thought about a Scripture Ray had written down and sent him in a letter. *And we know that all things work together for good to them that love God, to them who are the called according to his purpose.*

He thought he remembered that was from Romans chapter eight. Good stuff. Who knew God could use losing his father to lead him to the woman who would be his wife? He guessed he'd been too wrapped up in his own world before. Well, he still missed Dad, but at least something good — no, great — was coming out of it.

Margaret wondered if that business of breathing into a brown paper bag really worked. She felt like she was going to hyperventilate. Most of the town of Wise was out there in the community hall, and she wasn't sure she could face them. They'd know she wasn't pretty enough or smart enough for Henry Phillips. They'd know he was basically marrying a farmhand. And while she'd normally worry that her mother might come, now she was worried that everyone knew her mother wasn't there because she was at a clinic where she could work through her "issues." That's what Dad said when he called to let them know Lenore was checking into alcohol rehabilitation. He said Mayfair's illness and the loss of both daughters had been more than she could stand. Margaret wondered what had driven her to drink before all that, but she didn't say it out loud. She just made the appropriate comments and asked her father to let them know when Mom came home. Not that it mattered, but it seemed like the right thing to say.

Now she wished there were a place she could go and get away from everything. She'd been out there for thirty minutes, smiling and shaking hands, being hugged by women she barely knew. Everyone acted nice, but she couldn't help thinking they were looking at her with a critical eye. She'd been hiding in the ladies' room for ten minutes, hoping no one else would come in. She heard a hand hit the door, and her heart sank.

"Why, Margaret, what are you doing in here?"

Margaret tried to smile at Sadie — her future sister-in-law. She liked Sadie, who was a little on the plump side and very businesslike. She tended to get to the point, and Margaret actually believed her when she said she was glad Henry had the good sense to marry her.

"I'm feeling a little —"

"Overwhelmed. Of course you are. Mother never does things by halves. We could have just had a nice family supper, but she had to invite the whole town. Now they'll be mad if they aren't invited to the wedding, too." Sadie sighed and fluffed her strawberry blond curls in the mirror. "I can never get my hair to do right. You're smart, keeping your hair put up."

Margaret touched her hair, trying to smooth the waves and frizz she'd mostly tamed for the evening. She'd love to have actual curls like Sadie's. Margaret began to wonder if Henry would be willing to elope. She wasn't sure she could go through a wedding where there would be even more attention on her. And while she'd been excited about getting a dress, now she wondered what people would think of her choice. They'd judge and measure every little thing, and there would be no hiding in the background.

Panic rose in Margaret's throat, and she wanted nothing more than to run home and hide in the cowshed with Bertie. She started for the door, but as she extended her arm, the door flew open, and Perla stood there, looking flushed.

"Margaret, you'd better come. It's Mayfair."

Margaret rushed into the room she'd been trying to escape. Mayfair had been doing so well. Had she eaten too much cake? What if she went into a coma again? It could kill her.

Margaret stood in the main room, looking around desperately for her sister, probably lying prostrate on the floor. She never should have left her. Crowds were always overwhelming, and now she was having an episode on top of everything else. But instead of seeing her sister collapsed in a corner, she saw a room full of quiet people turned toward the small raised dais at the end of the hall. Mayfair stood there, looking pale, but perfectly fine otherwise.

"I have something to say." Mayfair's voice was soft but clear. Margaret felt rooted to the spot. "My sister is going to marry Henry." A smile crept across her lips. "And the best part is that I still get to live with them."

Laughter rippled across the crowd.

"I think they've had a hard time figuring out that they love each other." Mayfair ducked her head, but her voice grew stronger. "I knew it from the start, but sometimes I know things like that. Love is easy to see if you're looking for it. I guess I've always liked looking out for love." She lifted her chin and found Margaret in the crowd. "Margaret's always loved me, and I'm glad I'm not the only one anymore.

She's got a lot of love in her heart."

She let her gaze drift across the faces. Margaret feared that the magnitude of the crowd would overwhelm her baby sister. Would she faint? Run from the stage? But Mayfair didn't do either, and Margaret suddenly realized her sister was growing into a young woman.

"I just wanted to say to everyone that it's good for us to love one another. Like sisters or friends or family. You know, the way God loves us no matter what. It's the best thing there is, and I'm glad Margaret and Henry have it." She released her arms and tucked one foot behind the other. "Anyway, I can't wait for the wedding."

"Neither can Henry," came a masculine voice from the crowd. They erupted in laughter, and several ladies gathered around Mayfair, hugging her and kissing her cheeks.

Margaret wound her way through dozens of people who wanted to congratulate her until she finally found her sister. "That was a lovely speech," she said. "I'm proud of you for getting up in front of all these people."

Mayfair clasped her hands around Margaret's waist. "It's not so bad when love keeps you safe. It's even better than angels," she said.

Margaret closed her eyes and held her sister close. Another set of arms wrapped around them both, and she looked to see Henry holding them tight. She bit her lip hard and hugged Mayfair while leaning into the man she loved. Maybe no one had shown her what love between a man and a woman should look like, but this surely felt right. Maybe her sister was a miracle worker after all.

"Come with me." Most of the guests had gone when Henry grabbed Margaret's hand and tugged her toward the door. "I want to show you something."

Margaret thought she should probably stay and help clean up, but instead she let herself be pulled toward Henry's truck. He opened the door and helped her inside. They drove in companionable silence to Laurel Mountain Church. Margaret knew this is where they would get married. Maybe Henry wanted to talk about the ceremony.

They parked, and when Henry helped her down he didn't let go of her hand. His skin was calloused and warm. She let herself imagine what it would be like when he touched more than her hand. She flushed and steered her thoughts back to the wedding. First things first.

Henry walked right past the church and pushed open the gate to the cemetery. "Mom had Dad's marker set about a month ago. It's taken her a while, since we aren't sure which day Dad died."

Margaret had wondered about that. Would the stone say December 31, 1975, or January 1, 1976? Personally, she thought she'd choose the latter date. It sort of made Casewell's too short life seem longer. Like the difference between something that cost nine ninety-nine and ten dollars.

Henry walked past his grandpa John's grave. Margaret saw that Emily's name was already there, along with her birth date, October 30, 1895. Then, in the shadow of a cedar tree, she saw Casewell Phillips's still rounded grave, with a pristine stone at the head. She felt solemn. Maybe Henry wanted to share this moment in their lives with his dad, even though he was gone. That was nice.

Henry reached into his pocket with his free hand and pulled out two white stones — one smooth and one rough — which he placed on top of the marker. Click, click. He drew her close and wrapped an arm around her shoulders. "How perfect is that?" he asked, nodding toward the inscription.

Margaret admired the simple white marble. She'd never been fond of overly ornate memorials. The name Casewell Phillips was engraved in bold letters across the top. Then, "Date of Birth — Psalm 139:16." Margaret thought that was odd and asked Henry if he knew the verse.

" 'All the days ordained for me were written in your book before one of them came to be,' " he quoted. "But keep going."

The next line read, "Date of Death — John 3:16." She knew that one. And then at the bottom of the stone, "He has set eternity in our hearts."

Margaret furrowed her brow. "But it doesn't have dates."

"I know. Isn't it great? Mom decided that since she didn't know for sure, she'd use this as a way to remind people that Dad isn't really dead. He's just gone on ahead of us into eternity." He pulled Margaret into his arms and rested his chin on her head. "I was angry with Dad when he died — felt that he'd somehow abandoned me."

He tightened his arms, and Margaret felt as if peace were flowing into her through him. She snuggled closer.

"But now it feels more like he's blazing a trail for me. His whole life is like shiny white stones he's left along a path in the woods.

And here's the last stone and the verse that we can live our whole lives on. 'For God so loved the world, that he gave his only begotten Son, that whosoever believeth in him should not perish, but have everlasting life.' "

Margaret pillowed her head against the chest of the man she loved. They were going to have a good life together. She knew it now. And it didn't matter what anyone else thought. She also knew — at long last — what it felt like to love and be loved in return. Not only by Henry, but by Mayfair, by Emily, by Perla, and best of all, by God, who had blessed her without even being asked.

ABOUT THE AUTHOR

Sarah Loudin Thomas is a fund-raiser for a children's ministry who has also published freelance writing for *Now & Then* magazine, as well as the *Asheville Citizen-Times* and *The Journey Christian Newspaper.* She holds a bachelor's degree in English from Coastal Carolina University. She and her husband reside in Asheville, North Carolina. Learn more at www.sarahloudinthomas.com.